It's Just Sex…
Isn't It?

Nerys McCabe

ISBN: 9798674323143

Cover design by: Studio 6ix

www.nerysmccabe.com

NOTE TO READER

"If music be the food of love play on" Don't worry, I'm not going to get all English Teachery on you. But I am using this quotation for a good reason. It's a sort of caveat to my writing because music, words, literature, love - they're all linked and for me, the link is significant. Music is passion, music is love, music can stir feelings in a person so deeply that when they hear that song again, they are immediately transported back to that moment or that memory, whether it be heart-breaking or wonderful or both. So, I write about Love and I use music to drive it. I have always written: music, stories, even poetry sometimes and I have now found the perfect way to tie my love of all types of writing together. Songs play a part in my characters' stories because I see music as an essential part of life and one that can be used to evoke so much emotion. So, my recommendation is this: if a song is mentioned then, if you want to, have a listen to it. I have put it there to help the scene unfold or to get deep into the emotions of the character at that moment or to express just how significant that moment is to the character; maybe it will come back and haunt them, or hurt them, or help them. It helps when I write, and I really hope it helps to bring the characters to life for you. Enjoy.

"There is a charm about the forbidden that makes it unspeakably desirable"
MARK TWAIN

CHAPTER ONE

Thursday

I pull my last pint of the evening and make my way round to the other side of the bar for a drink and a bit of a wind down before I go home. It's been really busy tonight and I'm looking forward to getting into bed, so I won't be here long. I've been up since 6am and it's beginning to show. Mind you, it doesn't help that I have no make-up on. I'm surprised I've not scared the customers away! Although, maybe I have, there's only a couple left now. I've been doing a few shifts a week here so I can pay off my credit card. My last shift (and payment) is next week so I'll finally get my evenings back (and hopefully get rid of the bags under my eyes).

"Hi Kate," Matt Grove arrives at the bar, he's a chef, bit of a celebrity apparently, and comes in here after work sometimes. "You not working tonight?" he enquires.

"Just finished" I say and take a sip of my gin. I was hoping he wouldn't come in tonight, I'm going to have to ask him now aren't I? I've had some nice chats with him in the last few weeks but now his wife, who sometimes joins him on a Sunday, has asked me to check up on him and (in usual Kate fashion) I stupidly agreed.

"Can I get you a drink Kate?" he offers.

"No, I'm fine thanks, just having this one then I'm off home. Been a long day." I smile at him and try to build up the courage. He gets his pint and looks at me again.

"Mind if I join you?" he moves along the bar towards me and perches on the adjacent barstool. "How's your day been?" he asks. He's easy to talk to, seems different to the other men in here, actually treats me like a person rather than an object. He's a good listener. And you don't get much of that round here. But then, that's typical of

London! Strangers everywhere.

"It's been long," I reply, "Had to be at work early this morning and then straight here after so I haven't stopped. But you must know what that's like. Sounds like you have long shifts too." Matt owns a restaurant and it's doing pretty well from what I've heard.

"Yeah, it's been hectic, good to sit down and relax a bit." He takes a sip of his pint and I try to work out what to say. "Matt, I need to ask you something and it's a bit strange, to be honest, but your wife asked me to and I told her I would." He looks at me sideways,

"My wife?"

"Yeah, she asked me last week, I don't know why, I mean I hardly know her, and it's a bit awkward but…"

"Ok, I'm listening, ask away." "Well, it seems that she's umm…she's upset because she thinks you're looking elsewhere." I pause to test and look carefully at his immediate reaction.

"What does that even mean? Looking elsewhere?" his confusion seems genuine.

"Looking elsewhere for…" come on Kate, might as well just say it now, "somebody else…another woman… sex…" I say this a little too loudly but there's not enough punters left to hear.

"Oh!" his reaction is more worrying this time, no surprised tone and he looks down to the ground, in shame?

"You don't seem surprised" I say lowering my voice in disappointment. I think he maybe is having an affair, just from that "Oh!" my whole opinion of him has changed, he's gone from honest Matt to…his voice cut across my thoughts.

"I wasn't looking elsewhere" oh dear, emphasis on the 'wasn't', what am I going to tell his wife? Although, some people wouldn't blame him, she seems to rule their marriage with a rod of iron and nobody has much time for her in here, she behaves like she's too good for the place.

It's a strange match. His voice again…

"until I met you." What? What is he saying? Is he taking the piss?! What is he thinking saying that? Clearly not thinking or joking…

"Are you joking?" I ask, looking right into his eyes… Shit, he's not joking! No, no, no, no!

"No, not joking" Oh my God, my heart just did that funny thing, skipped a beat, and now it's beating way too fast…I shouldn't be reacting like this - what is my body doing? He's still looking at me with those lovely brown eyes (when did they become so lovely?) and I'm suddenly aware of my shabby clothes, my no make-up rule, my beating heart (be still!)

"No!" the word flies out of my mouth. Nothing else.

"No?" he repeats. "Don't you feel it too?" he steps towards me "Christ, you must, I know this isn't just me". He's almost apologetic in his tone, or nervous or perhaps embarrassed…

"What are you saying? You're married…I don't do that sort of thing" (do I?) "She's asked me to talk to you". I am breathless, mostly because I forget to breathe but also because he means it and it's making me happy - it's making me feel important for the first time in ages - he's looking at me and he's telling me he wants me, he likes me, he…back up here…Pause. Stop. Sort it out Kate.

"I can't help how I feel, Kate" he edges closer. I don't move away.

"Well you need to. You can't have these feelings for someone else, you have a wife… I mean… what are you expecting me to say" (help me, tell me what to say…)

"I don't know, I'm sorry, I shouldn't have said it but …I, I honestly haven't stopped thinking about you since we met and I know I shouldn't but I can't help it, I've tried and then there you are, with that beautiful, quirky smile and that quick wit and I'm hooked again"

Quick wit! I can think of better things to fall for or

more flattering comments…although 'beautiful quirky smile' I'll take that, beautiful anyway.

Bloody hell, what am I thinking? - reality please. Right, I compose myself. Deep breath…

"Listen Matt, this can't happen, we both need to accept that"

"We?" he smiles shyly, "so you 'do' feel it too?" Oh crap, what've I said!

"No, I don't, I'm just trying to…let you down gent…" His lips close on mine and his hand is on my cheek, Shit shit shit. Yes Yes Yes. Noooooo! What am I doing?

Oh God, I'm not stopping him, I'm kissing him back, it feels so nice…but I shouldn't be…but I can't stop…but…STOP! I pull away and I do the only thing I can do. I push past him and I walk away. As I get to the door, I open it and take a look back, he's standing staring at me, the apologetic look back on his face. And I feel like I'm seeing him for the first time, his dark brown hair, his gorgeous eyes, his strong arms and…I have to get out of here.

I'm walking along the street, quickly, heart still beating - oh my god that was exhilarating, amazing…Ahhhh! I'm in hell, what've I done? My phone rings. Shit it's his wife. What is this? I get to my door, put the key in, shall I answer it…what can I say? She'll want to know how it went, she'll want the reassurance she was looking for, the reassurance I was meant to get for her. I'll answer it…I push my door open and just as I'm about to answer the phone, he's there behind me, he's followed me from the pub!

"Kate" I spin round and look at him. My intention is to stop this right now but as I see his face again, those eyes, I realise my attraction to him. Was I internally suppressing it, until now? He's looking at me with an apologetic passion and my hesitation invites him to move closer, "Kate." His voice is gentle and the closer he gets, the faster my heart pounds. Then, once again, his lips are on mine and I am engulfed by his passion. His hands glide down my arms and our fingers entwine, connecting like they're made for each other … what… the… hell… am… I… doing… he gently backs me inside the flat, pushes the door closed behind us and I'm his, I can't stop this, I feel the wall behind me as he puts his arms around me and I melt at his touch…I want him and I'm going to have him…as we sink on to the sofa together I can still hear the faint ring of my phone but that just doesn't matter now.

CHAPTER TWO

What have I done? (shit!) what have I done? (smile)

He skulked away about 3am. Well, I say 'skulked' but it went more like this:

"Kate, I have to go. I don't want to but she'll be expecting me…" Wow, we've already gone to 'she' so that he can distance himself from her?

We were lying next to each other on my bed, we'd made it that far after the sofa, the floor, up against the wall (quite an impressive stance!) and then into the bedroom where we finally got out of our clothes and, after the fourth time, fell asleep…together.

It was just sex. Was it just sex? It was, it was just sex. I mean, just because we fell asleep together and I woke up in his arms, that doesn't mean anything. I know he said he likes me but that was just to get me into bed, wasn't it? But then, WAS it just sex? If all I wanted was sex, why choose a married man? Surely, if that was the case, I would've just gone and shagged anyone. Who am I kidding - as if I could get 'anyone' – I haven't had a relationship for over six months and the last one was barely that, it only lasted three months and he turned out to be a complete arse, even stole money from me (part of the reason for my having two jobs!) Does this mean I was so desperate for sex that I just had it with the first man that showed an interest? I mean, I had these feelings when he told me - excitement, fear, heart racing…was I just flattered?

"Kate, are you listening to me?" shit he's still here, stop fucking thinking.

"Yes sorry, I'm listening"

"This isn't just sex, you know" (Did he read my mind?) "I meant what I said and now this has happened, I want you even more." Not sure, but he sounds sincere - what have I done?

CHAPTER THREE

Friday

No regrets I'm sitting at my desk when the text comes through. It's 4pm and I've been sitting here doing nothing but regretting my actions all day! Then the text. It's as if he's reading my mind but probably just because he's feeling the same. I don't intend to reply so I put my phone down and make what must be the hundredth attempt today to complete this press release. It's only seconds before my mind is wandering again.

I sent Fay (Matt's wife) a text this morning to say that she was worrying about nothing. Double deceit. What am I playing at? I pick up my phone again and re-read her reply,

Thank you. My heart is beating too fast again but for different reasons than it was last night. What the actual fuck am I playing at? I had sex with someone's husband! This is huge, massive, ridiculous! Just as I'm going through the complete cock up again in my head (and trying desperately not to relive how bloody amazing the sex was) my phone pings again. It's Matt. Again.

I can't stop thinking about you xx

I thought the 'No regrets' had an air of finality about it but apparently not. And the way I feel when I read that text isn't good. I'm not thinking 'Christ, this can never happen again, it was a terrible mistake and a one off' what is actually happening to me is the fluttering heartbeat, the tingling skin and the memories of his hands on my face, neck, shoulders.... ahhhhh stop, good god woman, STOP!

I get a hold of myself and start to text him back...

This can never... no,
This was a mistake... ahhh

Please never call... ffs
This will never happen...
Bollocks to it. *Can we meet tonight?*
Yes comes the instant reply and then, *I'll come to yours at 7* Oh crap.

6.50pm

I'm trying desperately not to care if I look good or not, it shouldn't matter. In fact, it would be better if I looked terrible as then he'll decide he doesn't want me and will be more relieved than hurt when I tell him that we can't carry on like this.

6.53pm

I'm sitting on the sofa flicking through the pages of a magazine, the sofa where we made love, 'made love?' What am I saying? It was sex, just sex, it meant nothing, it was meaningless, pointless, stupid...passionate, glorious, amazing sex and... the doorbell destroys my next thought, quite rightly. He's early, I leave it a few seconds, don't want it to seem like I'm rushing to the door to see him...I take one more look at myself in the mirror in the hall, I'm looking ok, just the right kind of pretty to be confident and decisive. As I get to the door, the bell rings again as I answer it...

Shit, it's Fay! How does she even know where I live? Shit shit shit.

"Hi, what a lovely surprise" I say as she air kisses and fake hugs me. I look behind her, half expecting to see Matt bouncing up the path.

"What are you doing here?" I ask and hope it doesn't sound too unwelcoming. She has never been here before!

"I bought you this" she produces a bottle of prosecco, "to say thank you and ask you to...um...keep it all to yourself" she steps over the threshold (the threshold where Matt kissed me so passionately the night before)...

and I close the door behind us, taking one last glance down the path just in case he is there.

"I hope you don't mind my being here, I got your address from the landlord at your little pub, but don't worry I won't stay if you have other plans" she looks me up and down to suggest I am dressed for other plans, "Matt's working late at the restaurant so I thought I'd better pop over and make sure you don't mention it to anyone else."

Matt's told her he's working late, even bigger SHIT SHIT SHIT, Christ if he turns up now we're properly caught out! What am I thinking, I'm acting like we're having an affair… and we're not, I was about to end it with him, end what? The affair?

"Actually Fay, I do have plans, I'm off out for a drink, got a date" what am I saying? "Friend from work felt sorry for me so set me up with someone, never met them before, never, so don't really know what to expect but I need to go actually, don't want him to think he's been stood up" I smile, probably unconvincingly but she totally buys it,

"Oh my god, I thought you'd made a bit of an effort to be slobbing on the couch", she turns quickly and goes back to the front door, my heart is racing, she goes to open the door and I'm so petrified that he's going to be standing there I almost scream when he's not, "are you ok?"

"I'm fine" I breathe out, "just a bit nervous I guess, it's been a while since, you know..." my lies are coming so naturally, I had no idea I had this kind of acting talent!

"I wouldn't normally say this Kate but maybe have a small brandy before you meet him, otherwise you might come across as a bit desperate and…well…" she looks me up and down again, "…tarty!"

OUCH! She's really patronising! A bit fucking desperate! And tarty! Where does she get off calling me that! I mean, if she knew how recently I'd actually had sex and with...(maybe she's got a point!)

"Yeah you're right, I'll maybe do that." I usher her quickly out of the flat, grab my bag and slam the door shut behind us. Her car is parked right outside, I practically push her in and shut the door on her, waving her off as I pretend to start off in the direction of the pub. Wave walk smile wave walk smile, she's turning the corner she's gone. Jesus that was close, what if he'd turned up when she was there...what would she have said then? What would we have said?

I'm walking back up the path to my flat when Matt grabs me from behind,

"Hey gorgeous" he swings me round and kisses me as if it's the most natural thing in the world and it doesn't matter if the world sees, I come up for air and manage to catch my breath enough to say,

"What are you doing? Do you realise that your wife's just been here?" I hiss!

"I know, I saw her come to your door, was the other side of the road when she pulled up so I hid and waited."

Wow, we are having an affair! That whole speech was definitely the speech of someone having an affair! But I didn't say it, he did, and it came really naturally to him!

"Have you done this before?" I question,

"Done what?" He looks kind of confused,

"Cheated on your wife" I say it with such force he takes his arms from round me, stands up straight and takes a step back, there seems to be a moment of resentment or regret in his eyes. We just look at each other, an acknowledgment between us, almost as if we agree that we know what we're doing is wrong but that part of it shouldn't be mentioned.

"Do you still want to come in?" I ask, as I turn and walk to the door. He follows. We go in.

9.40pm

So much for ending it, I'm now in the shower while Matt makes us some food, apparently he always gets hungry after amazing sex. And I can't deny it was that. Last night wasn't just a fluke, we're actually really good together, at sex anyway, what does that mean? It's not like a sign that we're going to live happily ever after, probably more of a sign that forbidden sex is much more exciting and that actually, if this wasn't such an illicit situation, we would probably be really bored already? Maybe, but I have my doubts. The way he holds me and looks at me, it makes me feel alive and needed. Just as I'm about to step out of the shower, Matt steps in, naked and ready. He looks at me, deep into my eyes and kisses me, our eyes still open and that's when I know, I can't stop this, I don't want to stop this, I'm a bad person.

CHAPTER FOUR

So that was how it began. And how it continued and how it continues still.

Three years later. I'm still having an affair, Matt's still married, my life has become full of lies that I have to maintain every day but hey, don't judge me, sometimes we just find ourselves in situations that we can't (or don't want to) get out of.

So here I am, same job, same flat, same relationship, that's pretty impressive when you take the word 'affair' out of the equation. But I've come to a bit of a stalemate, I'm not moving forward anymore and I need a change. So here goes...

Friday 8.30pm

"But I thought we were happy?" Matt pleads with a pained expression.

"It's not that I'm unhappy, Matt, it's just..." "So why end it? We have fun, we have great sex, even after three years, and that's something you don't get with everyone, I mean me and Fay..."

"That's the problem Matt. You're married to someone else" he starts to protest, "and before you say it, I know that's always been the case but try to see it from my point of view, I can't plan a future with you, I can't plan to get married, have kids, I'm in limbo here" I sound a bit pathetic to be honest and it's not like I actually want kids right now but I need to make him see it for what it is.

"I'll leave her" he spits out, clearly not really considering the consequences of that statement.

"Will you?" I ask, "because that's not something we've ever discussed, this relationship hasn't been about that, and it probably shouldn't have gone on this long but it has, and it's been great" (it really has been great, why am I ending it?) "but I'm stuck in a rut, I can't move forward"

"Please Kate, I don't want to lose you, I don't want this to stop, you're the one good thing in my life, you give me something to look forward to, someone to share my feelings with." Why doesn't he do that with his wife?

The truth is, this relationship has been as perfect as it can be considering he's married. We have, for the most part, had a normal relationship. There's been the odd weekend away where we can actually act like we're a couple, we've even had a few meals in public because we're just seen as friends, no one suspects that gorgeous celebrity chef Matthew Grove could possibly be interested in plain little Katie Carlin. His wife seems oblivious to the affair and I don't think they actually talk to each other much for her to suspect anything. We're hiding our affair in full sight of everyone, paps included, I've even appeared in a magazine picture as 'a good friend of the chef, Matt Grove' and no one so much as raised an eyebrow.

"Is this really what you want?" He whispers. I hesitate. He sees my doubt, moves closer and kisses me. He still makes me melt, and he's right, how many relationships can say that after three years? Christ I'm so easy to his touch, he pulls me closer, his fingers gently caress the back of my neck, one hand then moves down my spine, he knows exactly where and how to touch me to make me submit and once again, I am lost in him.

CHAPTER FIVE

Saturday 7.30pm

I've decided to take a few nights off from Matt, even though we're carrying on, I need a bit of 'me' time so I'm out with my best mate, Rach. She knows everything about me, she knows about Matt, she doesn't judge but listens and supports me and is expecting me to be young, free and single again tonight so we planned a session. I haven't told her yet that I didn't actually finish it with Matt so she keeps saying things like, "You seem ok! Really positive, I thought you might need to talk about it all but you're so strong..." stuff like that that is somehow preventing me from telling her that I didn't end it and we ended up right back where we started, on the sofa!

We're at a bar called Luigi's. There's nothing particularly Italian about it, apart from a flag behind the bar and an old lambretta (or half of one) in the corner. Rach has bought us a cocktail each called 'Easy Rider' and I can't help thinking it describes me to a 'T'. I gave in so easily to Matt last night that we might as well have a red-room and just be done with it. Bit disappointed in myself.

Rach takes a sip of Easy Rider and pulls a face like she's sucked on a lemon,

"That good?" I laugh as I take my first sip and nearly spit it out. "Bloody hell, what is in this?" Apparently, it's three different vodkas, a shot of tequila and a splash of cranberry juice! Rach jokes,

"Must be called Easy Rider cos you..." she tails off as two men approach us and one of them, rather politely and in true cliché form says,

"Are these seats taken?" Rach and I glance at each other, we usually have a system for getting rid of unwanted advances but tonight she raises her eyebrows which normally means "let's go for it!" There have been a number of occasions in the last three years when I've been out with Rach and we've always turned down men like this but Rach seems more interested in setting me up. I try to shake my head but she refuses to see it and instead says

"Please feel free to join us" oh god, what's she doing?! Rach is single, six months now - (makes it sound like she was an addict and she's six months clean, though I would argue right now that you can get addicted to men!)

Wow she clearly wants the blond for herself as the flirting is outrageous, these two need to get themselves a room, or a cold shower! She's just leant across to him, whispered in his ear and made a very explicit hand gesture! Bloody hell Rach, make it a bit more obvious why don't you! I look to the dark haired one. His name is Sam and he's actually rather good looking, in a brooding, moody sort of way. He isn't saying much and clearly feels awkward about his friend's actions towards Rach, probably just as awkward as me so at least we have that much in common. A good place to start, I guess.

"Could they make it any more obvious?" I lean a little closer so he can hear me over the music. He looks at me then, (I don't think he's actually done that yet) and almost does a double take.

"Is your name Katie?" I'm sure I've told him this, is he stupid or taking the piss?

"Uh, yes" I look back confused at the question but as I'm looking, I see it, oh my god I know him! I went to Uni with him, Sam...Sam...

"Sam Peele" I shout it so loudly that Rach and her man stop flirting and pay attention for a minute, well about 5 seconds.

"Well shit a brick, Katie Carlin!" (I can think of nicer ways to remember someone!) his face has lit up though and so many memories come back to me. He was one of the hottest boys at Uni and omg I so would have! But never did! He always had a girl hanging off him, the high maintenance type with perfect hair and make-up and a constant rbf.

"Wow" I say nonchalantly, suddenly aware of myself and the inferior part I played at Uni, "I'm surprised you remember me, I always thought you pretty much ignored me" might as well say it like it is. He looks horrified,

"Ignore you?" Emphasis on YOU, interesting! "you were one of the hottest girls at Uni!" What the...?

"Are you taking the piss?" The words slip out of my mouth involuntarily.

"God no, loads of us lads used to talk about you all the time, you and your mate, Clare was it? You two together, steamin' hot!" Wow, not an expression I've heard for a while and it makes me feel good and bad all at the same time. Bad because this man sitting in front of me once thought I was 'steamin' hot' and I didn't realise anyone had ever thought that about me! I spent most of my Uni life working hard and thinking I was the dullest, ugliest thing alive – (I know, get the violins out). And good because I actually bloody loved Uni and he's just made it even better.

Chuffed, I down my drink and suddenly relax. "Can I get you another?" I feel like he's now coming on to me after his previous comments and... I like it....

"Yes please"

"What was it?" He says looking at my glass (oh shit I've just downed that cocktail!)

"That was an Easy Rider but I don't need another one of those."

"Is that because it's done its job?" He smiles at me, in a suggestive and cheeky way and I warm to him even more. It is more than likely the vodka talking but I reply with,

"Get me another drink and maybe you'll find out?" Oh dear, was that cheesy or even necessary? Doesn't seem to matter, he is off to the bar to get me a drink so can't be too offended (as long as he comes back!) I sit for a minute and think of my friend Clare, if she could see me now, flirting with Sam Peele, she'd be so jealous. He's back quickly, he sits much closer to me now and I like it. The warmth of his leg against mine is actually making me a bit horny and I'm starting to imagine where this night could go. Would that be cheating on Matt? I mean, in theory he's cheating on me all the time with another woman so surely it's ok for me...before my thought gets any further, I hear Sam repeating my name... "Katie, Katie, what do you think?" I look at him confused "do you wanna dance?" Oh blimey,

"That's not really something I usually do" sod that, "but as it's you asking, I'm dancing" more cheese but again he doesn't seem to mind it and so we are up on the dance floor. I'm pretty drunk and feel free for the first time in ages, no hiding away and being a good girl, I let rip, I'm enjoying the attention Sam is giving me and why shouldn't I? I suddenly feel like I deserve this and it's my turn to let my hair down and have some fun. It's not as if I've been living like a nun but I have this realisation that everything I've done in the last three years has been careful and considered so as not to draw attention to myself (and Matt) and now all I want to do is break free. And I am. Sam is getting more confident too and we are starting to touch each other as we dance, his hands feel nice on me, we move quite well together (played back in daylight I'm sure it would be a car crash but it's working for us right now). We get closer and closer until I can feel his breath on my cheek and then we're kissing, his tongue quickly finding its way inside my mouth and me returning the favour. I have no idea where anyone else is right now, they might be staring at us in disbelief or horror but I simply don't care. I'm in the arms of Sam Peele and it's like I'm back at Uni again, but with confidence and sass and fuck it, I'm loving it!

An hour later, I'm letting us in to my flat, he's come back with me for coffee (well why not) I mean I actually said that to him "do you want to come back to my place for a coffee?"

And so here we are. Giggling our way into the flat as I struggle to find the keyhole and then can't push the door open (so very drunk right now). We tumble through the door together and find ourselves kissing and tearing each other's clothes off (there's no point in small talk or coffee, we both know why we're here and we both know that it's a one-night stand with no strings, which is perfect for me right now).

It's strange kissing another man after all this time, it's weird how people kiss differently or touch you differently. I think of Matt, fleetingly, and how he would be touching me right now but my mind is quickly back on Sam as he undoes my bra (in a Joey from Friends moment) and he pushes me down on to the sofa. He's on top of me and I can feel how excited he is, it turns me on more and I push against him wanting him desperately but my mind is suddenly on Matt again and the fact that this is OUR sofa and I don't really want to ruin that (don't get me wrong, I am totally going to have sex with Sam, just not on the sofa.) So I expertly manoeuvre him into the bedroom and taking control, push him on to the bed and check out his muscly, shaved chest - his body is like an Australian surfer, a little fantasy of mine, thanks to Home and Away and the Braxton brothers! I run my hands all over his smooth skin and feel how much he wants me. I'm going to really enjoy this.

Sunday 8.15am

I'm lying on my bed staring at the ceiling. Sam left

about 10 minutes ago and I'm not sure whether to laugh, smile, go to sleep or cry! I feel exhausted, physically and mentally exhausted. What a night! After we'd had sex, we started talking about our Uni days and how much fun we'd had. It was so natural talking to him and lying next to him naked without having to worry about covering up my fat bits. We talked about relationships. He'd been in a long term one until about three months ago, mutual ending-of apparently but he was a bit messed up by it all the same, I think I'm the first person he's slept with since, so think I was a bit of a rebound shag, which is fine, I don't see it as anything more. He was very courteous and gentlemanly and said and did all the right things at the right time. Nice sex, not hugely exciting though. It was the talking all night that's exhausted me, that and my usual over thinking everything. The innocent and 'fun' me of my Uni days has gone and that's what happens when you grow up I guess. I didn't tell Sam about Matt. There were moments (including during sex) when I couldn't stop thinking that I was cheating on Matt. Like I'm now doubly worse because not only am I having an affair with someone but now I've cheated on the affairee which makes me a double cheat who is hurting two people, three if you count me too! Ahhh! Here I go, over thinking again, just switch off for a minute, get some sleep, it's Sunday morning, you're allowed! I close my eyes and just as I'm starting to drift off, my phone pings. I consider not looking at who it is, quietly contemplating whether it's Sam or Matt or Rach or... I pick it up, it's a text from Rach:

What the f happened to you last night? You and that guy were really going for it on the dance floor, thought you were actually going to start having sex at one point! Good going though lady, was impressed with your moves, hope he was too No such thing as a short text from Rach, she's an advocate of bringing traditional letter writing back!

I think about what to say and, to be honest, don't want to share too much. I'll turn it back to her,

Yeah, sorry, must've been that bloody cocktail, I was so drunk. How did it go with his mate? No mention of Sam, keep it simple.

Well..... the shortest text she'd ever sent, *I'm still with him now, amazing night. So, we both pulled! Not bad for two 30 somethings!* followed by several smiling emojis.

We arrange to meet up on Wednesday for a debrief. I start to drop off again and another ping. I look at my phone, it's Matt. Guilt.

Hey gorgeous, can I come see you? Had an early market run and have an hour before I need to get home *Depends* I reply, cryptically. Does he really think he can just squeeze me in for a shag between work and wife!

On what...? comes his expected reply. I'm feeling pretty angry with him. Not really his fault, just got myself worked up at the fact that I would normally drop everything for him to pop by, the guilt has gone though.

On whether you can face seeing me throwing up! I'm a bit green after my night out with Rach I lie. I don't feel hung over at all, just don't think it'd be appropriate for him to come over when I haven't even showered after Sam and he needs to know that I'm not just his bootie call. So what am I then? What do I want to be? What do I really want from Matt? I know he was in my head last night when he shouldn't have been, I know that I can't stop thinking about where we are going, so what do I want?

Ok, shame, was wanting to try out a new recipe on you for breakfast xx oh bugger, he wasn't expecting sex, he actually wanted to see me and ask my opinion and that must mean he values my opinion and values me…(careful where you're going with this!) and...another ping,

That and fuck you senseless!! oh, and there it is, as

I suspected, I'm his bootie call. I now wish I'd just told him the truth and said 'sorry Matt but I'm totally shagged out after last night with this guy I met in a bar, we were at it all night' but that might just open a can of worms I'm not willing to open just yet. I don't reply, sometimes silence says more, I fall asleep feeling a little incensed.

CHAPTER SIX

Monday

I've decided, I need to focus on me a bit this week. I'm always available for people (Matt) and need to make myself less so. Not to prove any points or make him try harder, just to bloody well be me. (I need to find myself again, stoned hippy voice over)

My Sunday pretty much consisted of sleep and trashy telly and (obviously) a lot of over thinking. Over thinking Matt, Sam, work, life, going round in circles really and longing for some sort of answer but coming up with sweet f.a. There is one thing I decided though, I need to find a new job or get a promotion. I am currently a marketing assistant for a small fashion label (which is completely ridiculous as I'm the least fashionable person I know). My job consists of me posting ads on social media, which means I'm always on it and that's probably why I have so many insecurities, and sending mail shots to potential buyers and customers. It's an exciting life, I even get to go to big opening nights or gala evenings (once!). But apart from that it's fairly dull. So, I need a new challenge! But what? Could change tack completely, try something new? But now I have experience in this job, it'd certainly be easier to remain in it.

"Kate, how long you gonna be with that latest update?" His voice cuts across my thought, (I haven't actually done any work for about 20 minutes, too busy day-dreaming about new horizons)

"Sorry Tim" he's my boss, "I'll get it sorted now, just a problem with the formatting" I lie! (Again! Becoming an easy habit?)

"Don't worry, I'm not having a go" he smiled at me, not really seen that smile before, what's happening here then? "Just wondering if you want to join me for lunch, think I'm gonna try that new place round the corner and need a bud to come with" he's a bit smooth, (or tries to be) speaks like he would have been a yuppie if born in the 80s, 'yeah man, like, you know...' posh and thick, although not so thick, he's doing pretty well in this business. He owns it with his brother, (bit of a nob) and they're doing pretty well with their designs. "What do you think?" He labours, "join me?"

"Why not" I say, "could do with a bit of lunch" I save the press release, pick up my bag and stand up to meet his gaze.

"You look lovely today" (oh crap, what is this about?) he's softening me up for something, am I getting the sack?

"Are you sacking me?" I blurt it out before we've even stepped away from my desk.

"What?" He chokes, "don't be silly, I mean, no I'm, well, I did want to talk to you..." awkward pause while I stare at him and he looks away, "actually yes, I'm really sorry but we just can't afford to keep you on"

I don't know what to say to that, I wasn't expecting to lose my job today!

"Do I have to leave now or are you still buying me lunch?" I try to joke,

"Well I never actually said I'd buy you lunch" wow he's a proper laugh isn't he! "I just suggested we go for lunch" alright, idiot, think you're missing the point! "Right, well..." Awkward! "...I'll be off then. Not sure you'd really enjoy lunch now anyway" bloody hell, what kind of a git is he! I know it's probably not nice to sack someone but give me a break here.

So, that pretty much conclusively sorted my idea that I need a new job. Be careful what you wish for! I'm sitting in the cafe down the road from work (old work ha!) drinking a bottomless coffee when what I really need is a big fat gin! What the hell just happened! They can't just sack me on the spot, surely there's a notice period and all that but I actually don't know, have never been in this situation before! I need to talk to someone and my first thought is Matt but he'll be busy at the restaurant right now so Rach it is.

My text to her is simple *just got sacked* her reply is quaint,

Wtf? And so after I've explained in a bit more detail we arrange to meet for a drink later so I can drown my sorrows. Feeling pretty deflated and unwanted to tell the truth! Need to have a word with myself, it's only a job! So why, then, do I feel like I've been rejected for the third time this week? First Sam (friend zone), then Matt (only wants me for sex) and now work, the universe is trying to tell me something. Or giving me a huge boot up the arse!

I'm about to get up and leave but I'm distracted by a bit of a fuss at the counter. There aren't many customers in the shop so it's quiet until the woman at the counter starts shouting!

"I can't afford that" she says, shocked, "all I wanted was a coffee." The barista looks unmoved.

"That is a coffee madam" bit of a patronising tone, "and everyone has to pay, we are not a soup kitchen" ouch! Bit uncalled for. The woman doesn't look homeless or anything but she's not budging on paying. I look round the other tables and everyone else is looking away, anywhere but at the woman, (if you can't see it, it's not happening!)

Should I help her pay? Maybe she's causing a fuss because she's embarrassed and actually can't afford it.

"Hey, would you like to borrow some money for your coffee?" not me but a man at the counter standing next to her. "or I'll just get it for you if you want?" the man is a bit sheepish, looks like he's challenging himself, he looks really uncomfortable and the 'piss off' look on the woman's face isn't exactly encouraging his good deed. "or not" he squeaks, confidence definitely lacking in this one.

"For god sake" the woman utters under her breath, reaches for her purse and eventually gives the barista the money before walking to the door. As she gets there, she turns round and locks eyes with me, she smiles and something in me wants to go with her. I was getting up anyway. I walk towards the door, she is still holding it open, and we both walk out, kind of together, it's a bit weird.

"I'm Lucy" she beams at me.

"Kate" I share. Shit, I think she's just picked me up! How is this happening?

"Sorry about the fuss back there, just wanted to get your attention, thought you might offer to pay for my coffee but that prick got in there first" I am dumbstruck, what the hell is happening here? Have I been hypnotised and she's going to steal my purse and flat key and leave me lying in a back alley while she goes off to live my life with my identity? Thinking a little too much again!

"So, Kate" she looks right into my eyes, "It's lovely to meet you, would you like to find a bar and have a drink with me?" Shit shit shit, she actually thinks she's pulled! I must look a little confused as she giggles, she has a breath-taking smile...what is happening? Did someone spike my coffee and I'm drugged up with rohypnol? Am I in a dream, maybe I'm not awake, I didn't lose my job today and I'm still drunk after Saturday night…

"Kate, are you ok?" I've stopped walking and I'm staring at the floor, the thoughts in my head are overwhelming but all I can really think about is getting another drink to numb the pain of losing my job and contemplating what the hell I'm going to do for money…

"Kate?" she's still there, "I'm sorry, that was really

forward of me, it's just, I saw you in there and you looked a bit down" she moves closer to me in a protective gesture "don't worry, I'm not a mad psycho about to bash you over the head and steal your bag" (people actually do read my mind!) I snap out of my day-dream and reply with,

"Do you fancy going to the Gin bar on Exeter Street? I really need a drink" these words fall out of my mouth so naturally, it must be what I want to do. So, we do.

Fifteen minutes later we're sat at the bar, better than a private table, (less awkward) and we're chatting like old friends. Lucy is a journalist. She works for a magazine in the City but is mostly freelance so works from home. She has a cat called Piper and lives with a girl who she occasionally shags when they're both feeling horny…apparently. She's very open about everything and it's kind of refreshing. Having spent the last three years being guarded about every part of my life, I envy her freedom to share her life with a complete stranger. I'm not so forthcoming. I do tell her that I lost my job and that's why I'm feeling so low but nothing else about how messed up my life is right now.

We down several gins in the space of an hour and I'm feeling drunk…again. Making a habit of getting pissed with strangers. I'm not really sure if she's interested in me or what she is expecting but I'm enjoying the attention so I'm going with it for now. Does she think I'm gay? Maybe she does…I'm not really doing anything to discourage her. I wonder what it would be like. She's very attractive. I mean, if I was gay, she'd definitely be my type (what am I saying? This gin is too strong!)

"You have the most beautiful eyes" again this is me talking and I'm not embarrassed by what I'm saying. I do think that though, she has stunningly beautiful eyes and I can't stop looking into them.

"Do you want to go somewhere?" her this time and now I'm a little more conscious…she must see the slight panic in my eyes as she back tracks a little "sorry was that too much too soon?" she sits back to put a bit of physical distance between us, she is so thoughtful and sensitive…I am so drunk.

"Lucy, look…I'm not…um…"

"ready for this…looking for anything serious…gay?" she finishes my sentence and to be honest it's not far from what I was going to say and then… "sometimes you just need to give things a go and see what happens". She smiles and I do actually get that feeling again, the fluttering heart, the blood pulsing…I'm actually thinking about it..

"Here" she hands me a piece of paper, "it's my number, if you want to see me again then just give me a call, no pressure" and that's it. She stands up, smiles at me one more time and leaves. Wow, she's good, she knows how to make someone want something they didn't even know they were capable of wanting, and then walks away leaving said person wanting it even more. Wow, what a day!

CHAPTER SEVEN

Tuesday 8am

When I got home last night, I spoke to Rach, told her about the pick-up and cried about losing my job and she told me to get a grip and start looking for a new one, job that is, not lesbian life partner.

So, that's my mission today. Get a job, whatever it is. It's an opportunity to try something new. Maybe I could be a barista, I do love coffee, I wonder if they're allowed to drink as much as they want. Maybe that's why all baristas are so lively, maybe they're completely…my phone pings and stops my train of thought. It's a bit early for a Matt text. I look at the screen, it's Fay, Matt's wife! I haven't been in touch with her for months. I'm suddenly nervous. Does she know? I open the message:

Hi Kate, hope you're ok, Matt told me about your job. A friend of mine has an opening in sales if you're interested. Just thought it might tide you over for a while. Let me know what you think xx

Kisses at the end strike the guilt chord with me. I haven't felt it for a while. It's easier to pretend she doesn't exist and act like it's a real relationship I'm having with Matt instead of an affair. I can't even remember telling Matt I'd lost my job so apart from the shock of receiving a text from her, it seems I drank so much I lost my memory.

I won't reply yet. It's quite sweet of her to try to help me but there's no way I can say yes. The last thing I need is to be beholden to Fay in some way.

My phone pings again, it's Matt.

Don't be cross but I think Fay is going to text you, I told her about you losing your job and she wants to help.
Bit late Matt. I'm pretty uncaring about these texts right

now, feeling pretty numb and a little hung over although I've got off lightly considering. I wander to the kitchen, phone in hand and make myself a coffee. I remember the coffee shop yesterday and Lucy and I smile into my cup, feeling flattered that someone was attracted to me. Then, I text Lucy. I put her number in my phone last night and have stared at it on and off all night. She's in my head. My text is simple:

Really loved talking with you yesterday, sorry if I was a bit drunk, Kate x

And then I sit and watch my phone. Waiting for an immediate reply as obviously she was so into me that she has been waiting for my text all night and will want to reply quickly so she doesn't miss her chance with me…. I keep staring at my phone…take a sip of coffee… nothing…I keep staring at it… nothing…

The words 'wake up and smell the coffee' hit me harshly in the face as I realise I'm in a stupid dreamworld and need to snap out of it. Who am I kidding! I go to the bathroom and take a shower, leaving my phone on the kitchen table so I'm not tempted to check it anymore. Feeling more stupid than attractive now, I get dressed quickly and try to get my focus back to job hunting (not very successful so far). There must be something out there I could do well. I've had quite a few jobs which probably doesn't look great on a cv, does it? I once worked in a chocolate shop but that didn't last long as I told a customer that they'd be better off getting a nice Dairy Milk instead of this fancy expensive stuff. Then I worked in a hotel as a chamber maid, shittiest job, shittiest sheets, (literally sometimes). Then I tried an admin job which was actually ok but it was temporary, covering for someone on maternity leave and that was that. Maybe I should do one of those career quizzes to see what I really want to do. Maybe I should be a bit more serious about my life, stop playing at relationships and jobs and actually grow up a bit. Is everyone like this? Or is it just me? I simply have no clue about what I'm good at. Maybe it comes from the insecurities of childhood, not knowing which path to follow, being a bit of a sheep. My degree is in Creative Studies. I mean, I did the damn degree for three years and I'm still not sure what I'm qualified for. Nothing?

I'm contemplating McDonald's when I notice my phone has a new message. Probably Matt, he gets a bit shirty when I don't reply straight away. It's Lucy. Feeling nervous again, I tentatively pick up my phone, I'm half expecting it to say 'really sorry but I have no clue who this is' but holy shit what it actually says is:

I loved talking to you too. Would love to see you again. Going to a friend's house-warming this Friday, would you like to come? I read a double meaning into the end of the text and then find my mind wondering to a place of pure fantasy about what it would be like to be kissed and touched by a girl, by Lucy. And I get the fluttery heart feeling again. Wow, she is good at this. I'm not completely inexperienced with girls, there was this one time at Uni when me and Clare were pissed off with men, had a couple of bottles of wine and ended up snogging for a bit. It was quite good but it never went any further. In a way, it cemented our friendship as we knew we had each other. But this with Lucy, this feels different. I'm sexually attracted to her, I want to know what it's like to be touched by her and what it's like to touch her. This is a bit crazy, it's just one of those fantasy things, if it were to happen ever, it would be short lived, and I would have fulfilled my lesbian fantasy. I think. I lie on my bed and thinking about Lucy in that way has made me horny, I slide my hand between my legs, close my eyes and imagine Lucy touching me. It's scarily good, my heart is pumping as I imagine her kissing me and flicking her fingers gently over me, I'm groaning with pleasure when my phone pings again…maybe it's her again…I look at the message and it's Matt which strangely takes away the horniness and brings me back down to earth. Oh well.

CHAPTER EIGHT

Friday

Is it a date? I can't decide what to wear. It's a housewarming, so casual should be ok but should I be trying to look good to impress Lucy? I really don't know what I'm doing. Am I leading her on? Maybe I should cancel. Maybe I should text and say I'm ill. Maybe I should…aggghhhh, maybe I should do something for myself and stop worrying about upsetting someone else all the time, why do I do that? I bet nobody thinks about me in that way, Matt included.

"Hey" I answer the door to her and as soon as I see her I feel more at ease. I've gone for jeggings and a loose fitting top with my denim jacket and a blue scarf, I feel good, maybe even confident and by the look on Lucy's face, I'm pretty sure she approves.

"You look great" she says, "come on, I've got a taxi waiting, you ready?" she really does have beautiful eyes and her smile…what is happening to me?

"So," she looks at me as we settle into the taxi, "how was the job interview?" I text Lucy on Wednesday to tell her I had an interview for an admin assistant at a Law Firm. It was a strange interview, nobody really seemed to know what they were doing, including me, it clearly wasn't meant to be from the start but I went on with it, trying to impress, lying through my teeth about my admin skills and smiling all the time to show how keen I was to get the job whereas in reality there was absolutely no way I would accept it even if they offered it to me. It was a creepy place, the kind of place you'd see in a Tim Burton film, little bit Willy Wonka/Beetlejuice minus the costumes, I felt like I would either be sucked up a tube any second or run out of the room followed by a man in a stripy jacket. It all just went to prove that job hunting these days is difficult and I hate it. So, no job yet.

"It was ok" I lie, "said they'd let me know next week." Don't really know why I didn't tell her the truth, just feel a bit of a failure when it comes to jobs and I don't want her to see that. She must sense my self-doubt because she reaches over and covers my hand with hers, it makes me look right at her and she smiles again, makes me feel the flutters again.

"Here we are" the taxi driver's voice cuts through our eye contact and Lucy lets go of my hand. She's nice, really nice. I'm seriously confused.

The house is beautiful and bloody big! I was expecting a semi in the suburbs but bloody hell, Lucy clearly has better connections than I have given her credit for. Not that I've really thought about it that much. Don't know a huge amount about any part of her life let alone what kind of friends she has. As we walk through the entrance hall (yes the entrance hall, not a porch an actual bloody entrance hall with hat stand and fancy tiles on the floor) I can hear the party is well under way, there's music and voices and laughter coming from a room towards the back of the house, the kitchen I think.

Lucy air kisses a couple of friends (bit pretentious) as we walk through the house. I can't help noticing the staircase and the oak doors throughout the hallway, so many doors leading to god knows where, it's huge and I'm suddenly feeling a little under dressed. Lucy must sense my trepidation because once again she grabs my hand,

"Come on" she reassures me, "it's not all that!" I smile and we walk into the vast kitchen, it's double the size of my flat, (like the whole flat, not just my kitchen), holding hands and it's bustling with people. I don't feel so ill at ease now as they all look fairly normal. Lucy drags me through the crowd to the sideboard where the drinks are and we help ourselves to a glass of wine each.

"Cheers" she says clinking my glass. "I'm really glad you're here" she smiles at me again, that smile.

"Me too" I reply taking a sip of my drink as I start to look round the room over the top of my glass and nearly spit my drink out as I see Matt and Fay coming towards us!

What the actual fuck! I'm suddenly frozen to the ground and feel like I've been caught out in more ways than one, the guilt floods in and I literally can't move. Lucy frowns as my expression changes and she follows my gaze.

"You ok? You've gone really pale." No shit! Take a breath Kate, calm down, nobody knows anything, nobody can actually read your mind. It's going to be fine. Shit, they've seen me and they're heading straight for us. What the hell is he doing here, of all the people Lucy knows, how the fuck can she know the same people as Matt? This world is uncomfortably small right now.

Fay speaks first and comes at me for a hug, "Kate, oh my god, I can't believe it's you, we haven't seen you for, like, ages!" You say 'we' but I was actually with your husband eight nights ago (shit has it been that long since I've seen Matt!) Fay hugs me (fake hugs me) and I look at Matt over her shoulder, he still has that effect on me, makes me tingle and feel breathless but right now I'm pretty sure the breathlessness is due to the lack of oxygen to my brain. How is this happening? Matt's expression is fairly normal, he's good at pretending everything is normal. It's Lucy that looks at him sideways while she observes my angst and then quickly looks back to me, she seems to read me really easily, maybe it's the inquisitive journalist look, maybe she's suss about everything?! Or, maybe once again, I'm just super paranoid.

Fay eventually lets go and Matt also hugs me. I suppose it would look a bit weird if he didn't. He smells good, I've missed his smell, I've missed him. And now he's here in front of me I realise just how much. Damn it.

"How's the job hunting going?" Fay enquires, "I was so sorry to hear you'd lost your job, wanted to help you out but you didn't reply, did you get my text?" she sounds a bit sour and I feel less guilt instantly, remembering exactly what she can be like and that tone she uses round me like I'm not good enough.

"Kate's had an interview this week for a top Law firm in the City" Lucy chips in when I say nothing, I'd almost forgotten she was there. Matt and Fay both look at her as if she'd suddenly appeared from nowhere…introductions, ummm…

"Sorry, where are my manners, this is Lucy, a friend of mine" I look at Lucy and hope she doesn't mind being described as a friend, (not sure how else I'd describe her, maybe: 'this is Lucy, the first girl I've ever wanted to shag' or 'meet Lucy, someone who gets me just as horny as your husband' or maybe just a simple 'this is Lucy, she's a lesbian and I'm contemplating giving that a go as your husband has been shagging me for three whole years and shows no sign of commitment' maybe not!) Lucy seems fine with my description and politely shakes Fay's and then Matt's hand. I can see Matt's eyes constantly flashing to me and I'm trying desperately not to make eye contact with him as I think I will blush and give the game away. To be honest, Lucy seems to read me so well, I think she can see it a mile off.

"So how did it go?" Fay asks me.

"It seemed to go ok but you never can tell, not sure I liked it to be honest" Fay puts a patronising hand on my shoulder and does the head tilt to show me sympathy for being so hopeless in life. Yep, definitely no guilt left in me now, more a desire to stick it to her in the best way I can so I say,

"What about you Fay, is Matt still working too hard

and making you paranoid?" wow where did that even come from? I've only had two sips of wine (nope, a look at my empty glass tells me I've been 'sipping' it far too fast and it's beginning to show!) Matt goes bright red and clenches his teeth making his cheeks ripple (so sexy) and Fay squirms a little, obviously remembering the fact she asked me to confront Matt about whether he was having an affair. Matt puts his arm round her and says:

"Paranoid? Fay? As if, why would I possibly look at another woman when I have this beautiful lady in my life?" he's looking directly at me when he says it and I'm genuinely unsure whether the beautiful lady he mentioned is me or his wife? She looks at him and there's an awkward moment between them, I don't think she believes a word he says. And, if I didn't know better, I'd say their whole relationship looks like an act right now. I'm starting to feel trapped, as if this conversation could bring out so many truths (or lies) and once again Lucy rescues me,

"Sorry, do you mind if I steal Kate away? I really want her to meet a friend of mine, lovely to meet you both," and she takes my hand and pulls me away from the most awkward situation I've ever been in. We make our way out to the garden through the French windows, the party has spilled out here and there are so many people here. I have no idea whose house I'm in but I'm starting to wish I had made my excuses earlier and not come.

Lucy pulls me over to a little wall where we sit down and she hands me another glass of wine which she must have grabbed as we walked away from the scene from hell. I down it, as she seems to anticipate and then just looks at me with a wry smile and raised eye-brows.

"What?" I say, she raises her eyebrows further and almost laughs…

"What the bloody hell was that?" she's smiling and clearly found the whole debacle quite funny which I guess is better than her being pissed off with me for virtually ignoring her. "Well? Are you going to share or am I going to have to guess? 'cos I've got my own theory about what just happened and I'm not sure you want me to share it"

"Sorry Lucy, I wasn't expecting to see anyone I know, let alone…" I shut down,

"Let alone someone you used to shag" she looks at me still smiling but a little shocked. I don't know what to say so I keep quiet. "And what was that line about her being paranoid? What the hell happened between you lot?" I still say nothing. "It's none of my business and to be honest, I don't really give a shit what you've done, but that was intense" I look at her and can't help but see the funny side of it, we both start to laugh and the reality of what just happened hits me.

"God Lucy, I'm so sorry" I'm still giggling and so is she.

"It's ok, it's ok" she reassures me and then, "You have such a gorgeous laugh." Of course that stops my laugh straight away as I become conscious of it (as usual) but she smiles and makes me feel reassured once again.

We sit and chat for about ten minutes as if nothing at all weird happened and then I head to the loo and she says she'll get us some more drinks.

I've been reliably informed that there's another loo upstairs as there's a bit of a queue for the downstairs toilet. I make my way up the very grand staircase, there are photos on the walls and I realise I still don't know whose house and party this is. Nobody looks familiar in the photos so hopefully I won't be embarrassing myself any further tonight. I find the bathroom but just as I'm closing the door a hand pushes it open, and Matt pushes past me, pulls me into the bathroom and shuts the door behind us. Oh fuck!

"What the hell was that?" he asks, he's really flapping "I've just had to spend the last fifteen minutes calming

Fay down, why did you say that? Why would you jeopardise my marriage in that way?"

Wow, did he actually just say that!

"Me, jeopardise your marriage, are you kidding me? You've willingly jeopardised your marriage for the last three years and you've got the nerve to say that to me?" he's clearly shocked by my tone.

"Kate, what the hell's got into you? Are you drunk? This isn't like you?"

"What isn't like me? The fact that I just stood up for myself? That I just did something that made you feel threatened? Or did you not like the fact that I'm out with somebody else? Do you think you're the only person who gets to spend time with me? Do you think I'm your possession or something? Who do you think you are Matt? All you ever do is shag me then leave, then send me a few texts to keep me interested and then I'm left with nothing but being alone and confused and wondering if that time was the last time and…"

"OK, ok I'm sorry, Kate, I'm sorry, what's going on?" I can feel tears pricking in my eyes, the last thing I want to do now is cry. Matt sees it too, "Oh Kate" he pulls me to him "I'm sorry baby" his arms around me make me melt into him, I've missed him so much but this can't happen, I need to be stronger. We don't speak for a few seconds and then he says,

"What do you mean you're out with someone else? Do you mean that girl?" There seems to be a little giggle in his tone. I stand back from him and look up at him. He's smiling.

"Yes Matt, I mean Lucy. We're on a sort of date" his face turns serious and then he frowns with confusion.

"Am I missing something?" then he smiles "Shit I think I'm getting a hard-on, you and her together"

"Oh my god, you complete and utter prat, is that all you can think about?" What a tosser, how is that the first thought he has, not jealousy, not concern but, Woah yeah I'd like to have a threesome with you two'. I mean at another time, on a night when I wasn't feeling quite so emotional, maybe that would have crossed my mind too because actually…wow both Matt and Lucy touching me, wanting me, it would be… OK enough, back to annoyed feminist stance.

"I'm sorry" he looks sheepish realising how much of a dick he sounded "Kate I'm sorry I…"

"So you keep saying" I interrupt. "Kate can you just let me speak?" I'm silent. "I'm missing you, you've been distant this last week and I don't know why. I thought we were ok, I thought we agreed to carry on as before and then I barely hear from you all week, what's going on?" I sit down on the edge of the roll-top bath and consider my answer. He suddenly looks broken, like I've hurt him. I feel a bit bad and a bit lost. I'm so desperately in love with him; it's pathetic. The song going round my head is 'sometimes love just ain't enough' and I have to bite my lip to stop myself breaking into it, that might be the final straw and I don't really want to lose him, do I?

"Matt, I'm sorry, but I don't think…" before I can finish the sentence he pulls me towards him and covers my lips with his, for a moment I let it happen but I find a strength and push him away, "No Matt, you can't just do that every time I try to end it" is that what I'm doing?

"Don't say that Kate, please, I love you." Fuck! We stare at each other with a kind of hopelessness.

"Do you? Don't you think if you really loved me you'd be moving heaven and earth to be with me?"

"You know it's not that simple, Kate, I have to consider so much more than you do" another heart string cut. And I know he's right, he does have more to lose but this shouldn't be how love feels.

"That's the problem Matt, we both expect too much from each other in a situation that's never going to change" god I sound quite sensible and switched on. "We've been having an affair for three years but that's all it's ever going to be, an affair, you have too much to lose and I just don't have anything to give anymore"

"I'll leave her, I love you"

"And what, come and live with me in my shitty little flat? Think about it Matt"

"I think about nothing else, I wish my life was with you,"

"But it's not. And unless you're willing to make massive changes, possibly lose your career and restaurant Matt, you know how vile the media can be, then this…us…just isn't possible anymore"

Silence.

He looks defeated. What have I done? Is this what I want? He moves towards the door and I think that's it. Should I stop him? Pull him back, tell him I was wrong and the truth is I never want to lose him…

"I'll never give up on us Kate" and with that comment, that hopeless hopeful comment, he walks out and I'm left feeling lost and alone once more.

I find Lucy chatting with a girl in the hallway. She sees me and smiles.

"Lucy I'm sorry but I'm not feeling great, I'm going to go home" she looks deflated. "I'm sorry" I repeat.

"I'll come with you, make sure you're ok?"

"Don't be daft, stay and enjoy the party, I don't want to ruin it for both of us". As we're talking Matt and Fay walk past us, making their way to the front door, I watch them leave as Lucy watches me.

"Let me come with you" Lucy insists, "if you don't mind, I'd like to". She smiles and I want her to stay with me, I need her to take me home.

Lucy takes the key off me and unlocks the door to my 'shitty little flat'. I can't quite believe I said those things to Matt, the conversation keeps playing over in my head, it's been a long time coming. I filled Lucy in on the way back, not all the details but enough to explain why I was no longer in the party mood.

She puts the kettle on and I slump on the couch. I'm feeling…glum…perfectly glum. There's no better word right now. It's weird, I know that ending things with Matt was the right thing to do but it doesn't feel good. Doing the right thing doesn't always make you feel good. That's what Lucy told me anyway. She's right, of course. She always seems to know what to say or do to make me feel better. She comes in with two mugs and puts them on the table in front of me.

"How you feeling now?" she says as she sits down next to me on the sofa.

"Like a fool" I reply.

"A fool for ending it?"

"No, a fool for letting it go on so long and a fool for messing things up with you tonight" I look at her hoping she's ok with all this. I'm not sure what I want from her right now but I like her being here and I'd feel even more lost if she were to walk away too. Again, she reassures me,

"You haven't messed things up with me" she sees my angst "you haven't" she smiles and touches my arm.

"What a car crash of a first date" I half laugh as I say it.

"Is that what this was?" she questions. I'm feeling a bit awkward now, perhaps I shouldn't have said that.

"I don't know" I retract, "Sorry, I'm so confused about everything tonight"

"Look Kate, let's be honest with each other, neither of us really knows what this is yet but I think we both quite like each other and whether that turns out to be a friendship or something else then let's not analyse it too much right now. You're a bit messed up about this Matt guy and need a bit of time and if you want me here to talk then that's cool. Ok?"

"I don't know"

"Don't know what?"

"I don't know if that's ok." She looks confused. "I've never had a relationship with a woman before and I don't want you to think that I know what I'm doing because I don't. I feel like you might like me and I don't want to lead you on but…"

"you'd quite like to experiment with me?" she smiles which makes me smile too.

"well kind of, yeah"

"That's pretty honest" her smile is contagious and she seems to appreciate me being up front with her, I think. "Can I just try something?" I feel a bit anxious now.

"I guess"

"Trust me Kate?" she raises her eyebrows and I nod. Then she moves closer to me on the sofa and places her hand on my cheek. I feel all sorts of sensations and I can't really make sense of any of them right now. Then, she leans closer and gently brushes my lips with hers. My eyes are open as I'm not really sure what I'm expected to do right now but I want her to do that again. "Close your eyes" she whispers, reading my mind again. So I do and I feel her breath on my lips as she moves closer again and kisses me. I don't really move, I just let it happen. And then she sits back. I open my eyes and she looks a little unsure now, maybe I should have reacted. This feels like a really long silence and I decide I don't need thoughts anymore. I look her right in the eye and I say:

"Do that again?" she smiles and as she moves towards me I close my eyes and my mouth opens as her lips touch mine and suddenly I'm aching for her to touch me; longing to feel her hands on my skin. I adjust my position on the sofa so I'm more in control and push my body towards hers so that I can feel her against me. Shit what am I doing? How did this happen? This is just a rebound and surely she must see that. Maybe she just wants sex so it doesn't matter how she gets it. Bit harsh. We start to lay back on the sofa so that her body is under mine and I can feel her pushing up towards me, jesus this is hot, I thrust my tongue deep into her mouth; she tastes of wine and…

"Kate" she starts to push me away. Shit. I pull away and look down at her. "You ok?" she says.

"umm" I ease myself off her and fall on to the floor. I'm so sorry, I just…"

"It's fine, I get it, you're a nought to sixty kind of girl" she giggled.

"No, I'm really not, I usually think far too much about something before I actually do it but when you kissed me I just wanted…well…I wanted you" I can't bring myself to look at her, feeling like I've done it all wrong and she's rejecting me.

"Kate, it's fine, you haven't done anything wrong" reading my mind again? "I just thought we should stop in case you regret it and that's the last thing I want, I want you but I want it to be right." Sounds a bit serious, not sure that's what I'm after?

"And I meant what I said, if I'm the person you choose to experiment with then as long as we're both cool with that, let's have some fun. But let's just take it a bit slower." Christ, I really like her, she speaks so much sense. It's like she knows me better than anyone. I turn round to face her and kneel up towards her.

"I'm sorry for coming on too strong" I touch her cheek and stroke her soft skin. "I think you're right, let's take it slowly".

Saturday

I'm lying awake on the bed next to Lucy. We're both fully clothed and ended up chatting for most of the night, (this keeps happening, a bit of a fumble with someone and then talking, rock and roll). We wanted to be more comfortable so came into the bedroom but I don't think at that point either of us had intentions of doing anything but talking and sleeping. So that's what we did.

I'm staring at the ceiling and listening to her breathe. I turn my head to look at her and she still looks gorgeous. One of those people who wake up with a perfect complexion and no smudged panda eyes. That's a skill right there. I quietly start to move but her voice stops me:

"Stay" she says in a dormouse tone, I'm not sure if she's actually awake, as this is my bedroom and I'm wondering if she's forgotten where she is and who she's with. I'm obviously not leaving as it's my flat. I continue to get up off the bed and she seems to have gone back to sleep, I tiptoe out of the bedroom and make my way to the kitchen to make some coffee.

I decide to have a cup in the kitchen by myself so I can check my phone. No messages from Matt. I really want to text him but I guess that won't do either of us any good right now. I open my texts from him and start to type…*hope you're ok* but as I do Lucy walks into the kitchen so I stop and don't press send. She doesn't say anything but looks at me and smiles,

"Wow, you still look gorgeous" what I thought about her. Maybe we just admire each other, it's probably just a mutual grown up admiration thing, right? She walks over to me, I'm leaning against the sink, she doesn't stop, she just kisses me, frames my face with her hands and I can feel nothing but passion and want and I'm suddenly horny again like I was waiting for this moment and didn't even realise it. I'm kissing her too and I can feel her hands making their way under my top and undoing my bra, (shit what is happening!) and then she's taking my t-shirt off and I'm naked from the waist up as she moves her tongue expertly in my mouth, flicking and pinching my nipples and then lowers her head to take my nipple between her teeth and nibbles at me gently but oh so sexily. I hear myself groan as her hand makes its way down my stomach and into my jeggings and gently but without hesitation her fingers find their way and start to stroke and flick. Oh my god, this is really happening and it feels amazing, I think I say this out loud as I hear her giggle and as she returns her mouth to mine she says 'I know' and it's like I'm in some insane fantasy that I never want to end, and oh my god, her fingers push gently as her thumb rubs and I come so hard that I go weak at the knees and nearly fall but she's there to hold me and keep me going, literally, for about five minutes, and I'm lost in her touch and I love it.

CHAPTER NINE

Wednesday

I'm finally catching up with Rach. We didn't meet last Wednesday because she had a date so we're at Luigi's again. I hadn't told her anything about Lucy before tonight and the look on her face when I start to explain what happened is incredulous. When I add Matt into the equation, and she realises I hadn't finished it with him the last time, she's a little put out.

"Sorry Rach, I didn't mean to keep it from you but I felt like I was disappointing you when I didn't manage to finish it with him before"

"Don't be daft" she rebukes "I'm not annoyed about that. I just can't believe Matt thinks you'd continue to wait around for him but more so, I can't believe that you've been with a girl" her face is in shock with a cheeky smile "did you actually…you know?" I giggle a bit at her intrigue and her embarrassment of not being able to say the words,

"Yes we actually, 'you know'" I reply "and to be honest Rach, I can't quite believe it myself and I have no idea where it's going but shit it was good." I drift off a bit thinking of the kitchen episode followed by the bedroom episode and then the shower, in fact we spent most of Saturday 'experimenting' as Lucy called it.

"So how did it end?" Rach questions.

"End?"

"Yeah, what happened when she left? I mean, I take it she left and you've not got her tied up in your bedroom or somewhere?" she smirks.

"Now there's a thought" I say and we both break out into laughter and don't stop for a minute or so. It's so good to talk to Rach again, we can share anything with each other and know there'll be no judgement.

When Lucy left the flat early on Sunday morning, we'd spent two nights together and I felt, at the time, like she knew me better than anyone else in the world. I've never felt quite so trusting of someone and it almost scared me how connected I felt to her, sexually and emotionally. Now, a few days later, I can see the reality of it all. It was great and I don't regret it but I have no idea what happens next and I'm not sure exactly what I want. Could it just be a sex thing? Could it be more? I can't see myself being in a relationship with a girl, that doesn't quite seem me. I suppose it's just added another element of confusion to my life. Rach asks the obvious question,

"Are you going to see her again?" and I have no idea of the answer.

"I mean, I guess, if she wants to…I'm not sure…I'm not sure I want to date her…"

"You mean, you just want to have sex with her again?" she looks a bit shocked.

"No, I don't"

"You don't want to have sex with her again?"

"Yes, I mean, no, well… arrgghh who knows what I want." Confusion is all mine today. "To be honest Rach, I can't stop thinking about Matt. He hasn't contacted me at all and I'm slightly gutted"

"Well, you did tell him it was over, maybe he's following your wishes for once" she bites back.

"Oh don't be like that, he's not all bad, he told me he loved me" that's what I can't stop thinking about. "Do you think he does?" I'm starting to sound needy and pathetic and it needs to stop. "Let's get drunk Rach. I need a friend who doesn't have an ulterior motive to be with me" just need some time away from confusion. Rach looks hesitant. "What? What's going on?"

"Well," she says gingerly, "I do sort of have an ulterior motive for meeting you tonight."

"What do you mean? You don't fancy me too do you?" I say laughing out loud while Rach giggles.

"No, but, look, I hope you don't mind but I spoke to a friend of mine, Rich, this bloke who used to be in the same company as me..."

"Look Rach I'm not up for anything at the moment, I know you think I should get over Matt quickly but..." she interrupts me,

"Alright, Miss Tickets on yourself, I'm not trying to set you up romantically, I'm trying to get you a job...well actually if you're up for it, I've got you a job!"

Wow, this is unexpected. I've been so lazy with job hunting.

"What do you mean, got me a job?"

"So, this guy, Rich, I used to work with is setting up his own company, same as we do, Event Management, and he needs an admin/secretary/dog's body sort of assistant so I told him about you and he'd really like you to work with him" She looks directly at me for approval. I can't quite believe it.

"Really? Without even meeting me, he wants to employ me?" Rach nods,

"I've told him how amazing you are at admin and organising and marketing" makes me sound great and I guess I am pretty good at all that, just had a bit of a knock in confidence recently, "and it might be as a sort of trial to start with to see if the two of you work well together but it's just up to you to say yes now." I'm kind of flabbergasted, not only at the thought of being employed again but at how wonderful my friend is for sorting my life out.

"Yes!" I blurt out. "Rach, thank you thank you thank you" I hug her madly and loudly screaming in her ear and getting a few funny looks from around the bar. "So when can I meet him, have you got his number, I could call him.."

"Well actually Rach, he's here, I told him to hang back so I could talk to you first but..." she looks over at the bar, there's a tall, well-dressed man sitting there with two drinks in his hands, Rach gestures him to come over and he gets up. He's kind of a young Jurgen Klopp but with shorter hair (quite hot actually... stop it!) and more of a swagger. Looks sophisticated in a hipster sort of way. He approaches us and hands Rach and me a drink each.

"Well? Has Rach talked you into working for an idiot like me?" he says slightly insecurely, "She's told me how wonderful you are and I think we'd work great together" interesting considering he doesn't even know me, Rach really has painted a picture of perfection to him.

"Are you sure you want *me* to work for you?" I ask, Rach punches my leg "You don't even know me!"

"Look, I've worked with Rach for two years and not only does she talk about you loads but she admires you and says you can turn your hand to anything so if you're willing to give it a go, then I definitely am." They're both looking at me, waiting for me to say 'yes', a smile creeps over my face,

"Yes, absolutely yes" I almost shout. This is the best news I've had for ages. Rach and him high-five in front of me like they've scored their own little goal and for the first time I notice a chemistry between them. Hold on a minute, what's going on here? She isn't just friends with Jurgen, there's more to this. Does this complicate things? What if the job doesn't work out for me? What if he dumps Rach or worse still, Rach dumps him. He might fire me then! Oh god, maybe this isn't such a good idea after all.

"Right, this calls for some champagne" Rich says as he returns to the bar. I look back to Rach who watches him walk away with a massive smile on her face, I mean she might as well have hearts for eyes. Am I some sort of pawn in their 'getting together game', oh dear, what is this?

"Rach, a question, are you and Jurgen, sorry I mean Rich, are you and him…an item?"

She looks away sheepishly, "Umm, not exactly" she says "but…"

"Oh shit, Rach, I'm not sure I should be taking a job with a potential boyfriend of yours, he's probably just taking me on to impress you and I'm not sure that's a good idea." Rich returns with a bottle of champagne and three glasses.

"Rich, Kate and I are just nipping to the ladies" (she said Ladies, she definitely likes him) Rach grabs my hand and pulls me towards the 'ladies' I guess so we can chat about it.

"Kate, don't see this as something I'm doing for me, I do like Rich but I truly think this job will be good for you. You two have great ideas and together you could really create something spectacular.

"I thought he just needed an admin assistant, not a creative director!" this job has suddenly become a whole lot more, which is fine as long as it works for everyone.

"He does, right now, but you're brilliant at this stuff, he needs someone to inspire him as he goes, to be exactly that, creative and sophisticated and I reckon that's you." She smiles at me "so yes, I do like him but my priority right now is helping my best friend out, whatever happens between me and Rich, I want you to be happy and this is perfect for you" I look at Rach and nearly start to cry, she's such a good friend looking out for me this way. We hug and I know she's right. I need this job and I'm going to take it.

Back at the table, Rich has poured us all a glass of champagne and we all toast,

"To new beginnings" Rich says and we all clink. He looks at Rach and winks, think he really likes her.

"So" he starts (will have to knock that out of him,

can't stand people who start every sentence with 'So…') Kate, I've hired a space down in Clapham, it's not much at the moment but it's got a computer and a desk and even a chair," he says with sarcasm " So." (ffs) "How about we meet there tomorrow and get started. First thing we need to think about is furniture, then marketing, which I know you're great at and then bagging our first customers. How about it?" He holds his glass up and we clink again,

"Can't wait" I say. And I can't, this could be the best thing that's happened to me in ages.

CHAPTER TEN

Thursday

Next morning and I arrive at my new work place at 8.30am. We arranged to meet in the 'space' he's hired and its pretty basic but definitely something to work with. Rich tasks me with the design of the place, it's basically an open plan large office. He says it's up to me how it looks but specifies that he'd like a cosy zone for clients; an office area; a creative work zone where we can bounce ideas off one another and a sales/marketing area where hopefully before long we'll be able to display all our 'look at the wonderful events we've created' photos. He's told me I've got £5000 to make it look like a fantastic, serious and friendly business and I'm in my element. I Ikea most of it, the cosy zone is my favourite, I've ordered an Orla Kiely Mimosa Large Chaise Sofa in charcoal, it's bloody gorgeous and just the right sophisticated look that says 'we earn lots of money because we do an amazing job'. I also get an Orla Linden Chair in dandelion, they look bloody lush together.

With the rest of the money, I buy some Ikea office furniture for all of the files we'll soon accumulate with all the business we're going to generate and I get a few bits from the antiques centre near my flat which really sets if off as unique and going somewhere.

The next thing I do is set up a photo shoot for Rich so that we can start the marketing campaign and he needs to be in the photos, a Jurgen Klopp look alike has got to be a winner. I also get some names off Rach of model agencies they use so that we can set up some party shots for the campaign. We can get them done in the next week so the photos will be on fliers as well as the sales area of the office. The only thing we're missing now is the sign to go on the front and this is because Rich can't decide on a name. I've got the sign writers all geared up but he's stuck between two.

I'm six days into this new job and I've not thought about anyone or anything else since we started. I even worked solidly through the weekend to get the place ready for the opening which we're hoping will be next weekend. Rich is a great boss, although we're more of a team than anything else. He's been working hard to secure clients and get the right companies involved, drinks and food suppliers, venues, staff... he's got a lot of contacts so he's been putting together contact lists and files for weeks now. And he's so enthusiastic, it's really refreshing to work with someone who loves what they do. Not sure what's happening between him and Rach. Honestly don't think he can have seen much of her as he has also been working every hour. I've text her a few times to say 'thank you thank you thank you' because I'm suddenly in a job I love and I'm finally moving forward and it's all down to Rach.

CHAPTER ELEVEN

Thursday

I get into work about 8am and Rich is already here. He's at his desk and says he's finally decided, he wants the company to be called "Rich Events."

"Fab" I say, "I'll get on to the sign writers straight away and it might even be done by Saturday." He smiles and leans back in his Lucca Executive chair and looks at the ceiling. "You ok, Rich?" I enquire.

"More than ok Kate, this place is amazing, I can't believe how quickly you've made everything happen, it's fantastic, it's exactly as I pictured it and it's all down to you."

"Well, me…Ikea…Next…and don't forget you have had just a little bit of input" I have literally no idea where his money comes from, he might have saved it, borrowed it, been given it by his parents…but we're not in a place where I feel I can ask yet and that's fine. He basically put £5000 in my account and told me to get on with it. I've got receipts for absolutely everything and actually, in the end, I have only spent 4245 pounds and 86 pence.

"Honestly Rich, I need to be thanking you, you've let me go crazy with your money, what more could a girl ask for?" He laughs and I join in. We do make a great team.

"Right, we've got to go" he stands up and stretches his arms to the ceiling like he's actually been sitting in that chair all night and is moving for the first time in hours, "I've got a meeting that could potentially be our first event. The chef there wants to relaunch his restaurant and he wants me to give him a quote. Bit of a celebrity chef so they say, although I've never heard of him. Not really into that sort of thing but I've done some research on him this morning so I'm all geared up."

I can't quite believe what I'm hearing, surely it couldn't be, no don't be ridiculous, celebrity chefs are two a penny these days it would be silly to think that it was...

"Sorry I should have said, he specifically asked you to come too, said he knows you" you've got to be kidding me "Matthew Grove? Seems like a nice guy. You ok Kate?" I'm not, I feel sick. For the first time in three years I finally felt like I was moving on with my life and what happens? Our first client is going to be Matt. And he knows I work here. How? I've had a couple of texts off him in the last week but I've not replied, figured it was better to just ignore so that perhaps he gets the message and makes it easier for me to move on. If he truly cared about me he would, wouldn't he?

"Kate, you've gone really pale, are you ok?" Rich's voice brings me back to the reality of this shit situation. What do I say, I can't refuse to go with him, this is our first potential client. Why would Matt put me in this position? Selfish shit. "Kate?" I bring myself out of the red mist and try to pull myself together, the most important thing right now is getting this job right and if Matt wants to play games then he's in for a shock. I will be the utmost professional and he will see that I have moved on, even if he hasn't.

"Sorry Rich, had a double espresso on the way in, think it's just hit" I giggle. "Come on then, let's get going." I enthuse about what a big deal this could be as I walk out of the office with Rich and hopefully he believes me about the coffee. Don't need to lose his faith in me now.

The Restaurant

I haven't been here for months and it brings back memories that I've been trying to forget. I certainly didn't expect to be here again any time soon. I feel sick again as Rich and I cross the threshold. It's quiet inside. There won't be any staff in yet as Matt likes to come in on his own to prepare his menu for the day's service. I look around the restaurant and see a few changes have been made since I was last here. The colour scheme is slightly different and there seem to be less tables than there were. Still looks pretty sophisticated though and I can see Rich is impressed. I hear Matt before I see him and it gives me shivers to hear his voice after so long. He has such a sexy voice, any woman would melt a little for him but it's difficult not to love the familiarity and comfort I feel at the sound of him.

"You made it", he calls out from the back of the restaurant, "I'll be there in just a second" oh god, I've missed him so much and my heart won't stop racing at the thought of seeing him again. Get a grip Kate, you're here on business, you need to show Rich that you're capable of wooing clients as well as all the other stuff, this is after all how we're going to make money. I think 'we're' as I feel I have an invested interest in this company now, I know it's Rich's baby but I feel a part of it, like I've thrown my heart and soul into it.

Matt steps out of the darkness and walks forward towards us. He's already got his chef whites on and he looks really well (I thought he might seem a little strained due to the immense stress of not having me in his life but no). And I suddenly think, this is just business, he actually does want us to arrange an event for him and he's no longer interested in me other than he's heard I'm helping to run an events company. It's just me that is stuck in the past then.

He goes straight to Rich first and shakes his hand, "great to meet you" Rich says.

"You too" Matt replies and continues "I've been hearing great things about your new company and it sounds like you might be what I need right now" he turns to me now. He hasn't looked at me yet and I'm shaking. They must be able to hear my heart or at least see it beating out of my chest,

"Kate, you look lovely, congrats on the new job, it's great to see you," he doesn't shake my hand. He keeps his distance. They must be expecting me to say something as both men are staring at me. For the sake of impressing Rich, I fumble together a reply in my head,

"Good to see you too" and then I get straight to the business side of things. "Rich says you're having a relaunch, giving the restaurant a bit of a new look?" I look directly at him. Don't waver Kate, keep focused. "So" I continue, "how can we help?" There's another pause as he just stares at me and says nothing, like he's trying to work me out, almost as if he's angry with me for being able to carry on without so much as a flicker of the feelings I once had for him (who am I kidding, the way my heart is beating and my palms are sweating, the feelings are still very much in place).

Rich takes over "This is a great place you've got here. Fantastic location." Matt takes his eyes off me and focuses back on Rich, he squints at him and then looks at me again and quickly back at Rich. What is he thinking? Rich starts wandering round the restaurant. Matt moves closer to me as Rich turns his back. He brushes my bare arm with his fingers and all those feelings come rushing back, he knows exactly what to do to make me remember his touch. I can't look at him, I won't. Why is he playing these games? I move away and join Rich at the front of the restaurant. He seems a bit agitated, but I guess we're not really making much progress and he's desperate to secure a client.

"I'll get some coffee and we can sit and discuss the ideas I have for the place and then you can both let me know what you think, sound like a plan?" Matt says, this time directing his words at Rich. Matt gestures to a table that has his laptop and some papers on it "please, take a seat and I'll be back with coffee shortly." He disappears into the kitchen and I feel relieved that he's gone, even if just for a moment, I can compose myself again and hope to god Rich isn't seeing my angst at being here.

Rich and I sit down next to each other on one side of the table.

"Blimey, this could be a great job for us" Rich whispers close to my ear. I giggle just as Matt comes back with the coffee and sees me and Rich in this position. Shit he looks furious and I suddenly see why he looked shifty before, he thinks Rich and I are together!

Matt puts the coffee in front of us and Rich says jokingly, "Careful Kate, you've already had a double espresso this morning"

"Double espresso?" Matt chips in, "I thought you always had a latte in the morning." He says it suggestively and Rich squirms a little, it's now his turn to look back and forth between me and Matt as if he is realising something? Please no. I frown at Matt as if to try and say, 'please don't ruin this job for me'. He looks slightly apologetic and has hopefully got the message.

"Anyway, before I start working with a new company, I like to know a little bit about them" Matt says in a very business-like tone. "So, how did you two come to start this business together?" Is that not a bit personal, I can't really tell because I'm so conscious of Matt's bare arms, they look even more muscular than before and I start to remember them wrapped around me and how safe I feel when I'm with him…shit Kate, get a grip!

Rich doesn't seem flustered by the question so maybe I am just being paranoid, "A mutual friend of ours introduced us and I offered Kate a job. To be honest though, she's the creative talent in this company, her ideas are amazing and she will make your restaurant look absolutely fabulous in a new campaign.

"I don't doubt it" Matt replies as he switches his gaze from Rich to me and smiles, taking me in with those eyes, making me relax my guard and I smile too. Feeling pretty flattered by Rich but I'm pretty sure it's sales patter to get the client. One sales technique I learnt early on is to praise the team you work with to others and if they hear it, they live up to it and become as good as they've been described. Also, the potential client trusts you as they think you make a good team.

The conversation continues and Rich and Matt start discussing dates and numbers and before I know it, they're arranging the next meeting. Rich and I are going to put some initial design ideas together for the relaunch and meet next week to see what Matt thinks. The meeting has gone well as far as Rich is concerned and that is all that matters right now. We get up to leave and Matt shakes Rich's hand. For all the possible ulterior motives Matt might have had in getting us here, he seems suitably impressed with Rich and is clearly serious about giving us the relaunch. Rich and I make our way to the door.

"Actually Rich, do you mind if I just borrow Kate for a sec, I have some ideas for colours in the back which I could share now to save time later." What's he doing?

"No, go for it. That'd be useful, in fact I have another meeting round the corner in 10 minutes so I'll see you back at the office Kate. Really good to meet you Matt." And Rich opens the door and leaves, leaving me and Matt alone together for the first time in ages. I turn to face him and decide I need to keep this business-like.

"Ok, so do you have those colour schemes?" I smile and make a gesture as if he should go and get them.

"I miss you" he says it so quietly I hardly hear him. He puts his hand to his mouth, rubs his cheek and squeezes his lower lip, he looks emotional, almost like he might cry. What is this? Another game? I don't know what to say so I just turn to leave but he grabs my arm,

"Kate, can we talk please?" he seems genuinely upset now. Like this is some sort of torture for him. He still has hold of my arm and I'm looking at his fingers as they start to let go, "Please, just talk to me." Ok, maybe this needs to happen. I haven't really stopped thinking about him since the party and he has tried several times to ring and text me but I haven't answered him so maybe that's a little unfair of me. We move back towards the table where we were sitting and he pulls a chair out for me to sit down. I don't know what to say, so I don't. I'll let him talk, he obviously needs to say something.

"It's so good to see you" he smiles. "When I found out you had this new job, I was so pleased for you…"

"So why risk me losing it then?" I retort. What difference does it make if he's pleased for me? He's not a part of my life anymore.

"What do you mean?" he looks dejected and confused,

"Why insist I come to this meeting, you could have met with Rich on his own, you didn't need me here, you've just made life really awkward for me, Rich is probably wondering what the hell my problem is"

"Kate, I just wanted to see you and it was all I could think of, you haven't returned my calls or my texts, it's like everything we had together means nothing to you and I can't just switch off my feelings so easily." He thinks he means nothing to me. If only he knew. But I can't tell him. We'll be back to square one and I've honestly been doing ok without him. I maintain my silence.

"Kate please say something. This is breaking me. I'm so lost without you" ('I'm all out of love' pops immediately into my head and I have to steel myself not to break out into song again just to ease the tension).

"Why?" I say

"Why what?"

"Why are you lost without me?" my tone is low and abrupt.

"Because I miss you, because I didn't realise how

much I need you, Kate, I love you and I'm sorry I haven't always shown that but it's true and it's taken you ending this to make me realise just how much I love you." I look into his eyes as he says I love you and I know I love him too, I know I need him too but I can't do this, I made the break and I have to maintain it. "Kate please" he reaches for my hand but I pull it away before he has the chance to make me melt again. I get up quickly, walk without hesitation to the door and I leave before he can say anything more.

When I get outside, I keep walking, the office is about 20 minutes away and I just need to keep walking. I look at the sky, I look at the shops, I try to take in everything around me as I pass it just so I don't think about Matt, beautiful Matt and that look on his face when he said 'I love you' I know he meant it and I know what he wants to do to prove it and I won't…can't let that happen, I will not be responsible for his marriage ending and his business failing when the press find out he's been having an affair. I will not be that woman. But shit, maybe, maybe I already am. I keep walking.

Back at the office, Rich is back at his desk.

"Thought you had another meeting" I question.

"Nah don't be daft, that was just to make it look like we're in demand. I just had to go to the cash point" he chuckles. "Did you get those colour schemes?" I panic a bit but then quickly say,

"No, he couldn't find them in the end. He'll get them ready for the next meeting".

"Fine." He looks inquisitively at me "Kate?" oh no, here we go, "how do you know Matt?" Tell the truth Kate,

"He's just an old friend of mine" that is the truth as far as anyone else needs to know. And I'm back to lying again even though the affair is over, I'm still lying. "Why do you ask?" silly question?

"He was just a bit...well a bit vacant, like he had something else on his mind, just wasn't sure what to make of him." He seems to be satisfied that that is the end of the conversation because he turns back to his computer screen and continues reading his emails.

I can't believe Matt has put me back here. I was doing so well. Why didn't I just refuse to go, seeing him has brought it all back, keeping my distance was the best way to get over him. And now I have to work with him. I wonder if I can make some sort of excuse to Rich.

"I was thinking, Rich, on the walk back"

"You walked back? Bloody hell, if you didn't have the money for a cab you should've said."

"Don't be daft, it's not that far and I fancied the walk" he looks a bit non-plussed. "Anyway, I was thinking, perhaps it would look better if you work with Matt by yourself, it's your business and people need to know you're the key factor in all this, the brains behind it all." I think it sounds like a sensible argument but,

"Now you're being daft. Kate, we're a team, I'm not arrogant and I know where my skills lie but, more so, I know where your skills lie and if I didn't tap into them I'd be a terrible business man. So, we're doing this together, ok?"

"Right" I smile back at him and head for my desk wondering how the hell I'm going to get through this.

CHAPTER TWELVE

Thursday Evening

I've decided to have a couch night. Just me, Inspector Barnaby, hot chocolate and some popcorn. Not even wine tonight. Wine encourages me to make bad decisions and I'm not going to make any more bad decisions. At least, not tonight, anyway.

I'm in the slobbiest, ugliest pjs but I'm oh so comfy as I slouch down into the sofa. I think it's a thing when people reach their 30s that Midsomer Murders suddenly becomes appealing. It's so cheesy but it's light relief and exactly what I need right now to take my mind off Matt. I haven't heard from him since this morning which hopefully means he's respecting my wishes and leaving me alone. It's for the best but my heart still hurts. Watch the telly Kate.

Ooh DS Winter is looking good tonight. Nice, dark suit and shirt reminds me of something Matt wore once when we… FFS Kate! DS Winter is nice but I'll always be a Jones girl, he was the best Barnaby sidekick. I take a sip of my ridiculously calorie filled hot chocolate and snuggle down further into the sofa. I reckon it was the pub landlord, he doesn't look anywhere near suspicious and it's always those characters that suddenly have a dark and sinister reason for killing someone. My phone pings. Matt's name appears on the screen. Shit.

I leave it for a minute. If I don't read it then I can't get annoyed or upset by it. But I know it's there and it's burning an inquisitive hole in my mind, I'm watching DS Winter chase someone across a field and obviously he catches him, watch him run, nice, and in a suit, that's impressive. I'm doing everything I can think of not to read the text but it's no good.

I'm sorry about today. I never should have put you in that position. It wasn't fair of me.

Wow an apology. My mind does its usual and considers the suggestion of the word 'position'. And my inner dialogue tells Matt he can put me in whatever position he likes. I look down at the sofa, our sofa, the sofa where Matt and I first really made love. It's true, we did. I know now. But it's too late. I consider not replying but I've made that mistake all week and look where that's got me. So, I reply with what I hope is a simple yet final response of

It's ok. No real harm done. I'm actually stupid enough to think that that will stop him saying anything else but one minute later my phone pings again,

Can we meet Kate? I really think we've got things to say to each other. If you tell me it's over one more time then I will believe you and I will try to move on but please just see me.

'If you tell me it's over one more time…' what am I meant to make of that? My head says just send a text saying 'It's over' then surely he has to live by what he has said? But instead, as that just feels too final, I say,

Matt, it's for the best that we don't meet, please try to accept that.

You didn't say 'it's over' no I didn't and then, *I'm coming round now* what? No no no, he can't do that.

NO YOU'RE NOT. You're at work and you can't just leave your own restaurant

Watch me

Oh shit. I'm in my slobby pjs, no make up, my hair looks greasy, I'm a state and… but that shouldn't matter if it's over, why am I still trying to look good for him? In fact, it's better that I'm looking like shit, he'll take one look at me and realise that he's wrong and he's not interested, he doesn't love me and it's just his dick doing the thinking, that and his pride for me ending it with him.

Don't Matt, don't come over I wait. Nothing. I wait some more. He won't, he can't leave the restaurant, can he? I wait for about 10 minutes and nothing, no more texts. It would take him 15 minutes to get here from the restaurant, so I keep watching Midsomer. Part of me hoping he's just being silly and another part of me (a big part if I'm really honest) is desperately hoping that there will be a knock on my door any minute. But I'm honestly not sure how I would react if I saw him right now. My heart is racing again as I look down at our sofa. Do the right thing Kate. Stick to your decision, no bad decisions tonight. Remember.

An hour later

No Matt so that's a relief, I tell myself. Midsomer has finished. Popcorn bowl empty. Heart broken. Why the hell am I so disappointed? I didn't want him to come over. In fact, I'm angry. This is typical Matt, says he'll do something and then let's me down (has he let me down?) this is exactly the kind of feeling I was trying to avoid and yet here I am, he has me in his control once again. I'm so stupid and gullible that…there's a knock at the door. My heart beats faster. God I desperately want to see him but what good will this do?

Another knock.

"Kate?" it's him, of course it is. He's here.

Another knock.

"Kate?" I get up and walk to the door. I look in the mirror and see my face is red from the warmth of my flat. I smell like hot chocolate and popcorn and my pjs have little elephants all over them and are too big for me. He's never seen me like this.

I open the door and there's my Matt. It's raining and his hair is wet so it's dishevelled and looks darker than usual. He has rain drops on his face and brushes one away from his cheek.

66

"Kate, I'm here. Can I come in?" I don't say anything, just nod and open the door wider so he can enter. He walks past me into the flat and I shut the door. For a second, I hold on to the door and steel myself again. Be strong. You know what you need to do Kate. Take this opportunity to end it properly so that you stop feeling so lousy and you can move on with your life. That has to be the most important thing.

We sit like strangers at opposite ends of the sofa. I think about the numerous times we've laid here together and I feel like I'm going to cry. Shit, how did this get so serious? Right here we go.

"Matt, I'm sorry I've ignored you but I can't carry on like this." I look at him and he's about to talk but I stop him,

"It's not fair that you get to live your life normally and I can't move on." I hear my voice and it's kind of monotone, when did I get so serious? Maybe I need to relax a bit.

"So what are you saying?" does he actually want me to say the words,

"This has to end Matt" he moves a little closer,

"You can't say it, can you? You don't want this to end just like I don't" Of course I don't want to stop seeing him, to not have texts from him every day, I don't want to stop feeling nervous and excited when he's with me and I hate the thought of never seeing him again but at the same time,

"I feel trapped Matt, I feel like as long as we're having this affair that I'm a liar. I lie to the people who know me because I don't want them to know that I'm in love with a married man".

"You're in love with me?" Shit, what have I said, that wasn't the plan, that wasn't what I was supposed to say, that's not the way you tell someone for the first time that you love them. "Kate" he moves closer and grabs my hands, "I love you too, you have no idea how happy it makes me to hear you say that"

"Matt no, you're missing the point." I get up from the sofa because as long as he is touching me, I can't think straight, I need distance between us. "It doesn't matter how I feel anymore, I can't live with the way things are, it just doesn't feel right or fair…to any of us" I look at him properly to try and gauge his feelings but I can't read him, he's staring at the coffee table as if he's processing, maybe it's finally sinking in.

"I'll leave her, we can be together then"

"Don't you dare leave her for me, if you have issues in your marriage, if you're not happy with that part of your life then sort it out, do something about it but don't you dare say you're ending your marriage to be with me because that pressure is way too much. You have no idea what that does to a relationship. You have no right to put that on me." Woah didn't even know I was harbouring those thoughts but I'm so right, see I can be sensible, I can think straight and rationally when I have to, pat on back Katie Carlin. But what I haven't actually realised as these words were pouring out of me so were my tears, and I'm now sort of sobbing rather than sounding sensible and rational and then,

"Kate, it's ok, I'm sorry, oh baby, come here" and Matt has wrapped his arms around me, his wonderfully strong arms that make me feel safe and I try to put up my hands to say 'I'm ok' but I end up with my fingers on his chest, trying just for a second to push him away but all I want now is him to hold me. So, he does. We stay here for what feels like minutes, neither of us speaking, I can hear his breathing as I feel his chest go up and down and he brings his hand up to cradle my head as I sob into him. How pathetic have I become? Right back where we started. Except maybe not. He knows exactly how I feel, I will not be the reason he ends his marriage. I move my

68

face away from his chest and lean back a little so that I can look at his face. He looks down into my eyes,

"Matt?"

"It's ok, I understand, you're right, it's not fair to put this all on you, I won't do that, I know I have to work it out for myself and I will without bringing you into it. I promise, I won't hurt you anymore, I'm so sorry." He places his hands gently on my cheeks and presses his lips to mine, I let him because nothing could feel more right at that moment. His kiss is tender and sweet and as he kisses me he whispers, "I love you so much" I pull away from him and look directly into his eyes,

"I love you too" this time I kiss him, gently at first but then something takes over inside of me and I'm pushing hard against his lips, the kiss becoming more erotic as I push him back towards the sofa, our sofa…

"Kate, Kate, Katie, woah, slow down…" he holds me away so I'm at arms' length and repeats, "Slow down baby" I feel a little rejected, not quite sure what's going on.

"What's the matter?" I utter, a bit pissed off.

"Kate, I want to do this properly" What does that mean?

"I want you to know that I don't just expect sex every time I come over, I mean don't get me wrong, pushing you away then was really difficult but it doesn't always have to be about sex and you need to know that" he smiles.

"Sometimes, I'd just like us to talk and hold hands."

"It's the elephant pjs isn't it?" I say half joking but worried that he's not attracted to me right now. He pulls me towards the sofa and chuckles as he sits and pulls me on to his lap,

"The pjs are sexy as hell! I want you more than anything right now Kate but I also want you to know how much I care about you. You don't have to 'put out'" he does the speech marks in the air thing, "every time I come over…Ok?" I smile at him and relax into his chest, he holds me and kisses the top of my head. Feels nice, really nice. We just sit like this for ages. He strokes my hair. I think he really does love me. I mean he's in love with me.

"Matt" I keep my voice quiet so as not to ruin the calmness of the moment, "what happens next?" He takes a big deep breath,

"I'm honestly not sure right now but I know what I want, I just have to work out how" bit vague but I won't push any further.

"Can you stay for a bit?" I sit up and look into his eyes.

"Yes beautiful I can." And I snuggle into him again. We breathe together and for that moment, everything is perfect. I could stay like this forever.

"Can I ask you something Kate?" sounds intriguing. I nod.

"What happened between you and that girl from the party?" I stiffen and squirm a bit awkwardly in his arms. I've never told Matt about stuff I've done with other people, he doesn't know about Sam either. I mean, I know I've not done anything wrong but why did he ask that now, in this perfect moment.

"Umm, I…" he lifts my head so he can see my face. He reads my expression,

"You didn't?" the expression on his face is shock but he's smiling. "Did you?" I just raise my eyebrows as he keeps staring at me "Wow", I feel him get hard against my legs.

"Matt!", I gently hit his chest and we laugh together, he's totally turned on by it which I guess is better than jealous or upset. Maybe not share the Sam story just yet. I'm praying he doesn't ask if there's been anyone else as I don't want to start this new understanding between us with a lie.

"You're so beautiful" he pulls my face to his and kisses me again.

CHAPTER THIRTEEN

The next few weeks plod along nicely. My job is going great. Rich and me work really well together. We've now secured three high profile jobs that, if we get them right, will secure us more business with any luck. Matt's is one of the three, we're working to relaunch his restaurant in the next few months so that he can time it right with the start of the Summer season. Rich has had a couple of meetings with him in the last couple of weeks but it hasn't been necessary for me to attend, and even though I would've liked to see him, it's probably for the best. I'm leaving him alone to sort out what he wants. I'm confident, after he came round that night, that he wants us to be together but he knows that I do not want to be the reason for his marriage ending. So distance is probably best right now. Having said that, we have text each other a few times and my heart still races when I see his name appear on my phone but I need to try and stay rational about it even if I have to wait, he needs to sort himself out before he can really work out what he wants. Sensible me. That's the head version anyway. My heart is missing him and I have constant moments of panic when I think it's just never going to happen. But his texts tend to make me feel better and get me past those moments.

My social life has been a bit non-existent, certainly in comparison to the weeks before, but that's ok. I've had a couple of nights out with Rach. I told her all about Matt, the fact that I didn't properly finish it with him (she was a little perturbed by me not being completely honest with her but as usual she has been supportive and just wants what's best for me – I don't think for a minute she believes Matt is best for me but as long as I believe he is, I know she will support me). Her and Rich are now officially an item and they're very cute together, in a bit of a pass the bucket sort of way, but I couldn't be happier for her, Rich is a lovely guy and she deserves that. So, our nights out have been pretty low key, no repeats of the Easy Rider night, and if any men have shown an interest, we have quickly put them off.

I got a text off Lucy last week, we have text each other a few times since our 'weekend of lady love' (as Rach likes to call it!) and I think she is becoming a good friend or I hope anyway. I haven't actually seen her since and that's my fault, or decision I should say. She has suggested we go out for a drink but there is a part of me that worries I will be leading her on (again?) and I genuinely don't want to hurt her. I would really like to see her. That weekend confuses me a little now. We had such a connection that I'm almost too scared to explore it further. Being with her was so different to being with Matt and I can't work out why (apart from the glaringly obvious physical differences but it's not that clear cut).

Friday

Rich and I decide to have a few drinks after work to celebrate how well the company is going. It's Friday, why not? We need to relax a bit as well. As much as I love the job, it has been pretty full on these last few weeks so I'm looking forward to chatting with Rich away from work. Of course, I've asked Rach to join us and I think she's bringing a couple of people from her work who already know Rich from when he worked there.

We're meeting at The Loft. It's a bar just off King Street and is great when finishing work as it's people wanting to unwind between work and home rather than get absolutely bladdered, so it's not full of nobs. Me and Rich find a table by the window and he goes and gets the drinks. I check my phone but there's no new messages. I still feel a little rejected when I don't hear from Matt every day but I've made it pretty clear I want him to sort other aspects of his life out before we can properly embark on anything, so I can't really have it both ways, can I? There's a knock on the window and I look up to see Rach, she presses her face to the glass with a big kiss for me. I laugh, breathe on the window and draw a little heart. I make some sort of hand gesture that is supposed to say, 'get in here quickly, Rich is at the bar and he'll be able to get you a drink if you're quick' but she just frowns and shakes her head, laughing before turning away and walking towards the door.

"Kate" she calls me from across the room. She has two men with her. One of them looks a bit too well dressed, shows all his insecurities by going way too far in the matching accessories department and the other is a bit shabby looking in comparison. Top button already undone, suit a bit creased but a bit more natural with more confidence.

"Kate, this is Seb" the insecure overly accessorised guy, "and this is Tom," the other one. We all say 'hi' and they start to make themselves comfortable round the table. Rach sits next to me on the little bench and gives me a massive hug. Rich is back with the drinks. He and Rach must have spoken on the phone or text, as Rich has drinks for everyone. Tom takes a seat opposite me by the window and Rich sits opposite Rach which leaves Seb on the end.

"So,"(why?) "how's today been? Did you get that client you wanted? She looks to me first and when I don't reply, she turns to Rich. "Oh, should I not have asked?" Rich smiles.

"Almost, they're just a bit hung up on the fact that we're new and they've not seen us do much yet. They're pretty honest about it all so I've told them to come and see the plans for our other events on Monday and hopefully Kate will charm the pants off them and they'll sign us up."

"She's good at that," Rach nudges me in the ribs, "charming the pants off people" she laughs and looks at me while I feign laughter, holding my stomach. I know exactly what she means and she's not referring to my business acumen.

Tom leans forward and joins in the conversation. "Clients like that just need reassurance that you're going to make them a success, they need you to show them that you know how to create the perfect event for them, it's all about the bespoke these days, not the corporate. Whatever they want, you've got to give it to them." He's got a really sexy Irish accent. One of those voices that, if he worked in a call centre, they would put him on the cancellations line as he could talk anyone round with those tones. Rach interjects,

"Bloody hell Tom, give it a rest with the work babble, it's Friday." He leans back,

"Sorry" he smiles, "can't always switch off straight away." He turns to me, "Kate, tell me something interesting that's not work related." Shit, on the spot much! I suddenly feel the pressure to sound interesting,

"Well," I start and I think Rach senses my panic,

"Bloody Hell, don't ask her she's just as work obsessed as you are, can't drag her away from the place most of the time." She looks at Rich and he is nodding in agreement.

"Actually," I say, "I could tell you something very interesting right now that is not work related in the slightest" they all look my way, "You see the woman at the bar in the red suit?" they all turn to look and then in unison say,

"Yeah?"

"Well in about 10 seconds, she's going to fake spill her drink on the guy to her left, she totally fancies him and has been trying to get his attention for ages. I reckon she's going for the turn around, throw drink all over herself after nudging into him so it looks like his fault and he offers to buy her another one" Rach joins in,

"Either that, or she'll pick up his drink 'by accident' so he has to start talking to her" we all watch in anticipation as she turns too quickly to her left and bam, spills the drink all over him. He reacts, she apologises and dabs him with a tissue, the start of a beautiful relationship?

"Wow," Seb chips in "how did you know that?"

"It was obvious, it's what I would have done" Rach says and quickly looks at Rich. "I mean, not for that guy, if I wanted to attract someone's attention, but not him, no he's…gross" Rich laughs as she squirms in the little hole she's dug for herself. "You know what I mean." She concludes, face glowing red, and sips her drink.

"Tom, how have you ended up here? I mean, that's not a local accent." I say making conversation and starting to relax a bit in the new company.

"Came to Uni over here and never left" he drawls and I think I'm a little bit in love with his accent. That's all though, he's definitely not my type in any other way.

"Talk some more" I say, "I could listen to that accent all night"

"Blimey Kate, killer chat up line, would you two like us to leave you alone?" Rach hollers. I'm sure it didn't come across like that, did it? Can't a woman admire a man's accent these days without it being a chat up line…

"If you wanna listen to me all night, that must mean we're going to be waking up together" apparently not! Everybody round the table starts laughing, which eases my unease somewhat as I don't want Tom to think I'm really flirting with him or trying to pick him up. I'm sure he's just joking, I know I am.

"Kate" someone calling my name from across the room stops the conversation and I look up to see Lucy walking towards our table. "Hi," she walks up behind me and I stand to turn and hug her, feels natural. "It's so good to see you, how are you?" I smile and say,

"I'm great thanks, how are you?" I'm aware that Rach is staring at me and she clearly requires an introduction, Lucy says she's fine and tells me she's just out with a few work colleagues.

"Me too," I reply and gesture the table. "This is Rach, Rach, this is Lucy" Rach is suitably impressed and nods as she shakes Lucy's hand, she looks at me and I know exactly what her look means.

"Lucy," Rach says, "why don't you join us? This is Tom, Rich and Seb."

"Hi, hi," Lucy does a little wave and she looks round the table but declines the offer. I'm actually disappointed she's not joining us. Thought I might feel awkward if I saw her again and if there was ever going to be a time when I felt awkward seeing her it would be with Rach there, the one person who knows just about every detail of what happened that weekend. But I feel fine, great in fact. And I really want to chat with her and catch up properly but she makes her excuses and goes back to her friends. After that, I keep looking over to where she is and I'm pretty sure she is doing the same but we never quite make eye contact. Rach questions me as soon as Lucy is out of earshot,

"Oh my god, Kate, did you know she'd be here?"

"Didn't have a clue."

"She really is gorgeous, I can see why you…you know" she still can't quite find the words for what happened between me and Lucy but then neither can I. I just know it was pretty awesome and felt right, at the time.

An hour passes and I haven't checked my phone since we arrived, it's too loud to hear it ping so I have a quick look and there's a message from Lucy.

Good to see you. and then a second text *You look

gorgeous* I look across to where she is sitting but her crowd has gone. Feeling a bit disappointed I head for the toilet. I need to get home soon, had a couple of gins in the space of an hour (and I didn't have lunch) so my head is starting to whir a bit.

As I enter the ladies, Lucy is standing at the sink washing her hands. She sees me in the mirror and smiles,

"You following me?" she quirks. I smile back.

"No, just need a pee", I go into a cubicle and wonder if she'll still be there when I come out. I don't know why but while I'm in there, I just have a quick check on my hair and make sure my tummy is pulled in when I walk out. She's still there, now leaning against the sink as if she's been waiting for me.

"Did you get my text?" she's straight to the point.

"Yeah, just, I thought you'd gone though". I wash my hands and study her in the mirror. It's a strange sensation being this close to her again, I'm still physically attracted to her, feels right and wrong all at the same time.

"You really do look gorgeous; I'd forgotten how much I fancy you" not bashful in any way. My face reddens and I'm not sure what to say. There's nobody else in the toilets so at least it's just me that's embarrassed.

"Thanks" I grab a paper towel off the side and dry my hands. "You look good too." Might as well say it, she does.

"Do you fancy going somewhere else for a drink and a catch up?" I really do but I can't, can I?

"I'd better not, was gonna head home soon, been a long week" She looks a bit gutted but says,

"Ok, no worries, just text me later if you change your mind, I'll still be out and about somewhere." She kisses my cheek and goes. I get the tingles as her lips graze my cheek. Blimey, it's a bit of an unknown territory for me. Feel like I could talk to her all night as a friend but not sure where that might lead.

I make my way back to the others and start to say goodnight to them all. Rich has moved round the table to sit next to Rach and they say they'll be leaving soon too. "Nice to meet you both," I say to Seb and Tom and then make my way to the door.

In the cab, I can't stop thinking about Lucy. Maybe I should have gone for a drink, what harm would that do? But then I don't want to lead her on. But then maybe she's not interested in me in that way now, although thinking about it, she did say she fancied me, bit of a giveaway.

I open my flat door and scoop up the mail on the way in. I'm going to get my comfies on straight away and have another little drink while I'm watching some Friday night telly. When I'm changed, I pour myself a glass of white wine and sift through the post. Bill, junk, bill… oh now what's this, looks and feels like a wedding invite, very classy envelope and beautiful writing in gold on the front. I love getting wedding invites and I haven't had one for a while now. In my twenties, it seemed like I was going to a wedding every other weekend, but it's almost like getting married has gone out of fashion a bit, people just co-habit these days and have partners rather than spouses. I can't think of anyone who could possibly be getting married, maybe another old school friend?

I open the envelope and pull out the expensive looking invite and my heart stops.

"You are invited to the Wedding Vow Renewal of Mr and Mrs Matthew Grove" What the actual fuck? Is this some sort of sick joke? So many thoughts are running through my head… is this a test? Has Fay found out? Did I misunderstand what Matt was going to do? Have I fallen for his fake charm again and he knew this was happening all along? My brain hurts and I'm furious. How can I have been so stupid…again? In my anger, I grab my phone, take a picture of the invite and immediately send it to Matt with *WTF?????" plastered underneath it. It sends and I can see it's delivered and… it's been read.

I grab my glass of wine, down the rest of it and refill it. I almost put the bottle back in the fridge but think better of it and take it with me to the sofa. My head is spinning as I look at the invite again.

"You are invited to the Wedding Vow Renewal of Mr and Mrs Matthew Grove. Even after 5 years of marriage, they are still so much in love and want to show the world once more, how much they mean to each other" Oh my god, I want to scream and cry and shout and…my phone starts to ring, it's Matt. I answer,

"What the f…"

"Kate, listen, I'm so sorry, I had no idea she was sending you an invite."

"What the fuck does that mean? Is this for real? Are you actually doing this?" He tries to interrupt me, he's making various protestations down the phone but I'm fuming.

"Kate listen, it's not what I want. It's complicated."

"Complicated? Seems pretty straight forward to me" I recite the words from the invitation, "Even after 5 years of marriage, they are still so much in love and want to show the world once more, how much they mean to each other?" the tone of my voice goes up at the end in disbelief.

"Kate, I know how it looks but I promise you it's not what I want." He sounds desperate but I can't get past the fact I've got an invitation to the vow renewal of the man who I love and stupidly thought I might spend the rest of my life with. I'm so ridiculous.

"I'm such an idiot for believing you Matt,"

"You're not, I meant every word I…"

"I can't believe I've fallen for your crap all over again, I'm so gullible."

"Kate please, let me explain. Just be quiet a second and let me explain, please."

"Go on then" I shriek down the phone.

"I told Fay that I didn't think the marriage was working, I told her that we should think about separating as neither of us have been happy for ages and…" he pauses

"AND?" I shout

"And she started accusing me of all sorts, saying I was a poor excuse for a husband, that I only had the business because of the money she initially put into it and that she made me who I am but then she started crying and throwing things. When she eventually calmed down, she said she didn't want to lose me and started talking about this wedding vow renewal thing, said a fresh start would help us, I disagreed with her but she just kept going on about it, I didn't know what to say, so I…"

"So you what?" I roar,

"I said that it's something we need to discuss, honestly Kate that was all I said and before I know it, she's having invites printed and sent out before I've even agreed to any of it. It's not what I want."

"So how come I've got an invite? Are you so spineless that you just let her dictate what you do?"

"Shit Kate, I'm trying to explain." He sounds dejected and a little angry. "You have no idea what she's like, she'd got them done without even discussing a date with me. I didn't even know they'd been sent until I got a call from a mate of mine this morning and I didn't know she'd sent one to you. I was trying to work out what the hell to do about it all."

"Will you go through with it?" I hear him take a breath "Matt, will you go through with it?"

"Kate, I…" oh my god, is he going to go through with it? He just said it's not what he wants…

"Matt, seriously? What's going on?" my voice sounds calmer but only because I'm scared shitless of what I think he's about to say…

"I don't know what to do Kate, I feel like she's got me over a barrel with the business and everything, I mean she owns half of it and I've worked so hard to get where I am today" Wow, wow, I can't quite believe I'm hearing this. The anger builds inside me again and I can't take anymore,

"Let me help you out here then Matt, you told me once if I said two words to you then you'd respect me and leave me alone, well here you go." I spit the words out, "Me and you, Matt, are finished, IT'S OVER!" I hang up on him as quickly as I can before I hear anything he has to say and I launch my phone across the room before I collapse on to the sofa, (our sofa) and break down, I can hear myself sobbing, and I can't stop it. I pull my knees up to my chest and cry until I have nothing left in me.

When I wake up, I'm still on the sofa and I can feel dribble running down my cheek. I downed the rest of the wine and it knocked me out, better not to think about pain, better to numb it. I wipe my face and adjust my eyes to the lights in the room. Then it hits me, what I've done. I've ended it with Matt once and for all. Again, I face an unknown future, a lonely future. Regret hits me and I remember that I threw my phone across the room, I quickly (and stupidly considering my wine intake) get to my feet and run to where I think my phone landed. It takes me a minute but there it is, screen smashed. I pick it up and it lights up so something still works. There are three missed calls from Matt from 5 hours ago, he must've tried calling me straight back, I didn't hear it and I wouldn't have answered it anyway. I can't believe he's going to go through with this ridiculous charade of renewing his wedding vows. He doesn't even love her, does he? I don't think I've ever asked him that. Maybe he does. He tried calling three times in succession and he hasn't since, no texts either, think that's it. I said the words and now we both have to live by them. It's over.

CHAPTER FOURTEEN

Over the next couple of months, I throw myself into work and decide to take a vow of celibacy (see Matt, we can all take vows). I love my job and thank god I do. I've been working so hard that there hasn't been time to wallow in any kind of self-pity and actually I feel stronger now. I took control. I didn't let him decide, I did it. And let's face it, if we can't make decisions for ourselves, particularly when we get into our thirties, then what can we do? So, I feel refreshed, assertive and ready to draw a line under that particular chapter and start something new. But no relationships. Not for the time being anyway.

I have managed, single-handedly, to bag Rich Events seven new clients over the last few weeks. Through the small events that we've already done, I managed to make a few contacts and because we worked the events at short notice, other companies were impressed by the speedy and succinct organisation and presentation. In fact, we now have events lined up for the next eight months so it's all go.

Of course, the elephant in the room is Matt's event. It's next week. I've so far managed to avoid any further meetings, mostly because of all the other clients we've secured (and partly because I've arranged meetings with new clients knowing that they'd clash with Matt's meetings) but I know I can't avoid the event itself and I will have to see him. I don't think Rich would be pleased if I refused to go to our first major client's relaunch when he knows there will be people there that I should be schmoozing for business. So, it's inevitable and I need to put my job first.

I'm sitting at my desk, working on a guest list for a

Company Award Ceremony (all the fashion these days and quite right too. Why is it only the actors and musicians of this world that get awards, anyone who works hard deserves recognition) when my phone pings. It's Lucy. We've text each other a few times over the last few weeks but I haven't seen her since that night in the bar. For a few days after I finished things with Matt, I was so tempted to invite her for a drink, but it wasn't fair on her, I would have been doing it for the comfort and attention and it would have been a definite rebound. Some of the texts we exchanged suggested this would be fine with her (get the feeling she's not really into commitment) but I resisted and feel better for it. One of us would have ended up hurt and I'd like to keep her friendship.

Saw this and thought of you attached to the text is a picture of a coffee cup from the café where we met. I smile and remember that day, the weird feelings I was having and the fear at having no job. I look round the office and feel so grateful for Rich and this job. And for Rach for setting it all up for me. Not sure where I'd be without them right now but I don't think they see it like that. We've all benefitted in some way out of this. But I will always be grateful.

I think about my reply to Lucy wondering what she's expecting and in the end, I say what I'm actually feeling which is:

Fancy a drink later? I think we've come far enough down the line of friendship and texting to meet up without wanting to rip each other's clothes off and I could do with another person to chat to. Someone who has a life outside of my safe little work bubble.

*Yeah great. The Loft after work? *

Fab, see you there about 5.30

It's not Friday but there's something rather liberating about going for a drink mid-week. It allows you to see your day in a different light and to realise, I guess, that life isn't all about work. I have done nothing but work these last couple of months and it's been my salvation. But there's more to me than that and I can't let what happened with Matt turn me into a spinster. Eventually, I need to get back to…I don't know…dating? Anyway, right now, just a drink with a friend would be the perfect way to get me out.

5.15pm

I get to the bar early as there wasn't much else I could do at work. I made a few more phone calls but most people had gone home so it was a case of leaving messages. I order two Brockmans and tonic and take a swig of mine at the bar before I head off to find a table. I'm feeling quite nervous about seeing Lucy. Texting is one thing, you can easily hide behind messages, but face to face, am I definitely ready for that? I'm about to find out as she walks in, sees me and smiles, that smile.

"Kate" I stand to greet her, not sure if it's going to be a hug or a 'hi' so I let her take the lead and she kisses my cheek, "so good to see you, how are you?" I sit down as she takes her coat off and sits on the bench next to me.

"I got you this" pushing the gin towards her, "it's what we drank in that gin bar the day we met" careful Kate, sounds like a chat up line, "figured you'd be ok with that".

"Thanks" she says and takes a sip. "I've drunk so much of this since that day, it's my new favourite" this feels like a little slight, suggesting that it's not that special to her but then I didn't really intend it to sound like it was that important to me either, just fact I guess (stop analysing!)

"So, what's been happening with you? It sounds like you haven't been out of that office for weeks" she looks right at me and seems genuinely interested. It always surprises me when someone genuinely wants to know how I am, and with the recent 'confidence knock', my self-esteem hasn't exactly blossomed.

"Pretty much work, work, work. The company is really starting to take off so I'm enjoying it. Never thought a job could be quite so much fun to be honest. But it probably does seem like I'm a bit of a workaholic." She smiles and nods and lets me talk, the connection between us is back straight away, "that's really one of the reasons I fancied a catch up with you tonight, feel like it's time to enjoy a bit of a social life again before I have no friends left" I flippantly laugh but I'm deadly serious. I don't have many friends. Since Matt and I started, I kind of got consumed in the lies and it was easier to back off from people. Rach has been my only constant and that's because it's unconditional, and there's not many friendships you can say that about.

"Well I'm glad you asked me to have a drink with you, it is really nice to see you" she frowns a little when she says this, almost as if she's wondering if I think the same. I don't let her down,

"I'm so glad I suggested it, I've missed you" too far? "but I was always a bit afraid to see you because of what happened" wow, sometimes my mouth just gets right in there, (so to speak!) Lucy raises her eyebrows a little, not sure she was expecting such frankness this early in the evening, but she's always been upfront with me so I might as well follow suit.

"Do you think about what happened between us?" she moves her head a little closer to me. "I wasn't sure how you felt about it all, I know you were apprehensive and when you didn't really keep in touch, I thought you might have regretted it?" her tone is gentle and I hope I didn't hurt her.

"I think about it a lot, it was…" I consider my words carefully, don't want to appear like I'm coming on to her again but also want her to know how amazing that weekend was for me. I look directly into her eyes and remember how she made me feel and my mouth takes over again… "it was so fucking hot" for a second we just stare and then at the same time we smile and laugh and at last the tension is broken. Being that honest has made me feel better and like I could tell her anything right now. Our emotional connection scares me but I love it.

We talk for ages, about her job (she's currently working on a lifestyle piece for modern teenagers whatever that means) about my job, about the two women she's been seeing and neither of them knows about the other (she's so proud of this, likes to live dangerously I think), we've had several gins by this point and eventually she says:

"Kate, I still fancy you so much, you just do something to me" she leans forward and puts her hand on my leg and I get those tingles again and even a bit of a throbbing between my legs, "I'll totally understand if you don't want to do this, but I'm going to nip to the ladies, meet me there." She smiles, gets up and walks away. Now I really am throbbing as I can imagine what she's thinking, but I don't know what to do. I do really want to go but am I just ginned up again? Does it matter if I am? I'm not great at making decisions when I'm sober let alone half cut. Fuck it, I head to the ladies.

There are three cubicles and two of the doors are shut, shit which one is she in and what am I actually supposed to do. Then my phone pings

I'm in the left hand cubicle I push the door open tentatively and there she is.

"Hey" she whispers. I go in. I can feel my heart pumping and I feel flushed. I didn't intend this to happen, I just wanted to catch up with her, (didn't I?) She locks the door and I turn to face her. "You ok?" she asks, I must look nervous. I nod,

"I think so". And I suddenly realise, this isn't about

feelings, no, it's about pure sex. And right at that moment, I begin to think, there's nothing wrong with that. She pushes me back a little so that I'm up against the wall and she moves one hand over my breasts, my nipples harden at her touch. She keeps moving her hand down towards my stomach and beyond, all the time just staring into my eyes and smiling, it's intense. Her mouth is close to mine but we don't kiss, I can feel her breath on my lips and that sweet gin smell is making me want her more. Her hand has found its way under my skirt and into my knickers and I'm standing, staring, smiling, feeling her discover me all over again. The main door to the ladies opens and closes, we hear someone enter a cubicle and lock the door, Lucy is still caressing me inside and out and we smile at each other as if the fact that we're doing this in the close vicinity of someone else makes it so much hotter. I take a sharp breath, the sensations I am feeling made more intense by the fact that we're just staring at each other, and my whole body is consumed by my climax. The person in the other cubicle flushes the toilet and we hear the door unlock, the taps run, the hand dryer and then they're gone.

"Fucking hell" I say as Lucy makes sure my knickers are replaced and my skirt is properly pulled down.

"You still ok?" she smiles at me. She knows I am. "Come on, let's get another gin." But I want more, I haven't finished yet so I say,

"Wait" and I turn her to face me, push her back into the corner of the cubicle, expertly (or so I tell myself) undo her jeans and practise what she has so expertly taught me.

We eventually find our way back to our table and I, once again, feel strangely liberated. No awkwardness, no desire to get out of there as fast as I can, I just feel… well, fine. We've been back at the table for about ten minutes when,

"Kate? It's Kate isn't it?" I look up and see someone I think I recognise, "It's Tom. I work with your friend Rachel" the penny drops,

"Oh hi Tom, how are you?" he seems a bit sheepish,

"I'm fine thanks. Could I get you ladies a drink?" I'm not really sure what to say as I'd rather he didn't join us.

"Oh thanks Tom, but we were just about to leave when we've finished these" Lucy looks at me in surprise, we weren't leaving but I can't be bothered making polite conversation with anyone other than Lucy tonight.

"No problem, just saw you and thought I'd ask. Have a good night" He skulks away.

"He is totally into you!" Lucy murmurs under her breath.

"Don't be ridiculous" I reply

"Seriously, you can't see it? What the hell did you think that was?" Oh god maybe she's right, oh well, we had better leave after all.

Outside I grab a cab and Lucy says she'll text me soon. I'm fine with that, I didn't expect us to go home together tonight and neither did she. I think we both got what we wanted, for the time being at least. (The Beatles song Something is going round my head, she attracts me like no other lover.) In the back of the cab, I smile to myself at the thought of me and Lucy in the ladies. So much for celibacy.

CHAPTER FIFTEEN

Saturday - Day of the Relaunch

It's 8am and I'm standing in Matt's restaurant. I've brought the photographer here early to catch the restaurant looking at its absolute best, with the new layout and design, before the party begins later. It's been closed for the last week while the decorators have worked their magic and given it a look for the new decade. I have to say, it looks fantastic. Blends the homely but modern style perfectly and it's all down to Matt's eye for detail. He knows what he wants and he makes it happen (in his work world at least).

I know that Matt isn't due here until 10am, when he will become a part of the photo shoot, so I'm safe for now and it shows-willing to Rich that I'm on board with everything today and not shirking away from it. I've 'unfortunately' managed to book myself an appointment with a potential new client at 9.45 so 'unfortunately' won't be able to walk Matt through the shoot, so Rich is going to take over at that point.

Just as I'm guiding the photographer round the sparkling kitchen, I hear a voice from the front of the restaurant, I peer through the porthole window and it's Fay. Shit. Was hoping I wouldn't have to see anyone until later when the place is full.

"Matt? Are you here?" she clearly thinks its him that has opened up. I'm about to show my face when she says "Matt? Jesus Christ, where are you? It's enough that you didn't come home last night but at least be up and ready for today..." I contemplate, waiting and listening, to see if she has anything else to say as that has intrigued me (is Matt not going home? already off with another woman, playing away, maybe it's just what he does and my whole involvement with him was just 'another one of his affairs'), the thought breaks me a little bit but I must stay strong, today of all days.

I make my way out and act as if I haven't heard a word of what Fay has said,

"Hello?" I feign seeing her "oh hi Fay, how are you? We're just getting some shots of the kitchen and the restaurant while it's still gleaming."

"We?" she repeats suspiciously,

"Yes, me and Jamie, the photographer" he appears out of the kitchen just at the right moment, just in time, as it turns out, I think she thought that I was back there with Matt. Interesting. Stop thinking Kate.

"Oh sorry, Kate, I'm a bit flustered this morning" she approaches me now and air kisses each cheek, "I'd almost forgotten that it's your company running this today, you've done a great job. Thank you."

"It's our pleasure Fay, it's a great business to be involved in" aren't we nice to each other, very professional, which is important today. She starts to walk towards the office,

"Just need to sort a couple of things out in the office, don't let me stop you, do carry on." And she let's herself into the small room at the back by typing a code into the silver keypad. The door shuts behind her.

Jamie, the photographer, is still happy snapping at various parts of the restaurant as the door to the restaurant opens again and what appears to be a huge box with legs walks in. Trouble is, I'd know those legs anywhere, shit! He's not supposed to be here yet. But then why did I assume he would arrive dead on 10am? He can't see me for the box he's carrying, a massive white cake box which he's being very careful with. For a split second, I consider ducking into the toilets so he doesn't even know I'm there but then,

"Hello, can someone give me a hand? I can't really

see where I'm going and if I drop this bloody cake I'll never forgive myself." I look around in vain for help but my professionalism kicks in, thank god, and I approach him quickly,

"It's ok Matt, just go left a little so you avoid a table," I'm right next to him now and at the sound of my voice he seems to have frozen.

"Kate?" the box says in what sounds like shock. I place my hand on his arm and guide him between a couple of tables, he puts the cake down carefully and spins round to look at me. "Kate" he repeats but this time it's not a question, more like a relieved sigh. I see a small smile form at the corner of his mouth.

"I wasn't expecting…I didn't…I mean…shit" he is so flustered I feel the need to help him out,

"I'm here with the photographer, didn't think you'd be here until later, sorry if I've…"

"There you are" Fay's voice brings us back to earth and reality hits once again. "I thought you were holed up in your office again" Matt looks to her and then back at me like he can't breathe "you won't believe him Kate, sometimes he sleeps in that bloody office, he works way too hard…either that or he's trying to avoid me" she laughs and we all fake laugh together, there's something very surreal about this conversation. And the fact she is telling me that Matt sometimes sleeps at the restaurant makes me wonder what the hell is going on.

"Right Kate," it's Jamie, "I'm going to get some shots of the façade, ok?" I welcome his interruption and quickly make my way outside with him. Jesus, I knew I'd have to see Matt at some point today but not like that. To see him again has brought it all back, those feelings, the heartache, the love I still feel for him. I feel pathetic and crazy for him all at once.

I'm standing on the pavement outside when Matt and Fay both exit the restaurant,

"We're off to pick up the new menus, Kate" Fay shouts across to me, "Oh and I still haven't received your RSVP, you know, for the Vow Renewal Ceremony" I look to Matt, he looks to the ground. Enough said.

11.30am

I'm back at my desk having just finished my 9.45. I don't think for a second the guy will hire us, everything was about money. He seemed to think we'd do it all for free and if it was a success he'd pay us, we're not a bloody profit share scheme, bloody idiot. But then, to be honest, at least it went on long enough so that I didn't have to return to the restaurant. Rich is back and says the photo shoot with Matt went well.

"Saw some of the shots" Rich shouts across from his desk, "They make the guy look incredibly handsome" steady Rich, "but I guess he is the kind of guy who the ladies would go for?" He looks to me for some sort of reassurance.

"Can't say I've ever really noticed" I lie through my teeth, "not my type" shut up now Kate, "not ever really looked at him in that way" I fear the lady doth protest too much! Rich looks right at me and his frown smiles so I redirect his thought process, "and anyway, don't bother me with your gay fantasies, if you like the guy tell him" we both laugh and turn back to our computer screens. I think Rich's eyes are still on me though, have I given the game away?

5pm

Rich and I arrive at the restaurant together. We have a few last-minute checks to make and ensure all the staff have arrived so the evening runs smoothly. Thankfully, there's no sign of Matt. Officially, the time on the invites is 6pm so this gives us time to make our checks and get a few final social media posts sorted ahead of the evening. Matt aside, I feel really proud of our little company for achieving such a high-profile gig, so, when we've got everything sorted, I grab two glasses of champagne from the bar and go over to Rich. He's been talking to the staff (event staff, just for tonight as Matt wanted his staff to be able to enjoy the launch, personally I'm not sure if this is good business or the sign of a push-over boss but that was Matt's decision).

Rich finishes his briefing and steps towards me, I hand him a glass of the Ayala Blanc de Blancs, (pricey stuff but I'm pretty sure Matt's been given this by a famous chef who will be endorsing Matt's brand by attending tonight) and we have a moment of nodding and looking round the room.

"Well done us" Rich declares quietly "We make a good team Kate, cheers," we clink glasses "here's to a successful evening"

"And many more Rich, well done" I beam at him. It's unfortunate that our first major event is overshadowed, for me, by the obvious but I'm so pleased with our achievements - the place looks amazing, we've got the press where we need them and we've got a guest list that could literally be on The Late Late Show with James Corden. It's amazing who you can get to come to the relaunch of a restaurant if they think it will help boost their career a little bit by having their pic taken with the up and coming celebrity chef. At the thought of Matt, and having to see him again soon, I take a too-large sip of the Ayala and then another, and then another. Just to calm my nerves.

"Right" Rich says, "Let's get this party started." And so it begins.

Guests arrive thick and fast, apparently it's not trendy to be late anymore. It seems everyone wants to be the first to step into the newly refurbished space and claim it as their own. Matt's entrance has been planned, he will be arriving (red carpet style) at 6.45pm so that the paps can get their shots outside and go home happy. The private photographers will then continue with the internal shots; we have managed to get one from Hello magazine so hopefully, all being well, (and barring any more Royal weddings) we should get a good spread. He arrives in a limo right on time. I can see it all happening through the window, Rich is standing outside to oversee everything but it all goes pretty smoothly. He and Fay get out of the car, he helps her out and they hold hands until they get to the door, waving at the paps on the way and looking like the perfect couple to everyone else. I guess they are, they have everything they want, and this launch will definitely put some more money in their pockets. Thanks to me. There's some sort of irony in there somewhere, I think, never been great with irony.

The evening appears to be going well. Matt has given a quick speech to thank everyone for coming and Fay is schmoozing the night away. I have been running around making sure everyone's glass is always full (not actually part of my job description for the evening but it keeps me busy). Rach is here as Rich's plus one. We couldn't decide if, as the event co-ordinators, we were supposed to have plus ones but Rach pretty much set us up in business by introducing us so it only seemed right that she attend. Rich also invited a couple of his old friends from where he used to work with Rach. That Tom guy is here, looking quite smart, and another guy who I don't know. I can see the four of them across the room and Rach gives me a quick nod to make sure I'm ok. She's the only one here who knows about my relationship with Matt (apart from Matt of course) so she's looking out for me. I give her a quick nod back and raise my champagne glass as she looks away. I then throw my head back and down the whole glass. Just need something to keep me focused. Although, that last glass has made me feel a little wobblier than I intended.

I can see Matt talking to a journalist and I just stare at him. God he looks good. He's wearing a Hugo Boss blue checked suit that clings to his gorgeous arse like… "Kate?" I'm brought out of my daydream by Tom who is now standing right next to me, I turn to face him and have to steady myself on his arm as I feel the champagne kick in.

"Oh hi Tom," I lean in to kiss his cheek, "It's so nice to see you again". I instinctively look across to Matt and he is looking directly at me, teeth clenched and cheeks rippling. Careful Kate. I don't let go of Tom's arm and I'm pretty sure he takes that as encouragement, why wouldn't he?

"I have to say Kate, all this is very impressive" his arm creeps around my waist as we stand and look at the party together. I don't discourage the closeness, I just shoot another look at Matt but he's looking away now, talking to another small group of partygoers.

"How do you feel?" Tom is still talking and I can feel his breath on my temple, maybe that's a little too close now, and if I'm honest, I feel like I need to sit down.

I try to get a little distance from him, stepping away, but I feel myself wobble some more and suddenly I'm heading to the floor, Tom reaches out to catch me but in his effort to grab me I end up pulling him down on to the floor too, shit shit shit. I'm suddenly aware of his body lifting away from me as if someone is picking him up and I see Matt pushing Tom away from him, Oh crap…

"Maybe you should keep your hands to yourself mate" Matt says as he straightens his jacket. But Tom has also had a few too many and doesn't appreciate Matt pushing him away. "What the fuck was that?" Tom shouts and the whole room seems to go quiet. FFS. What have I done?

"Just leave it Tom" I hear myself say as I attempt to get up off the carpet. Both of them are looking down at me and it's Matt that grabs my hand and pulls me to my feet. Rich and Rach have arrived and I can see how horrified Rich looks. He makes light of it,

"Everything ok Matt? Tom?" Matt and Tom have a stare off over my head as I'm sandwiched in between them and I haven't a clue what to do.

"Everything is fine" Matt speaks calmly, "but this gentleman was just leaving" Jesus, Matt is fuming. Why is he so cross? It was all just a misunderstanding. We're definitely drawing attention to ourselves. Fay is walking over. I look up at Matt, he's still staring at Tom like his clothes are going to burst off him at any moment and he's going to turn hulk.

"Everything ok over here?" Fay echoes Rich's words, she looks calm but is desperately trying to diffuse the situation. I just can't seem to move. I look into Matt's eyes and he finally takes his eyes off Tom and looks back at me. He looks so confused. I have no idea what he's thinking but I find my focus through him and my survival instinct finally kicks in.

"I'm so sorry everyone, I knew I shouldn't have worn these heels, never could get away with a stiletto." I look round at their faces in the hope that I have eased the tension and Rach helps as usual,

"But they are killer heels Kate" she winks at me and I hear Fay say,

"Is that all it was? Matt you are so chivalrous" she looks at me, pointedly as if to say, 'come on Kate, sort it out' and then she leads Matt away, making Matt even more the 'star of the night' as they go,

"My husband, always jumping in to help poor little damsels in distress, what a hero!" She looks back to me and I swear she's thinking 'I'll sort you out later bitch' but I'm sure (hope) it's just my imagination.

"Oh my god" Tom spits, "What is that guy's problem?" Rich stops him,

"Tom, can you just calm down, we all think he's a bit of a dick but can you just let it go, this evening is really important for the company" he pleads. Tom looks at Rich and then to me.

"I'd watch your back with him Kate, I've seen him watching you all evening" which makes me think maybe Tom has been watching me too? "pretty sure he fancies you and he's not the kind of guy who'll take no for an answer" I don't like Tom's words and insinuations and the alcohol kicks in again,

"Hold on a minute Tom, you can't just go saying that about people, Matt is one of the kindest people I know and...

"Oh I get it," Tom retorts rather bitterly, "you fancy him too, in fact the two of you are probably already shagging" Jesus, what is going on? Tom's voice gets louder and he's clearly drunk as well as pissed off, "Well this is going to look a bit awkward in Hello magazine..." Suddenly, Rich grabs Tom by the arm, and forcefully walks him into the kitchen, Tom puts up a bit of resistance which once again gets some attention from others around the room, including Matt who turns quickly and seems ready to come back to assist until Fay holds his arm tightly and manages to keep him rooted to the spot. My eyes meet Matt's again and I think I'm going to cry. Rach grabs my arm,

"Kate, focus on me, you've got to snap out of this, you're going to mess up the whole evening if you're not careful" wow, words of wisdom? She's right. If I'm not careful, everything I've been working for over the last few months, the business, getting over Matt, is going to come crashing down around me and I'll be back to square one all over again, what am I playing at? I needed Rach's reality check. I pull myself together. Blink my eyes a few times in an attempt to sober up and more importantly to stop looking at Matt.

"Rach, help me to save this"

"It's ok, nobody significant has really noticed. The photographers have been busy with Mary Berry. You might need to do some repair work with Rich though." I look at her and sigh. I'm such an idiot. Of all the nights to drink too much…

Rich returns from the kitchen minus Tom.

"Rich," I say, "I'm so sorry, I'm just nervous and let the pressure get to me. Don't worry. It'll be fine"

"You're right Kate" he says half looking at me and half smiling across the room at various people as if everything is fine, "Rach, can you put Kate in a cab and get her home please" he says very matter-of factly "and Kate, can you walk to the door without falling over anyone else and leave discretely" It's not a question, it's an order. He's really pissed off. Rach frowns and looks like she might try to defend me but Rich looks at her, pleadingly, and she nods.

"Come on Kate, let's get you a cab". She takes my arm again and guides me across the room. I can feel Matt's eyes on me as I walk through the crowd but I daren't look at him. I'm ashamed of my behaviour and I think I've lost my job. I need to just get out of here now. What a fuck up!

Outside, Rach hails a cab and puts me in it.

"Shit Rach,"

"It'll be ok, Rich is just focusing on the evening, he's got his business head on and he needs to make sure this is still a success"

"Which means he thinks it won't be a success if I stay" She just shrugs and winces,

"It'll be ok, just get yourself home, it's just damage

limitation" wow, that says it all, I have well and truly messed up. Rach tells the driver my address, shuts the door and the cab pulls away. I sit back in the seat and for the second time in as many months sob my heart out.

CHAPTER SIXTEEN

Sunday

I wake up in bed and feel quite surprised that I managed to make it this far considering how much I had to drink yesterday. My head aches. I start to relive the events of the evening and I feel like a complete idiot. I put the duvet back over my head, if I can sleep some more at least I don't have to think about it all. But unfortunately, the world has other plans for me.

I'm woken about an hour later by someone knocking at the door. I ignore it to start with, I really can't face anyone right now but then I hear my phone ringing too. I follow the sound of my phone to the floor at the side of the bed, stretch down to pick it up and see Rach's name flashing on the screen. Normally, she'd be my saviour at times like this (Times like this? As if I've ever had a time like this before!) but today she might be super pissed off with me considering I've messed up the job that she got for me with her boyfriend. What was I thinking last night? It could have been so different if I'd just managed to keep sober. But then, Matt didn't have to come over, I mean, he didn't really do himself any favours by intervening the way he did, did he? The phone stops ringing but starts again immediately and then another knock at the door. I answer the phone,

"Kate, it's only me at the door, I'm on my own, so come and let me in?" she sounds ok, not too irate, I don't think. I peel myself off the bed, wrap my cosy blanket round my shoulders and make my way to the door. "Bloody Hell Kate" she scoffs, "you look like shit!"

"I know, I feel it too" I walk away from the front door, Rach comes in and closes it behind her.

"Have you had a coffee yet?" She asks, making her way past me and towards the kitchen, "I'll put the kettle on now". I make my way to the sofa and dump myself on to it like a sack of potatoes which is pretty much how I feel: ugly, lumpy, smelly.

Rach places two coffees on the table and sits down next to me. She has that look on her face like 'well that was an interesting evening' a sort of grimace/smile without really knowing what to say so I start,

"How's Rich today? Is he going to fire me?" I look at her to gauge an instant reaction, I know Rach can't lie to me. She immediately shakes her head.

"No, of course he isn't going to fire you. He's not stupid Kate, you've almost single-handedly created a client list for Rich Events which he couldn't have, he just doesn't have the schmooze ability like you do." (not always a good thing it turns out!) I do feel a 'but' coming…

"But," (yep) "he does want you to take a bit of time off. You see, Kate, the thing is…I told him." She told him what? That I can't hold my alcohol, that I blag my way through everything in life…that…oh shit no, "I told him about you and Matt" She looks at me, and flinches, almost like she thought I might have lashed out at her.

"Shit Rach, that's big" I guess she had to.

"It was the only way I could explain last night, I mean, if he thought that you were going to behave like that at every event you put on then he probably would have thought about firing you. When I told him about Matt, it's like everything clicked into place for him. He said there was a weird tension between you and Matt and he could never work out why so when I told him you'd been in a relationship with him, Rich understood why you were so reluctant to go to the meetings."

Wow, I guess she was right to tell him. Makes me feel pretty awkward though.

"Look Kate, you know what Rich is like, he's a nice guy, he understands that you've been hurt and the last thing he wants to do is fire you. In fact, he even joked that if it wasn't for the affair then Rich Events might not have got the business from Matt and things might not be quite so successful right now" she chuckles but then stops when she notices how much my eyebrows have risen.

"Ha" I say with some dead-pan sarcasm, but Rich is probably right. Matt asked for the meeting in the first place so he could see me so who knows where we'd be now without that. That's so messed up!

"What about last night?" I ask a little hesitantly, "How did it all end?"

"It was fine, nothing more was said about Tom being asked to leave, there were a couple of journos there who asked what happened but Rich just explained that one of the guests had enjoyed a little too much of the free champagne and felt it best to leave. Your good sense at inviting the higher-end magazines was fortuitous as there were no gossip mags around. Matt's wife made Matt out to be some sort of hero when he came to your rescue. I guess she knows how to make the best of a bad situation." Ouch! Was that a dig at me?

"What about Tom, is he going to keep his mouth shut, he was saying all sorts about me and Matt." Rach puts her calming hand over mine,

"It's fine, I've already spoken to him this morning and thankfully, he feels a complete twat and sees it all as his fault so he won't be repeating what he said. He's gutted as he thinks he's blown it with you" she sees my furrowed expression, "You must know that he totally fancies you?" I shake my head.

"Lucy did say something about that, but I just thought she was being silly. Bloody hell, this just gets worse doesn't it?"

"Or better," Rach is always optimistic, "Tom's a nice guy, you could do a lot worse." That's so not what I want to think about right now, so I just look away and Rach gets the message.

"Anyway, Rich thinks you need some time to sort your head out a little bit. He says he can run the office for a while, your next event is virtually set up and it's only a champagne breakfast so he can handle that." She starts to smile, "So," she sings the word, going all the way up and down a scale as she says it, "he suggested that me and you book ourselves a girly holiday" not exactly what I was expecting her to say.

"Really? He wants you and me to go away on a 'girly holiday'?" I'm not sure he understands the consequences of girly holidays, Rach and I have been on several before.

"Well let's call it a grown-up girly holiday. A beach holiday, somewhere lovely where we can both relax."

"And you're ok with this?" She hasn't wanted to spend a second away from Rich since they became official.

"Hell yeah, I think it's a great idea. I'll miss Rich, of course, and I don't intend to do the kind of things we did in our twenties but a holiday in the sun, on a beach all day, lounging round with my bestie? What's not to love?" When it's put like that, sounds perfect. I'm starting to warm to the idea.

"And Rich thinks this would be good for me?" I question.

"Absolutely, he thinks you haven't had the chance to get over Matt properly before the relaunch happened and he wants you to take some time so that you're properly focused when you get back. He needs you to be a reliable part of the business, so this makes sense to him." And put like that, I think it makes sense to me too. In fact, I actually feel a little bit excited about going. I haven't had a holiday for ages. My phone pings on the table in front of us and Rach sees Matt's name come up before I do.

"Kate?" she sings "I thought you and him were over"

"We are over" and I mean it. I'm more surprised than

she is. What the hell does he want? "After everything that happened last night, me nearly wrecking his relaunch, it's probably a barrage of abuse towards me" I secretly hope that it's not though and am wondering what lovely Matt words are now sitting waiting in my phone. I resist the temptation to look while Rach is still here. I direct our thoughts back to the girly holiday and we start to plan when and where. She needs to make sure she can get time off work too but all being well, we're going this week! Arrgghh I'm so excited, I think this is just what I need. And to be honest, this outcome is a million times better than what I was imagining.

Rach leaves about 30 minutes later and I virtually run to my phone to see what Matt wants. I take a deep breath and open the text. It's long.

There's so many things I want to say to you. I'm sorry being the most obvious. I'm an idiot. A real idiot. But I'm only an idiot when it comes to you, Kate. You have always had that effect on me and you always will. I can't believe I jeopardised all our hard work with the restaurant last night, not to mention your job and for that I'm sorry. You've made it clear to me that it's over and I've struggled to accept that. I'm still struggling. But I know we can't go on like this. And I don't want to hurt you anymore. I'm going to delete your number from my phone, so I am not tempted to text you anymore. I respect your decision to end our relationship, but I just want you to know that I will always love you and I will never regret anything that has happened between us. I love you Kate, Matt xx

Fuck.

CHAPTER SEVENTEEN

Friday – The Holiday

Five days later and I'm sitting on a sun lounger on the Costa Del Sol. We found the most perfect beach: hire a sunbed for the day, swim in the sea whenever we like, nip for a quick bite to eat on the strip, back to the sun lounger. It's heaven here, a million miles away from the chaos of my life back home. The last couple of days out here with Rach have made me realise that it's me that makes my life complicated and so it's me that can uncomplicate it. Trouble with me is (where do I begin?) that I become emotionally attached to every single thing I do or any person that I meet. I allow myself to be led but also confuse matters by occasionally putting my own opinion into the mix. That's when confusion ensues. There's only three people that have really been able to work me out, Rach, my oldest and best friend; Lucy, who just got me straight away and decided my way was ok; and of course Matt, the days and a few weekends when we had been alone together, few and far between, were perfect and I won't regret them either but we're done, finally. I did reply to Matt's message but it was plain and straight forward and said very simply: *Ditto* I didn't hear from him after that and I deleted his number from my phone. Rach thinks this is hilarious, she reckons I can contact him any time I want to through work or by just turning up at the restaurant and thinks I'm kidding myself a bit. This all came out at the airport. And I know she's right. If I really wanted to, I could see him or ring him but at least I'm trying to move on and away from the situation.

I lounge back on my sun bed and stretch my arms up. Just to be able to relax like this is fantastic. No work, no relationships, nothing complicated at all. The hardest decision is deciding what to eat. It's bliss.

"Here you go" Rach hands me an ice-cream, "It's a mango and strawberry sorbet, the guy said you'd love it because you loved that lemon and mint sorbet yesterday." The fact that it tasted like a mojito had nothing to do with it. I use the tiny spoon to get a taste of the sorbet and it's amazing, just what's needed when you feel this hot but this relaxed and I finish it quickly. Rach plonks down on her sunbed next to me. She's been a bit grumpy today. I think she's missing Rich more than she thought she would. She's never really been in a serious relationship before and I think the strength of her feelings for him has surprised her but in a good way. Now she's away from him, for the first time since they started seeing each other, she's a bit lost. Which is sweet in a frustrating sort of way. I'd like my fun friend right now so we can really kick back and enjoy this place.

Just then, there's some screaming and shouting in front of us on the water and Rach and I both turn to look at what's happening. Some lads have hired a pedalo and seem to be going round in circles with it. I put my hand up to my forehead to shield my eyes and get a better look. There's a slide on the back of the pedalo that you climb up to and then slide down straight into the sea. It looks like great fun and those lads are certainly enjoying it. I look at Rach,

"Let's hire ourselves one of them and have a proper fun day in the water." Rach looks at me, quizzical,

"I don't know, it looks a bit crazy"

"Exactly, come on. Let's get crazy". I jump up off the lounger and pull Rach up and towards the pedalo guy at the edge of the water. I strike a quick deal with him, pay him, we jump on and he pushes us out into the water so we can get our pedals working. It's actually quite hard work. My leg muscles are aching before we've gone ten metres. Rach and I look at each other with a bit of a grimace and a giggle, our faces say it all, maybe we've bitten off more than we can chew, but we keep going. We're not too far out and decide to stop and float for a bit. Rach has found her sea legs, if you call them that on a pedalo, and she's climbing the steps up to the top of the slide. I watch her and decide we should take it in turns, otherwise the pedalo might get away from us, although I'm sure the guy hiring them out must have had to swim out for a few of them in his time.

Rach whizzes down the slide and flies off the end, up into the air before basically arse slapping the water. She maybe needs to work on her entry technique. It's like something off You've been Framed and I really wish I'd filmed it. Rach resurfaces to see me laughing ridiculously at her misfortune. She bobs up and down in the water and if looks could kill, she's not happy about my hilarity.

Just then something hits the pedalo and I'm jolted forward slightly.

"Shit, what the.." I look round to see another pedalo has ploughed into ours.

"Woops, you idiot Chris, I told you it was too close". It's the boys from the other pedalo but I'm pretty sure from their fake acting that they totally intended to crash into us. Rach grabs the side of our pedalo and attempts to haul herself back on board with little success. She tries again and starts to giggle, you know that kind of giggle where all your muscles and bodily functions stop working. After a while she's laughing so hard at herself that she's lost all ability to do anything.

"Oh my god, I give up, I'm swimming back" and she's off, leaving me with a bloody big pedalo to pedal back all by myself. Another shunt and the boy's pedalo crashes into ours (mine as it turns out!) again.

"Hey, where's your friend gone?" one of them shouts across. I look across at them properly now as it turns out

I might need a hand. The guy that spoke has dark hair and looks young, fresh-faced I guess you could say. (And it's quite a nice face too!) He stands up and their pedalo wobbles a little. The other two are on the pedals and make it rock a bit as he stands and has to get his balance.

"Ha ha funny you guys" then he skillfully steps from his pedalo to my pedalo and sits himself down next to me.

"Um hello" I say, secretly glad he's there as I manifested a hero right at that moment, but it won't do any harm to play the innocent naïve heroine.

"Looked like you needed a hand" he turns to me and smiles (killer smile, perfect white teeth and cheek bones to die for but friendly too, not a cheesy smile). We hold each other's gaze for a few seconds before I say,

"I could have managed," yeah right, "I mean I'm not some weak woman that needs rescuing",

"Ok" he makes to get up and leave but I place my hand on his arm "although now you're here" and I do my best flirty smile. (omg Kate, you're incorrigible, you never stop!)

"Right, now the best way to get this going is to push down into the pedals, use your thigh muscles, right here" he pats the tops of his legs and I can't help but notice his defined muscles through his wet shorts, nice, very nice. (Kate, enough!)

Suddenly, with his help this thing is easy to pedal and we're gliding smoothly through the water back towards the shore.

"My name's Chris by the way" he looks at me

"I'm Kate"

"Really nice to meet you Kate." Gosh he's young but so polite and a gentleman.

"Really nice to meet you too Chris". And we smile at each other, one of those holiday smiles that might be totally innocent but might be totally loaded with promise and innuendo. I'll make my mind up about that one later.

He gives me a hand down on to the beach and boy is he strong. Almost lifts me off the pedalo and places me gently on the sand. Oh here come the flutters. And why not, I'm here to have fun, aren't I? As always, Matt flashes into my mind and a tinge of guilt momentarily consumes me, like even having those thoughts are cheating on him. But, I'm young, free and single and I can do what I want. Have some fun Kate, that's what you're here for.

"Might see you later" he says as he lets me go, I do a sort of twirl round as I'm walking away,

"Maybe" I smile and try to be as sexy as possible but fail miserably, nearly getting one foot wedged in the sand as I spin round. But, as I walk away, I'm pretty sure he's still looking at me. Should I turn again? No, just keep walking, cool and calm.

7.30pm

Back at the hotel, Rach suggests we try a new bar tonight, we've been to the same one for the last two nights as it's not too flash or full of idiots which suits us but she's heard about this other place called Monroe's from the ice cream guy so we're going there.

Rach seems to have perked up a bit. She facetimed Rich when we got back to the hotel and she seems a bit more up for a good time now. I think she's realised it's ok to miss someone and still have fun.

I decide to wear a white denim skirt and an almost off the shoulder little shirt that both show off the start of my tan nicely. And, being honest, make me look a little younger. I mean, not like mutton/lamb younger but Rach says they definitely give me a fun, youthful air, and I'm all in for feeling young right now. Rach looks stunning. She hasn't even tried (what's the point when she has Mr Perfect back home) but she always looks gorgeous. She's wearing a pink maxi dress which would make me look like a sack of potatoes, but she looks sophisticated and classy, two things I'll never quite pull off.

We arrive at the bar about 8 and it's nicely buzzing, not too busy but not embarrassingly quiet. Rach orders us a cocktail each (should have learnt my lesson here) mine's orange in colour and potent in flavour, could not tell you what's in it but it's definitely alcohol. We make our way to a high table close to the glass fronted mezzanine and perch delicately on the stools. I say delicately, because if I did anything other than perch in this skirt then I might look like a high-class prostitute looking for business. (high class, who am I kidding!)

"Thanks for today Kate" Rach looks at me a bit sheepishly. "I was feeling really low this morning and you made me realise that we're here to have some fun, sorry if I was being a dull cow" she smiles,

"Don't be daft Rach, I know you miss Rich, I get why, it is allowed you know".

"I know, but I don't want to spoil the holiday for you, we're supposed to be here so you can get over Matt, and me moping around doesn't help" and neither does mentioning Matt, I suddenly feel different. Just his name is enough to make me want to cry. Need to be stronger Kate, need to move on. Quickly. Rach must have seen my face drop as she says,

"Shit sorry, didn't mean to bring him into it" she ponders this and then "…but I guess there's no point in pretending it never happened, part of getting over someone is acknowledging how you used to feel about them and moving away from those feelings" words of wisdom or just a stark reminder that I haven't got over him yet? Haven't I? Why not? Just move on Kate.

Rach looks down over the glass barrier and waves at someone below. I look down to see who on earth it is and for a split second have a little panic that Rich has flown over to be with her because they miss each other so much and maybe this is why she has perked up since this morning… but I look just in time to see it's not Rich (thankfully), it's Chris from the pedalo. I quickly look back at Rach who's now looking at me with a grin on her face but she quickly turns her gaze elsewhere.

"Rach?" she looks at me innocently, "what have you done?"

"What do you mean? I haven't done a thing" but she smiles cheekily into her glass and I fear a set-up. Just then Chris appears at our table,

"Hi Kate" his eyes are on me straight away, kind of searching mine to see if he's welcome. I look back to Rach whose raising her eyebrows at me as if to say, 'say something then!' I look back at Chris and bite my bottom lip, he looks down at my mouth and I start to get the flutters. (He is so good looking). He's wearing a blue shirt and beige tailored shorts and I suddenly realise I'm giving him the 'up and down' like I'm really checking him out (which I am) so quickly return my gaze to his face and he's smirking a little bit as he obviously realises what I'm doing but he's still looking at me, waiting for a reply… shit speak Kate,

"Um, hi Chris" I'm flustered now, not at all cool "I'm sorry, just surprised to see you, you not with your friends?" he looks to Rach who is just starting to giggle. I look at her too. "What's so funny?" I ask, but only as I don't know what else to say, this isn't the easiest few seconds of my life…

"Actually Kate, I'm really sorry but I'm not feeling great" Rach says this with a smile on her face the whole time, not feeling great, my arse! "So, if you don't mind…"

"Rach, don't you…"

"Sorry Kate but I really need to lie down, but look, Chris is here now so you stay out and have some fun," I try to interrupt her again but she knows exactly what she's doing as she grabs her bag and slides off the stool, "sorry again you guys, have fun!" and she's gone.

I watch her go and then turn to Chris. (He is so attractive). He's smiling at me.

"Is this ok? She said you'd be up for a drink with me but I didn't realise that maybe you didn't…um…know… anything about it?" He's really hesitant and it's really endearing. He seems so naïve and that's so sexy. The top two buttons of his shirt are undone and I can't take my eyes off the golden skin underneath, almost rippling as he talks and I remember just how good he looked on the pedalo without his shirt on. Back in the room Kate!

"Kate?"

"Sorry, Chris, I'm just a bit surprised. I was expecting a girly night out and…"

"I turn up and ruin that for you?" he apologises. (So good looking)

"No, you haven't ruined it," I'm not sure what to say to him, maybe that doesn't bode well, "I'm not sure what you've done to be honest" he laughs and so do I.

"Look, let's just have a drink together and then I'll walk you back to your hotel, I don't want to make you feel awkward, Kate." God I love the way he says my name. He's got a slight Scottish twang, a little touch of Richard Madden in his tone. (he actually looks a bit like him too) And who would say no to that? I get my head sorted and say,

"Let's have a drink, and then just see what happens, is that ok?"

"Sounds great" he smiles again. Flutters. And so it begins.

Two hours later, I'm walking along the beach with Chris. I've taken my shoes off and it feels lovely to have the still-warm sand between my toes. We've basically been talking since Rach left. I think we've shared quite a lot in such a short space of time. I know that he's 24, originally from Glasgow but left there to go to Uni in London and has lived there ever since (only five years, even though he tries to make it sound like he's older and wiser than 24!) His degree was in business and he now works for one of the corporate banks. He's pretty switched on and knows his stuff, he's easy to talk to, quite intelligent but quite sensitive, I think. Maybe he's just good at 'being on the pull' because who wouldn't be attracted to all of that?

We're getting closer to the water and it's so peaceful and quiet. For a moment, I sort of forget Chris is there and just enjoy the moment. This is what I needed, to be away from the crapness of reality for a while so I can realise that life isn't so bad.

"Kate, you ok?" I turn to look at him and just take him in, his face, his arms, his hands and I move closer to him. I put my hands on his arms and feel my way up over his shoulders and then on to his chest. He tenses under my touch and breathes in and I can feel his muscles flex a little. When I look up at him, he relaxes and starts to lean towards me. His lips are soft on mine and his arms wrap round me. He slides one hand up my back to my neck and the other finds the curves of my bum as he pulls me closer to him. It feels nice. It feels like it should. Like I'm a single girl on holiday, having some fun. His naivety disappears as he expertly explores my mouth with his tongue and I hear him groan a little as my hands find his bum and give it a little squeeze. I smile under his lips and he pulls back from me.

"Want to come back to my room?" he whispers and I know that that is exactly what I want.

CHAPTER EIGHTEEN

Saturday 8am

My phone goes off and I pick it up to see Rach's name on the screen. I'm lying in bed next to Chris, he's asleep.

I take it you went back to Chris's and you're not lying dead in a ditch somewhere?

Nope I'm dead, some friend you turned out to be leaving me alone with a psychotic killer

You had sex then ;-) You're always funny when you've had sex not quite sure how to take that but I guess she's right. I'm definitely more relaxed when I feel like there's someone in this world who is attracted to me and I guess being relaxed brings out my funnies.

Breakfast at Mango at 9? an hour gives me time to freshen up and say goodbye. If indeed that is the etiquette of holiday sex. I probably should have left by now. I'm pretty sure it's the job of the person whose room it isn't to leave before the person whose room it is wakes up and therefore if any embarrassment might be had by either party it is quickly and easily eradicated. But, I'm still here. Maybe Chris is actually awake too and is pretending to be asleep to give me that chance to leave. I will. I look round the room to try and spot where my clothes ended up so that I can pick them up quickly and quietly without waking him. I spot my denim skirt on the floor next to the bed and I think that's my knickers sticking out from underneath it. I look a bit further and see my shirt slung over a chair, I'm hoping my bra is close by but I can't see it so will have to take my chances.

Slowly and quietly, I start to pull back the sheet and edge myself off the bed. I turn to look at Chris. He's still sleeping. For a moment, I drink him in. He's kind of beautiful lying there in white sheets, tanned body, muscles rippling under the sheet as he breathes in and out. And I give myself a metaphorical pat on the back, 'good job Kate, in your thirties and still attracting the Chrises of this world'. I smile, feeling proud but I have lingered too long and he's stirring, shit. I lift myself off the bed, pick up my clothes and nip into the bathroom before he realises. Phew. While there, I look in the mirror, just as well I'm leaving before he wakes, think he might realise he's pulled a granny. I get dressed, splash some water over my face, get a bit of toothpaste on my finger and swish it round my mouth and then slowly open the door back into the bedroom.

"You sneaking out?" Chris is leaning up on one elbow, still lying in bed, sheets now covering his bottom half only. God he looks good like that.

"Um, I was just, I mean, I thought maybe…" completely arsing this up,

"Do you have to go?" Oh, I wasn't expecting that. "I mean, you could come back to bed and keep me warm" he flashes that smile at me once more,

"Yeah, 'cos it's so cold here!" I say with sarcasm and what I'm hoping is a flirtatious smile on my face.

"It is so so cold," and he pulls back the sheet to reveal his bottom half, "I'm completely frozen stiff." And there's not too much I can say to that so I stay…and I warm him up.

9.37am

"Sorry sorry sorry" I say as I run into Mango and rush to the table we have frequented for breakfast these last three mornings.

"I should think so too" Rach just smiles and looks pleased with me or for me. Maybe both. "So, I've ordered us the usual, hope that's ok?" She takes a sip of orange juice and indicates that I have one too. I take a sip and nod.

"Come on then, how was last night?" She leans forward and looks expectant, she wants details.

It was good Rach, it was great." It was, "And this morning wasn't bad either" Rach's jaw drops and she laughs,

"Nice, well done you, he was hot" she smiles and leans back again.

"And it's definitely true what they say about men in their twenties and sexual prime" I wink at her.

"Jesus Kate, enough now",

"You asked!" we laugh and I decide that's enough detail. But I meant it. Chris is really fit; we were at it most of the night and if I hadn't insisted that I was meeting Rach for breakfast...

But anyway, I feel like a new me today. Like I've laid some ghosts to rest and I'm moving on. I feel liberated. And we've still got 3 days left!

CHAPTER NINETEEN

A few hours later and Rach and I are back on our sunbeds, the same ones, creatures of habit (and it makes it easier for Chris to find me again should he come looking!) My phone pings and I slowly come out of my sleepy stupor to see who it is.

"Don't read it," Rach starts "if it's not me then it's not important." She says in a sort of dreamlike voice, we're both sun-drunk. I squint at my phone and try to focus on the screen.

I miss you. I'm not sure I can do this

I'm suddenly brought out of my daydream. WTF? I sit up and look at the number, there's no name. which can only mean one thing. It's Matt. He hasn't deleted my number, as I have his, and he's going back on what he said about respecting my decision to end the relationship. I'm angry, no I'm fuming. I look across at Rach but her eyes are still closed and she's none the wiser to my disgust (and confusion). The selfish bastard. It's not even been a week since his sincere text and…ignore it, delete it. I go to press delete and find myself reading it again. *I miss you. I'm not sure I can do this* God I miss him too. I momentarily imagine what it would be like if we were properly together as we'd planned and we were on holiday together as a couple for all the world to see.

Stop. Don't go back there. You're doing fine. I delete the message, put my phone down and close my eyes, making a little tear run down my cheek.

I must have fallen asleep because when I open my eyes again, there's someone sitting on my sunbed, I squint and shade my eyes with my hand to see who it is.

"Hey beautiful" the sultry subtle Scottish tones

completely seduce me in two words, I feel the corners of my mouth turn upwards involuntarily but I don't mind him seeing my delight at his presence.

"Hey yourself" I say, in an attempt to sound young. His hands are on my ankles and he wraps his fingers round them in a playful and familiar way.

"Do you fancy joining me for a swim?" he raises his eyebrows and I'm wondering exactly what he means by a swim as it sounds a bit loaded. I look across at Rach, she's reading her book and without taking her eyes from it, just says,

"Run along you two." Chris jerks his head as if to say 'come on'. And he takes my hand and we walk towards the sea.

The beach is less busy today. It's Saturday. Rach and I booked a midweek to midweek holiday so for us it's the middle of our holiday but most people are on their way home or on their way here I guess. I thought Chris might have been leaving today but him and his mates are here for ten days, they leave the day before we do.

Chris leads me out deeper into the water until I can hardly stand, think he was serious about the swim. He's a good few inches taller than me so he's still gliding through the water as I start to swim. He turns to face me and puts his hands on my waist before leaning in to kiss me. As I can't touch the ground anymore, he lifts me and I wrap my legs around him. His skin feels amazing against mine and he's already excited. He pushes himself against me and I start to realise what his 'swim' actually means. Though, I'm a little self-conscious and really not sure it's a good idea. I pull back from his kiss but keep my legs wrapped round him.

"We can't Chris, not here" I whisper, smiling at him.

"Why not? Nobody is around us, no-one's even noticed us" His hands move down over my bum and into my bikini bottoms. I'm starting to throb for him again and there might be no going back soon. "Do you want to stop?" he says, as his hands stop caressing my buttocks. I look at him and then look back towards the beach. There's nobody around us. And it feels so nice to be in his arms again, feeling his skin on mine… I look back at him and shake my head. I lean back in to kiss him and feel him get harder. He softly pulls my bikini bottoms to one side and guides himself into me. It's not exactly like you imagine in the movies, it doesn't exactly go smoothly, getting the right angle is a lot more tricky than some actors/directors would lead us to believe but, oh my, once we're together, it's just like the movies. He's so strong to stand in the water like this while its pushing us back and forth and we start to move with the waves, I tighten my legs round him so that I can keep pulling him in further and further and at that point it honestly doesn't matter if anyone can see us because nothing's going to stop us now. (Starship's song starts playing in my head and I have a little inward giggle to myself because it's true).

So, Chris and I spend the next couple of days together, in and out of the water. I like his company; as holiday romances go, he's up there. Rach is happy enough to lounge on the sunbed all day while Chris and I do our thing,

"This is why we came on holiday Kate, so that you can have some fun" Rach tells me when I share my concerns at spending too much time with Chris. She's fine with it. Although she did have a go at me for the sea episode, "Unprotected sex Kate, are you kidding me? How old are you? You should know better!" She was right of course, it was stupid of me. I know I can't get pregnant but I should have been more careful. STIs are rife and on holiday… I spoke to Chris about it and he tried to reassure me that he'd also never had unprotected sex with anyone before, he just couldn't help it with me, or words to that effect and it was a bit late to worry about it after the event. I'd just have to trust him and never do it again. Idiot. So apart from that, Rach was fine with everything.

Chris's mates weren't too happy and seemed to put a bit of pressure on him but it didn't bother him and we spent the rest of the time as a sort of couple I guess. Both knowing that once the holiday was over, the relationship was too. Which was fine, he's far too young for me but it's been fun.

CHAPTER TWENTY

Tuesday 2pm

Chris's flight is at 6 tonight and they're leaving for the airport soon. We're sitting having a final drink together to say goodbye.

"Kate, I know we said we wouldn't but..." oh no, "can I have your number?" oh dear. "It would be good to keep in touch, wouldn't it be a bit weird now if we just say goodbye and never see each other again?" I try not to frown,

"Or it would be good, we say goodbye and look back on this as a really lovely holiday romance." I try to be emphatic in my tone but I'm not sure it's working.

"But the truth is Kate, I don't want to not see you again" he takes my hand and recognises the angst on my face

"Don't get me wrong, I'm not in love with you" a little ouch "but I would just love to see you again, we don't live that far away from each other and it would seem a real shame if we didn't continue with all this amazing sex back home....wouldn't it?" he places his hand on my thigh and lets it slide higher up, giving me a few tingles. He does sort of have a point but things always get complicated and I'm supposed to be uncomplicating my life.

"I think it's better if we just say goodbye here" he looks down and I feel the need to reassure him, "this has been such an amazing holiday for me, because of you Chris, and I want to remember it like that".

"Ok" he says, "it was worth an ask though" he smiles. "I'm going to miss you beautiful Kate." We stand and he pulls me to him, places his lips on mine one last time, looks into my eyes, smiles and takes a deep breath. "Have a great life gorgeous" and he leaves.

Tuesday Evening

Rach and I decide to enjoy our last full evening in the bar we started in a week ago. This holiday has been a breath of fresh air in many ways. I've realised a lot about myself. I can be strong when I really put my mind to it and I do have the will power to say 'no' to someone. Like Chris and his number. I feel super liberated and a little bit empowered. I made the decision and I stuck to it. Pat on the back, Kate.

I still feel a bit guilty for spending so much time away from Rach although I think her and Rich have been endlessly texting (or sexting judging by some of the giggles I've heard coming from Rach's room).

So, this evening, is our evening, me and my bestie. No phones. No texts. No men. Just Kate and Rach.

We're sipping cocktails and I notice Rach's eyes on me.

"What?" I ask, smiling

"You look different!" she beams.

"In a good way or bad way?" "Definitely good. You look like a weight has been lifted. I think Chris was good for you" and then under her breath "even if he was a child" I slap her arm and laugh

"Oi, you said age doesn't matter"

"No, it doesn't, Kate. It's fine" she's still laughing "Mrs Robinson" I slap her again and we both laugh.

"What about you," I say, "You and your phone seem to be having a rather close relationship at the moment" I raise an eyebrow, "there's definitely been some interesting noises coming from your bedroom. What will I tell Rich when we get back?"

"I think you'll find he was with me all the way" she says with a wry smile.

"Ok that's enough." I plead, "That's my boss you're talking about." And we continue laughing while downing our drinks.

"What about that? Going back to work with Rich? You feeling ok about it, even though he knows everything?" I take a deep breath and feel the Matt pang again. I suppose I need to admit to myself that I can't just forget him. Those memories are going to stay with me for a long time, forever maybe, so there's no point denying them, I just have to learn to live with them I guess.

"It'll be fine Rach, I trust Rich, he's not the sort to hold it against me or use it in anyway. In fact, I'm glad he knows, it might make things a bit easier if anything comes back after the relaunch. At least he knows now it would be better for him to deal with it. I'm honestly just looking forward to getting back to work. I've missed that part of my life." I say sincerely.

"Have you missed any other part?" I know exactly what she means. And I try to be honest.

"I do miss Matt, Rach, but it's over. It's more than over. I've had this chance to move on and..." (pangs again) "...he'll be happily remarried to his beautiful wife by now so it's more than over."

"Don't want this to sound cheesy or patronising Kate, but I'm so proud of you" she takes hold of my hand, "I know you loved him". And I did, do. But,

"Some things have to end Rach" enough said.

We spend the rest of the night giggling at our past indiscretions and then eyeing up a few men around the place. None of which will be coming back with either of us tonight. I really do need a night off after Chris. And it's lovely to actually spend some quality time with Rach again. We decide to go back to the hotel about 10.30pm as our flight is at 9am and we need to be leaving about 6.30am. We've already packed, Rach's forward thinking in case we got drunk, so we just chill for a bit on the balcony with some water (Rock and Roll) before we go to bed. I take a last look out over the beach, still bustling with drunken people and the lovely sounds of holiday, breathe it all in and make my way to bed. I'm ready to move on.

CHAPTER TWENTY-ONE

Wednesday

Our flight back was fairly uneventful. I slept a lot and Rach continued to text Rich. He can't come to the airport to meet her as he has a meeting with a new client (one I don't even know about yet!) and he says it's too big an opportunity to miss. Rach seems fine with that as I think she's got big plans for their 'reunion' and from what she's said, it'll definitely be better if they're alone for that!

We make our way through customs and I'm feeling totally refreshed and ready for my next chapter. Matt fleetingly skips through my mind but, to be honest, it's a positive feeling, I've empowered myself to be in control again and I know I can do this. My thoughts are rudely interrupted by Rach suddenly pulling at my arm and away from the shops,

"Alright," I say laughing, "I was only going to get a bottle of water" she's still pulling at me, hauling me across the concourse, what's wrong with her? "What's going on Rach?"

"Nothing, I just want to get out of here, let's just get a taxi and get home" blimey she really does have big plans for Rich, she keeps tugging at my arm and I can feel her nails going into my skin,

"Rach, for god's sake, will you just…" and then I see it, the newspaper stand outside, Rach was desperately trying to steer me away from it, it can't be, it must be someone else, mustn't it? I mean, why would, why haven't I, why??? The headline reads:

'CELEBRITY CHEF DITCHES WIFE AT ALTAR'

I stop stock still and Rach knows I've seen it.

"Just ignore it Kate, keep walking" but I can't. I can't even move. I don't know what to think. I can hardly breathe. What do I do now? Shit shit shit.

Rach hauls me into the nearest bar, I hear her ask the bartender for a straight whisky as I stand in dismay, staring and fidgeting and feeling numb and scared and excited (nooo!) So many questions are flying round my head! Has he left her? Has he done it for me? Does he want me? Does anyone know about me? Have I been named? Oh my god! What if I've been mentioned? Shit shit shit.

I manage to free myself from Rach's grip. I down the whisky she's put in front of me in one swift movement and slam the glass back down on the bar.

"I need to read that article" I say as I turn and run out of the bar before she gets the chance to restrain me and I find my extreme desperation to find out what the hell has gone on propelling me to the news-stand. I throw some money at the guy (I think it might have been a tenner, judging by his shouts after me as I return to Rach in the bar).

"Another whisky" I say to the bartender as I stare at the headline. I feel Rach's eyes burning into me. "I just need to see what it says Rach, that's all." I look at her now, almost pleading to let me read it without trying to stop me. She sees my need. I'm visibly shaking.

"Ok, but let's read it together" I grab the whisky and we make our way to a table.

The strapline says that Celebrity Chef Matthew Grove, who was supposed to be renewing his wedding vows to his wife of 5 years left her humiliated in front of all their friends and family when he stopped the ceremony and ran out. Apparently, Hello magazine were there covering it and will eventually tell the full story but for now all that's known is that he's gone into hiding to avoid the pressure of the media. His agent has said that 'it's a difficult time for Matt and his wife and they need some time to work out what happens next'. What the hell does all that mean?

Rach finishes reading the same time as I do,

"Kate, stop thinking, this is not about you. You cannot go back to thinking that you have a chance together, you have moved past this. Don't let it set you back again."

"But, what if, what if he couldn't go through with it because of me, because he realised that me and him..." she stops me.

"Enough Kate. I will not let you put yourself through this again. Christ, you could have any man you want and you're seriously considering Matt again? After the week you've just had, making yourself get over him, you have to stick to that Kate, you have to. You have no idea what is happening between them and if you let just a little bit of false hope cloud your strength and judgement now then you'll get hurt again. That's all Matt has ever done, he hurts you Kate and I for one will not let that happen again. You're worth so much more than that."

Wow, speech! I take a deep breath and feel my shoulders relax a bit. Rach is right. For one, Matt and Fay might be together right now, they might have worked it all out and the whole 'ditching' debacle might have scared Matt into realising that he can't live without her. On the other hand, they might be over. He might be wanting to see me to see where we...Shit, the text he sent.

"Rach, he text me when we were away" I confess.

"What? What did he want?" she sounds so disgusted

"He said that he missed me, he said that he didn't think he could do it and I assumed he meant that he didn't think he could go through with our split but shit what if he meant he couldn't go through with the renewal?" I think about the day it came through, it was Saturday, it must have been before he ran out on her.

"Did you reply? I thought you'd both agreed to delete numbers?"

"I did delete his number, and I didn't reply to the

message, it made me mad, I was so angry after the so-called respect he'd promised me so I deleted it quickly before I could reply". Rach smiles,

"You deleted it, it didn't matter what he was doing Kate, for once you put your feelings first, you didn't even consider what was happening with him like you have in the past, you put yourself first and that's exactly what you should have done. You totally did the right thing." I know she's right. When I got that text, I was so angry with him for being selfish it didn't even cross my mind that it was the day of their renewal. I had tried desperately to wipe that event from my mind completely and it must've worked. And I have put him first for the last three years, I've put his feelings before my own and that's pretty pathetic. But he thought of me and he couldn't go through with the renewal. What does that mean? Forget it, Kate. I try to remember how I felt when I walked off that plane less than an hour ago. I need that feeling back. I need strong Kate. So why is there this part of me that wants to talk to him and just see what has happened? I need to know if they're still together. I need to know he's ok. But I can't. I won't get in touch with him. Right now, I wouldn't know how anyway, especially if he's gone to ground to hide away from the papers.

I push the newspaper and the whisky glass away from me and look towards Rach.

"OK?" she questions,

"OK." I reply with an air of finality. "Let's go home." Rach smiles and we get up and make our way to the taxi rank.

I open the door to my flat and it's bloody freezing. I shiver as I quickly walk in and slam the door shut behind me, dumping my case in the hallway as I head for the kitchen to get the kettle on and turn the heating on. It's only 1 o'clock and I'm not due back at work until tomorrow so I'm going to have a cosy 'me' afternoon. It's raining outside anyway so not much point going out anywhere and that suits me fine just now. I need to keep my mind moving though so I decide to unpack my case straight away and get a wash on. I put the case next to the washing machine and start to unload all my holiday stuff. I smile to myself when I pull out the bikini that I wore the day Chris and I had sex in the sea. Thinking about Chris makes me feel wanted and a little bit sexy. I need to remind myself of Chris when I feel low and ugly, I know it was only a holiday romance but he made me feel really good about myself and that gave me confidence, a confidence I want to hang on to. I smile to myself, thinking about him and the fun we had.

The last thing in my case is the book I was supposed to be reading. Not that I actually read it, I started to but then Chris happened. I smile again. I throw the book on the table and as I do I notice a bit of paper fall out of it. I pick it up and I'm about to screw it up when I notice a phone number on it. I take a closer look and to my absolute delight/horror it says the following:

'I knew you wouldn't let me have your number, so here's mine, if you want to meet up again, now you know how to find me, Chris xx' I can't help but smile and for a second I consider throwing it in the bin and keeping the memories just as that, memories. But things have changed and maybe, just maybe, it would be good to see Chris again. Why shouldn't I have a bit more fun? So, I type the number into my phone, add Chris to my contacts and quickly put my phone down again. I have no intention of contacting him right now (how desperate would that look!) but I might, one day. Soon.

CHAPTER TWENTY-TWO

Thursday 8am

I'm first to arrive at the office in the morning. I want to make sure Rich knows my mind is completely on the job following the holiday. So that he knows it was the right thing to do and I'm over it. I assume that he too has seen the headlines about Matt and I'm sure Rach will have filled him in on it if not, so I need to show him I mean business and that I will not let that affect me anymore.

The office looks different. Rich has swapped some of the displays around. There's a new board in the middle now taking centre stage and as soon as I approach it my stomach flips. Right in the centre, the photo of Matt standing outside his restaurant, arms folded, chef whites on and that smile beaming from his face. (I miss that face, those arms...) It's ok, I should have expected it. The restaurant relaunch is our biggest event to date so of course Rich would use it as a promo. It's slightly shit that I have to walk into my place of work and see the man that I love and can't have every day but hey, I'll just see that as a positive – an incentive to work harder to get bigger and better clients. Then we can replace Matt's (gorgeous, beautiful) face with someone far more lucrative to the business and he will be yesterday's news. So there. He's my yesterday.

I didn't really sleep much last night for thinking too much. I really want to know where Matt is, what he's doing, are he and Fay still together? Have they worked it out? I had a scan over a couple of newspaper headlines on the way to work but nothing about Matt. He's small fry compared to what's happening elsewhere in the world at the moment and with the new privacy laws kicking in soon, the tabloids won't be able to publish anything unless they have complete and absolute proof.

I must try harder not to think about him. Why couldn't he have just gone through with the renewal like he said he would, then I would still be in empowered with my new found independence and I wouldn't be thinking about him. I'll get that back, I will. Starting now.

I sit at my desk and there's a note from Rich.

'Welcome back partner, I have a meeting first thing so won't be in until 10.30am. There's a list of potential new clients on your desk' I have a quick scan down, some interesting names but nobody to scare me this time, 'could you chase them up and arrange meetings for this week?'

I'm pretty sure Rich doesn't have a meeting this morning, not of a business nature anyway. Rach text me last night, just to check I was doing ok, and she let slip they were planning on having a romantic breakfast together. Very sweet (where's my bucket emoji!) And it gives me a chance to find my feet in the office again so I can look completely efficient and irreplaceable when Rich does eventually get here.

I make myself a coffee and look back to the list of new clients. Let's get started.

My first phone call is to Taylors, a small pharmacy company who want to organise a team building/fun day for their staff. The girl I speak to sounds young and a little unsure of herself. She is the contact for this deal but she has to keep checking with someone else about the answers to my questions. For example: Can we meet with you this week to discuss the event further? After significant umming and arring, she still wasn't sure and put me on hold only to return to me telling me 'yes' but no date or time and, to be honest, no common sense whatsoever. Eventually, I manage to arrange a meeting next Tuesday at 11.30am. I have strong doubts as to whether it will actually take place based on her complete vagueness and lack of ability to communicate but here's hoping. Can see why they need the team building!

Phone call two is slightly more promising. This one is a hair salon, opening a new branch in Soho and they want the whole razzmatazz opening, celebrities where possible, red carpet job, they do have (so they say) quite a famous client list, mostly B listers but still, if we can get some of them to the launch, it would look impressive. So that's quite an exciting one. I arrange a meeting for both Rich and I to meet with Elaina Sanchez next week.

Next up is an award ceremony for a corporate bank in the City. The guy on the phone, is suitably vague about what they want but they would like to meet to discuss it anyway. They will need a venue and they want us to come up with a potential three that might be suitable and they will judge us based on our selection. There are words that I could use right now to suggest what I think of the man at the other end of the phone but this is business and I must keep a professional head at all times. It might be lucrative if our selection of venues meets their way of thinking 'then potentially we could put a lot of business your way, bear that in mind and make us your top priority right now, kapish?' seriously?

So, three meetings scheduled for next week, all sorted before lunch time. I'm back. Time for another coffee and another metaphorical pat on the back. Go me. As I'm settling back down at my desk, the door opens and Rich walks in.

"Hey stranger," I say as I walk over to him. I'm going in for the hug even if he's not.

"Good to see you Kate" total return of hug, result, he's not angry with me.

"How are you?" He looks directly into my eyes when he asks with a slightly furrowed brow but my reply is swift and positive,

"I'm great, already got us three meetings sorted for next week so I'm getting through that list pretty quickly" and he looks relieved.

"God Kate, I'm so glad you're back, I mean, it's been ok and everything but I don't know how you deal with some of the dickheads that ring up. They're so full of bullshit some of them." I laugh and smile and tell him about the latest phone call.

"You're definitely coming with me to that meeting Kate, I might end up punching him if he talks to me like that, kapish?" we laugh and settle back into our work for the day.

Rich is working on a job for a small catering firm, it's a team building weekend and he's managed to get a brilliant venue. The boss of the company wants to take his employees away for two nights and, as it seems that money is no object, Rich has booked a hotel with conference suite in the Lakes. They want physical activities that 'scare and excite' and a conference/ classroom for the work-related activities. Rich has got an old colleague on board to sort the work activities but the venue is an outward bound centre so I think the employees will be getting pretty muddy. It sounds great, one of the activities is a jungle run through mud slides and dense rhododendron bushes, I want to go too!

Just as Rich is finishing telling me about this, my phone pings. I look at the screen and it's just a number. Matt. Shit. I try to continue the jolly conversation with Rich but my mind is on other things now. What does Matt want now? Why hasn't he deleted my number? It was his idea. I don't want to read the message but it's burning away again and I know I won't be able to think about anything else until I've read it. But I don't want Rich to suspect anything, I owe him for giving me this second chance. He needs to know I won't mess it up.

"Rich, I was thinking of trying that new sandwich place down Venn Street for lunch, can I get you anything while I'm out?" I'll take a walk so whatever the message says, Rich won't see my reaction to it.

"Yeah go on then, surprise me, I don't mind what."

"Ok" I say as I grab my bag (and phone) and head for the door, "back in a bit."

When I get outside, I wait until I'm round the corner and then stop in a shop doorway. The unknown number is still showing on my phone, maybe it's not even Matt, maybe it's just a random sales text. I take a deep breath and open the message...

Hi Kate, I want you to know something. Fay and I have split up. I couldn't go through with the vow renewal. I am not expecting anything from you and I understand that you have moved on but I needed to tell you. I figured you deserved to know, Matt xx

Shit. I mean, shit. I don't know what to think. I feel pretty angry with him because he's still messing with my heart but at the same time, I really wanted to know what was happening with him and now I do. How do I feel? Like I still want him? Yes. Like we can be together now? No. It's just too messy. Complicated. Selfish of him, selfish to text me. Why can't he just leave me alone? What actually is the answer to that question? Thanks Matt, another head fuck.

I decide I've stood here for long enough and need to get moving to the sandwich shop. Rich will start wondering where I am if I'm too long. And work is my priority right now, I can't let Matt make the rest of my life fall apart again. I pick up the sandwiches and feel strangely calm considering. The news of their split is starting to sink in and I feel like there's maybe some sort of closure there for me. Maybe it doesn't matter to me, maybe I have moved on. Maybe I don't love him anymore. (Except, there's too many maybes in those thoughts!) Jesus, why can't I just be badass and not feel so much or think so much or worry so much about hurting others. I honestly need some training for switching off emotions and moving on. Or maybe there's another way round this…

You free for a drink later? I press send before I change my mind and put my phone away. I get a whirl of excitement in the pit of my stomach and really want him to reply straight away. I don't want him to think I'm desperate but I just need a positive right now. My phone pings in my pocket…

Please let this be you, beautiful Kate? Just what I needed.

Yes Chris, it's me :-) I'm excited and worried all at the same time. That really was a quick reply and I'm reminded how young he is. But hey, it's not like he's in love with me, I can't hurt him, we just have fun together. *Would love to see you again but can't do tonight, can do tomorrow?* Oh, playing a little bit hard to get, quite like that. Maybe I should play that game too…

Can't do tomorrow no instant reply this time. Hmmm, maybe I should say something else? No, leave it Kate, don't be desperate. I'm almost back at the office when my phone pings again.

Tonight it is then. When and where? Wow, wasn't expecting that. I wonder what just happened?

We arrange a time and place of my suggestion and I walk back into the office with a smile plastered across my face,

"Woah Kate, those sandwiches must be good, judging by the look on your face" Rich raises an eyebrow inquisitively, but I give nothing away,

"Haven't tried it yet, just soooo happy to be back at work" I joke and he laughs knowing full well that my jovial mood is nothing to do with work.

The rest of the day goes pretty fast. I manage to make several more appointments for the next few weeks and source a couple more potential clients in the process. I also get started on finding the three 'venues of the century' for 'kapish' man.

I'm meeting Chris at 7 so I leave work at 5, giving myself time to get home, get showered and decide what to wear. I'm excited about seeing Chris again. Part of me is wondering if this is a mistake. Holiday romances tend to be pretty non-romantic when back home. Maybe they'll be no chemistry between us, maybe he'll realise how old I look in the dreary British weather and leave before I realise he's there. Maybe I should cancel, maybe… for goodness sake Kate, get a grip and just let it happen. I try to regain my holiday confidence as I look at myself in the mirror. I've decided to wear my little maroon dress, it's my confidence wear. Shows my waist off nicely but also suggests I have half decent legs if I wear the right apple catchers and hold-everything-in tights. I can't breathe or pee all night but damn I look good.

I've booked a taxi to take me as it's a little bit further away than I'm used to plus it's raining and I've straightened my hair to within an inch of its life and I don't want the frizz look, not tonight. I've been in the taxi for about 5 minutes when my phone pings. It's Matt's number again. I haven't replied to his earlier text. So that's two texts he's sent me now that I have in theory ignored. I feel empowered by that fact alone. The old Kate would have replied straight away and given into whatever he wanted. So pathetic. But not now. I consider not reading it again but as usual, it's burning away in my mind and I don't want it to taint my night out with Chris. I'll read and delete.

I'm going away for a while, need to get my head straight. Can I see you first? I miss you xx

He's going away. Why is he telling me this? What does he want me to say? Maybe nothing based on the fact that he probably thinks I won't reply. Why does he miss me? I miss him too and I suddenly wish that it's him I'm meeting tonight. I wonder if he would meet me later tonight if I asked him. I wonder if he'd meet me right now? Stop it. Stop it. Stop it. What am I doing? I think about getting the taxi driver to turn round and take me home but just in time I get my holiday Kate back. I delete Matt's text. I focus on this evening and Chris. That is what needs to happen.

CHAPTER TWENTY-THREE

I walk in and see Chris standing at the bar, his back to me. Oh wow, he is so nice to look at. (And that's just the back of him). He turns as I get closer and actually takes my breath away a little bit. He looks more like Richard Madden now than on holiday. I smile and he smiles back. I'm not sure either of us is sure how to greet one another, a hug (seems a bit too friendly after knowing him so intimately); a kiss on the cheek? (bit too like a first date); a kiss on the lips? Before I get the chance to ponder this one,

"Kate, you look beautiful" and he kisses me gently but confidently on the lips. The kiss lingers and I don't mind, suddenly feels like I've done the right thing and I'm right where I need to be.

"I got you a gin, hope that's ok?" he gestures the drink on the bar. Wow he's shaping up pretty nicely.

"Perfect" I say. I look at him. "That was a pretty cheeky move, putting your number in my book!"

"Worked didn't it?" he has a smile for a toothpaste ad, I can almost see the 'ting' coming from his teeth. I think he's actually a bit too good looking, is that possible? We move over to a table and sit opposite each other. I suddenly feel a bit awkward, what do we talk about? On holiday it was just fun and games and cheekiness but now we might have to actually talk about life!

"Are you back at work yet?" he asks, quite naturally.

"Yes I went back today. Had a good day. I love my job so I guess I'm quite lucky and my boss Rich is great so I'm really lucky." (think I just said that, oh dear, feeling nervous now). "What about you?"

"Not back until Monday so I've had the rest of this week off. Been nice."

"Done anything exciting?" I'm trying to sound flirty but not sure it's working, he's going to work out any minute now that I'm not cool, I have no idea how to socialise and I'm ancient.

"Well," he elongates the word and leans towards me, "until about midday today I was visiting my family in Glasgow but then this gorgeous girl text me and asked me out for a drink" he smiles at me. Oh my, he's travelled down from Glasgow for this! Shit that's a bit serious. Or romantic. Oh dear, what's he after? Wow, thinking about it, I'm actually really touched. This man has travelled from a different country (steady) to see me? I wonder if I'm just a really good shag or whether he really likes me. I've obviously been quiet for far too long because,

"Kate, you ok? You look at bit shocked",

"Um, yeah, sorry, are you serious?" I think I smile when I say this, trying not to look too stalked,

"Yeah, I wanted to see you. I was coming back today, just caught an earlier train, don't panic" he sees straight through me.

"I wasn't panicking, I was just feeling bad for making you change your plans." I sort of lie. I feel a bit guilty for saying I couldn't make tomorrow when in reality I could have. That's what you get for playing games. But then, I used to always take things at face value and that never worked for me either. There must be some middle ground somewhere?

"If I'm really honest Kate," straight face, "I haven't stopped thinking about you since I left Spain. And not in an obsessive way but more like in a 'me and you are good together' way, like we get each other. I was hoping you'd contact me but at the same time I just thought what's meant to be will be." He really does have a lovely smile. And a way with words. And I'm starting to lean in closer, hanging on his every word, think he might have hypnotised me or something with that Richard Madden voice. "Kate?" I can't take my eyes off him and all I want to do is kiss him. So, I do. I lean right across the table and I kiss him. Full on snog. A complete public show of affection. He's not stopping me either and I'm pretty sure people must be starting to look so I stop and lean back in my chair again. I just smile at him.

"So, what did your family think about you leaving early?" He's surprised by my calmness after that kiss. But it's all I can think of to say.

"Oh, they were fine with it, they're used to me coming and going so it's not a problem" he giggles to himself, "I can't believe we're sitting in front of each other again. I did think that maybe you'd just throw my number away, you seemed pretty sure that it was just a holiday thing when I left."

I feel a bit awkward again now, the only reason I text him when I did was to take my mind of Matt but I probably shouldn't mention that. Although, I did save his number, so I was thinking about doing it at some point, just not this quickly. It's only been three days since we said goodbye in Spain.

I really must stop thinking and try to enjoy myself.

"So, what happens now, Kate?" he's got such a flirty, no, sexy smile on his face that I can almost read his mind about what he wants to happen now. If we were still on holiday we'd be getting drunk, flirting outrageously, and then heading back to his room. He smiles at me as these thoughts go through my head, like he's reading my mind, I think my face must give it all away.

"Let's enjoy this drink and pretend we're still on holiday" I raise my eyebrows now and I'm pretty sure he understands what I'm saying. I have pretty much spelt it out. I down the gin quite quickly then, need a bit of courage and confidence.

"Shall I get us another drink?" he asks, he's already finished his Jack and coke.

"Please," I nod and watch him as he walks to the bar. I check my phone, haven't looked at it since I got out of the taxi and there's a missed call from an unknown number, Matt, 12 minutes ago. I look to Chris at the bar and wonder if I should text Matt now and tell him to leave me alone, what if he keeps trying? No just ignore, it's better that way. Easier not to enter into a dialogue with him, I tell myself.

Chris is back with the drinks. He sits next to me this time. We're on a bench in a booth so our legs are touching and I'm getting the tingles. His muscles flex under his trousers and I remember him sitting next to me on the pedalo when we first met. I know his body so well and if we weren't in public right now there's every chance I would be ripping his clothes off. Pretty sure this is what they call animal attraction.

Our conversation is more natural after a couple of drinks and it really does feel like we're still on holiday. Maybe I could just keep feeling like this, go to work in the daytime and then meet Chris now and again pretending it's still a holiday fling! Maybe?

As we've chatted, we've got closer and closer together and Chris now has his arm resting on me and at times he twists my hair between his fingers. Anyone looking at us would assume we're a couple. Either that or they'd be thinking 'shit, she's punching above'. Chris is now running his thumb along my naked collarbone, he knows I love that, and I'm desperately trying not to show how turned on I am.

"Do you think you will get this big client then?" I've been telling him about 'kapish' man as well as a potential singer on our books.

"Hope so, it would be great if we did, would really put the company on the map" my brain goes into business mode and I'm already thinking about possible venues. I talk a few through with Chris and he seems genuinely interested as we discuss the pros and cons.

After a while he says, "Kate?" I look into his eyes and I can see what's coming next, "will you come back to mine tonight?" I take a deep breath, I have obviously been thinking about this but now he's said it I'm not sure what to say. Although, if I say 'no' then it will make this seem like a date and that wasn't what I wanted, I mean what I wanted was sex with my Richard Madden and it's being offered to me on a plate so why am I still thinking. I find myself not wanting to hurt Chris. I'm worried he's got more invested in this than he's letting on. "Kate?"

"Not sure, will I have to do the walk of shame in the morning?"

He giggles,

"I promise I will get you a cab so you don't have to be seen walking the streets" makes me sound a little like a prostitute, I'm sure that's not how he meant it! "Or I could do the walk of shame instead of you, if you invite me back to yours?" and that's what we decide to do.

Within 10 minutes we're in a cab on the way to mine, and as soon as we climb in the back, Chris starts kissing me, it feels raw and passionate and I feel a little bit swept off my feet, oh dear, are there feelings involved here? Mine or his or both? Not sure. It's probably just the booze thinking. His hands are up under my shirt and I can feel my nipples getting hard under his touch, shit he's good. I feel a bit conscious of the cab driver so start to pull back a bit. We're nearly back at mine so I use that as an excuse to start giving a few instructions to the driver and Chris gets the message. We pull up outside my flat and Chris pays the driver as I walk up the path to my door. He's back with me quickly and puts his arms around me as I unlock the door, I turn to kiss him and feel my phone vibrate in my pocket, bit late for messages. Chris and I make it inside, there's not much talking, just kissing, and that suits us both.

"Do you want a drink?" I say, as his lips move down over my shoulder and find their way to my nipples, making me groan a little,

"No, I just want you…" I lead him into my bedroom and push him down on to the bed. My room is immaculate, I tidied before I went out, pretty much knew where this night was going to end up. I straddle him and can feel how hard he is against me. I unbutton his shirt and kiss his naked chest as he lies back on the bed. I move down slowly to his jeans and start to unbutton them; he's groaning and writhing about like he's completely lost in me. We undress each other slowly and I feel like I've never wanted anything more than I want him right now. I have no idea what is happening, this suddenly feels like a tad more than 'just sex' but I want him desperately and this is no time for thoughts, just actions.

Naked, skin shining with perspiration, our bodies move together and I'm kissing him slowly and we're moving slowly. He expertly manoeuvres us both so that he is now on top and I want to feel him inside me so my body naturally pushes up to meet his, taking him in and he moans with pleasure and…this isn't sex anymore, I think we're making love and he's looking into my eyes as our bodies succumb to each other and I bite my lip and make an involuntary little whine and I'm starting to come without even trying or thinking about it and it feels right as we come together and his face looks beautiful and I realise… I've just spectacularly complicated my life once more. Knew I would. Always do.

CHAPTER TWENTY-FOUR

Friday 7.30am

I'm sitting in my kitchen drinking coffee, with a serious smile on my face. Caught halfway between the great sex with Chris last night and worrying that it is now more than sex. I was perhaps a little bit flippant when Chris left.

"I'll call you" I said, mostly because I was worried about how I was feeling about him. I don't want to fall for someone right now, this was meant to be fun. This was meant to be just sex.

"Kate, are you ok? You seem a bit distant?" he replied, looking a little confused.

"Yeah I'm fine, sorry, just tired I guess. And I need to get ready for work." I sounded distant too.

"Last night was great Kate. It was really good to see you again. And… will you?"

"Will I what?" I snapped as if he was asking me to marry him…

"WILL you call me? Only I get the feeling…" his voice trailed off. I was finding it hard to even look at him to be honest, maybe because his good looks scare me and draw me in. I tried to snap out of it but still don't think I sounded particularly convincing.

"Yeah of course I will." And with that, I sort of ushered him out of the door and said "bye then".

Not my greatest moment. But my 'thinking post-alcohol brain' often takes over and I just can't get a hold of myself. So, I'm sitting in my kitchen contemplating last night and think I better text him just so he doesn't think I'm a complete bitch but I have no idea where my phone is. After a few minutes of searching, I find it under my bed, must have fallen there in the melee of us underdressing one another last night and I find a smile back on my face remembering his hands on my skin and just how that makes me feel: giddy, excited, sexy.

As I make my way back to my pot of sobering coffee, I glance at my phone and notice there's a message. I have a tiny recollection of it going off last night but I had other things on my mind. Perhaps it was just as well as the message is from Matt and was sent at 11.26 pm. Shit…

Shit Kate, I'm outside your flat. Just seen you go in. I guess you really have moved on

Shit shit shit. He saw me get back to the flat with Chris? Yes of course he did. Why was he here? What was he doing lurking in the shadows waiting outside my flat? Why didn't he call me if he was coming over? What was he thinking? I'm striding round the flat like a mad woman. I suddenly feel like I've blown it for good with Matt and that breaks my heart and that in itself confuses me and I don't know what I feel and for who? Oh why did Matt have to be there? I try to get a grip and sit myself down on the sofa. Deep breaths. In…out…in…out… I can feel tears rolling down my face and I try desperately to be strong, independent Kate but my heart is beating too fast.

I look back to the message expecting there to be more that I've missed or another message. Did he drive away? Of course he did. But just to make sure I look out through the window and see if his car is out there. It's not, of course, and that makes me feel the emptiness again. Like I've lost him. Like him seeing me last night has helped him to 'get his head straight'. What have I done?

Without thinking, (makes a change!) I write a reply and hit send straight away.

Why were you outside my flat? I wait. I stare at the phone. It's delivered…still staring…he's read it. The reply box is flickering, those three little dots, he's writing something, but then it disappears, and then it's back again and then…

I wanted to see you. I didn't want to see you with someone else

What right do you have to judge me for being with someone else?

I'm not judging you. I don't blame you. I've treated you badly

Shit Matt, you have no idea what you've done to me

I'm so sorry Kate I'm not thinking at all as I send these texts, but I'm in contact with Matt again and it's making me feel good, just knowing he's at the other end of this phone and he's thinking about me is making me feel better already.

I'm so angry with him. I'm so angry with myself. Why am I letting him get to me so much…again? He has me completely. What kind of love does this to you? Is this normal? Does he care about me? I wish I could say something to make him realise how I'm feeling, just so that he gets an ounce of this bloody pain.

Kate? I haven't replied for a few minutes, he must think that's it. Maybe it should be but…

If you're sorry, why are you still hurting me? Why are you sitting outside my flat?

The last thing I ever wanted to do was hurt you. I came to your flat last night because I couldn't leave without seeing you

Leave? What is he saying? I suddenly remember he said he was going away for a while. But this sounds more final…permanent. And all I can think to say (in desperation) is:

Don't leave Matt and I wait and read my words over and over, he's not replying. Damn. I stand up and start to pace again. I really have no idea what I'm doing. My phone pings.

I won't be gone for long. I think we need some space So not permanent but he wants space away from me. I suppose he wanted that anyway, even if he hadn't seen me with Chris. My phone pings again:

Need to ask you one thing. Was he a one night stand or are you in a relationship with him? Well, that's a good question, I wish I knew. Can't really reply with that though. Not sure Matt has the right to ask that anyway:

I know I don't really have the right to ask, just want to know if I'm still in with a chance Wow, that text makes the heart flutters return. I think he still wants me. He must if he's saying that? I don't really know what to say in reply but I don't want to lie so I don't:

Not just a one-night stand, we met on holiday, but not a relationship and even as I press 'send' I'm wondering what it is I have with Chris. He's young, free and single and is really into me whereas Matt is complicated with a lot of baggage and has never been able to commit. Who would you choose? If only it was that simple!

Ok, thanks for being honest. Is it ok if I ring you when I get back?

Yes. How long are you away for?

Not sure

As vague as ever. And there's my pang of doubt. Right there. Will he ever completely be mine? Based on our relationship so far, maybe it's just impossible for him to really commit to a relationship. Maybe he'll go off and find someone else now. Maybe I'll always have these doubts. Another ping, an after thought?:

But I'll ring you as soon as I'm back xx

And that's that. I don't reply again. No point. I'm right back where I started. I'm left waiting for him to ring me. I'm such a fool.

CHAPTER TWENTY-FIVE

The weekend grinds by so slowly. I don't want to bother Rach with my latest dilemma as she's so fixated with Rich, having spent a week away from him, but I really need to talk to someone. I consider Lucy. She understands me and she knows about Matt. But would that be cruel? I think she's a friend, albeit a friend with benefits. But I definitely don't need those benefits right now and I don't want to lead her on. Not sure.

It's Sunday afternoon. I haven't contacted Chris since he left. What with the debacle of Matt texts I decided to leave that alone. But I feel guilty about the way I said goodbye and I don't want him to be hurt by me. Maybe I'm reading too much into it once more. I wonder what he's thinking about us. Us? Is there an 'us'? He's so lovely. And there's definitely feelings there, a connection. If I was over Matt, would I be contacting Chris now? Is Matt holding me back again? I'm bored with my thoughts. I need to do something. I need someone else's input. In fact, I need to stop thinking about these problems and do something else. Just for me. I haven't been for a run for ages. That's it. A run in the park is exactly what I need to blow these man cobwebs away.

It takes me a while to find my running kit. I find one of my trainers under the bed and eventually find its partner at the bottom of my washing basket! Not sure, don't ask. A few stretches before I leave the flat. Need to try and look like I'm not the worst runner in the world, or the most unfit. Rach says when I run, I'm a little bit arms and legs everywhere, a bit Phoebe-esque but I try not to let this bother me today. I close the flat door behind me, press play on my phone, and begin my run straight from the door. I'm pretty lucky as the park is only one street away so I don't have too much pavement pounding to do before I feel like I'm in a safe haven of other runners and walkers.

It feels good to be running again. I stopped doing it regularly pretty early on in my relationship with Matt as it was my Sunday morning thing and then…well…he became my Sunday morning thing. I'm listening to a running album – a load of songs put together to run to. Some of it's a bit lame but it pumps me up and keeps me going. Although the remix of John Newman's Love me Again is a little too close to reality for me right now. But it's fine. Running is giving me power. I'm taking control. I can make my body work for me and me only. Wow I'm starting to sound like a Nike ad. Clearly still thinking too much. I try to switch off by giving myself a little sprint test. I speed up and feel my breath becoming shorter but it still feels good. I haven't pushed myself like this for ages.

I run for about 40 minutes and though I feel knackered, sore and my boobs feel like they're going to fall off (couldn't find my sports bra, ouch!) I feel fantastic. Just to do something for me for a change without worrying about other people's feelings was great and I make a pact with myself to keep my Sunday run 'a thing'. I put the radio on loud in the living room so I can hear it in the shower and Walking on Sunshine blasts through the flat reflecting my mood at this moment. I'm not really sure why I feel this good and to be honest, I'm trying not to analyse it. So I'll just go with it, enjoy my shower and enjoy the music. Feel like I'm getting my holiday Kate back. Oh shit, Chris. Better text him.

An hour later I'm sitting on the sofa with my second glass of wine in one hand and my phone in the other. Right, what to say…?

*Hi Chris, how are you? Just thought I'd text to

say…* nope delete,

Hey, hope you got home ok… nope he obviously got home ok he's a grown adult.

What am I actually feeling? Just say it.

Hey Chris, it was really good to see you. In fact, almost too good which is why I probably seemed a bit weird when you left. We sort of went from holiday romance to something else, not sure what. It phased me a bit. Sorry Bit long? It says what I'm feeling. Just press send. My thumb lingers over 'send', I take another swig of wine and think, 'sod it'. SEND.

I read the text back and realise I didn't put any kisses on the end, maybe that's ok. It was instinctive so I'll just go with it. I stare at my phone for a while but realise the text might need some consideration, so he probably won't reply straight away. My glass is nearly empty again so I get the wine from the fridge, might as well just take the bottle in. Antiques Roadshow is on the telly and some posh guy has just been told his father's watch is worth between £100 and £200. Most people would be quite happy with that but his face says he was definitely expecting more. Poor bloke, might not be able to afford his Bolly this month. My mind is totally on my phone even though I'm pretending to myself that I don't care what Chris is thinking. I do. I suddenly feel like I might have blown it with him too and that makes me feel a bit sad. I can't have everything though. Do I want Matt or Chris? Do either of them want me? My phone pings. It's Chris. Deep breath, I wonder what he made of my text.

Chris: *It was great to see you too. It did feel like you were kicking me out but I suppose in the cold light of day, holiday romances don't really last* Ouch! That was unexpected. Is that it? Another ping…

Chris: *I guess we just need to work out if this is a holiday romance or something else* Crikey! Slightly less final. Ummm, what do I say to that? Be honest. As I'm contemplating my reply, another ping, he's keen. Oh, it's from Matt. I've put his number back into my phone so his name comes up and that always makes my heart race.

Matt: *I miss you xxx* brief and to the point. I decide to focus on one man at a time and even though Matt's text has made me smile, I decide not to reply, not straight away anyway. I return to Chris's text and start to type,

I think that's what scared me. Do you want it to be something else? Immediate reply from

Chris: *Why scared?*

Me: *scared because we had something good on holiday and why ruin that?*

Chris: *If the other night was anything to go by, I'm pretty sure nothing's ruined!!*

That makes me smile. The memory of him in my bedroom makes me a bit horny, we do have great sex but that was the other scary part, it wasn't just sex the other night. On holiday, it's different, you can pretend to be a couple and have great sex because you know there's an end to it, that's why those types of relationships work because each party knows what they're getting into and exactly when they're getting out of it. But seeing him on home ground has changed things, I knew it would. It's complicated everything. I'm not really sure I should encourage Chris with this flirty behaviour so I say,

Me: *It was a good night Chris but maybe we should leave it there*

Chris: *Is it the age thing?* good point and that's one of the issues. I can't tell him about Matt,

Chris: *Or is there someone else?* or maybe I should tell him about Matt? At least he can't get too hurt if he knows it's nothing personal. I consider my response again. This is the beauty of texting. You can think about what you want to say. If I was in a face to face conversation with Chris right now I'd be blurting things out left, right and centre. (whilst staring at his lovely thighs and then ripping his clothes off)

Me: *Aren't you worried about 'the age thing'?* I put it in inverted commas to try and make a point that it's obviously a problem if that's what he's calling it.

Chris: *not worried at all* so I go in for the reality of it, well he did ask,

Me: *There is/was someone else. I'm not sure I'm properly over him which is making my feelings for you confusing* just as I hit send, and I have no idea how I've done this, I realise I've sent it to the wrong person, I've sent it to Matt! Oh shit, I read it back, what the hell is he going to make of that? I start shaking and realise Matt has sent me another text which must have automatically opened and I didn't realise I was typing the message to him instead of Chris. Oh Shiiitttt. What an almighty fuck up! I said I'm not sure I'm over him which suggests it's over, doesn't it? Has Matt read it? Yes he has. I read the second text he sent me which says:

Matt: *Can't stop thinking about you and how good we are together* Oh crap! Why do I mess things up so bloody well? I'm the queen of this shit, I totally bring it on myself. What is Matt thinking? Will Matt think it was meant for him? I suppose it's possible.

Matt: *Kate, what do you mean there was someone else? Was that text meant for me? Are you texting someone else right now?* FFS I think I might just turn my phone off and go to sleep. My lovely Sunday has just become a complete car crash. Right Kate, damage limitation now.

Focus on Matt.

Me: *Sorry Matt. That wasn't meant for you. Really sorry* not much else I can say.

Matt: *Don't play games with me Kate, I can't handle that right now* where does he get off saying this stuff, he's completely messed me around for the last few months and he's now expecting me to be at home waiting for him to call. Well he can…

Me: *I'm not playing games, it was a genuine mistake* I'm trying to sound calm. Like there's nothing to worry about but…

Matt: *Are you seeing someone else? Is it that guy from the other night?* Christ, how many men does he think I've got on the go? Rude.

Me: *I'm honestly not sure it's any of your business but no I'm not seeing anyone else, I'm texting someone else*

Matt: *And sleeping with him* oh dear he's angry. And so am I to be honest. We're in the same old same old. He literally thinks I'm sitting at home waiting for him to call. Although, I suppose in a way I can't blame him as that is what I did for three years! Maybe it's time he realised that if he wants me then he needs to fight for me. Fighting talk, you go girl (can't get away with that can I!)

I decide not to reply to Matt. He doesn't deserve a reply. And I can't even remember where I was with Chris now. Oh yeah, the text I sent to Matt. Shall I still send it to Chris? Damn this is confusing and I've just finished the bottle of wine so that's not helping the clarity of the situation.

Me: (to Chris, just in case you're as confused as I am) *Let's just see what happens* vague and non-committal, it's all I've got left right now.

Chris: *sounds good to me xx* Oh kisses that time. Stop analysing Kate.

I put my phone down on the sofa next to me. I have no idea what I want from either of them and I'd just like to be left alone for a bit.

I fall asleep to Countryfile and wake up three hours later, my mouth dry, the after-effects of the wine kicking in. Bedtime I think. I turn the tv off, pick up my phone and make my way to bed. I look at my phone but there are no more messages. Good. Sleep.

CHAPTER TWENTY-SIX

It's Monday and I'm so relieved I have this job. It gives me focus when my mind (and emotions) can't cope. I haven't heard from Matt since the stupid texting and I can't stop wondering what is going through his mind. Is that it now? Has he decided it's over? Was it already over? Is he angry with me? Why am I so stupid? The last question is a chorus between all the other questions, a constant doubt and feeling of stupidity. Thing is…I know in my heart, however stupid I am, that I love Matt, am in love with him and that isn't going to stop anytime soon, at least I'm sure of something though, hey?

Rich has a meeting this morning with the 'kapish'. He decided to hire us after we presented him with some 'really sophis ops', (really sophisticated options – incase you're wondering, I really hope you are!) he said he likes our 'attention to the niche market of bespokism!' I mean, is that even a word or a sentence? Anyway, there's heaps of money in it so…

While Rich is out (point blank refused to go with him!) I'm starting to make plans for a couple of key events we have coming up. Which is why I'm sitting and thinking. Right Kate, back to it. I, inwardly, remind myself of how lucky I am to have this job. Not just because my best friend got it for me in my hour of need, or because I have a great boss who values me and my input but because he gave me a second chance when most people would have sacked me on the spot. I can't mess him about again, I might not be so lucky next time (please don't let there be a next time).

I bury my head in planning. The first company is the Hair Salon. I grab a budget planner and contract and put them in the file to take to the meeting later in the week. I then settle down to brain-storming ideas for the event itself. The salon is called Serenity. It's not just hair, they also offer beauty treatments and complementary therapies – this is the new string to their bow, hence the new branch, so this is something we need to place centrally in the marketing (I think).

So, the meeting needs to cover the guests, caterers, drinks, music, products and incentives. Lots to discuss and I'm actually really excited about it. Love getting my teeth into stuff like this. I continue to write down my initial thoughts on how the event might look and what kind of theme they might want based on the name and their new treatments when (you guessed it) my phone pings. Maybe I should make a rule that I don't have my phone on at work, although that would be impossible as that's my main point of contact with Rich and I use it so much for other work things too (I kid myself as I casually glance over to it).

It's Chris. I smile but also feel a little disappointed that it's not Matt's name on the screen. But still, Chris, he's gorgeous and he's texting me so I'm not complaining.

Would love to see you this week? How about lunch one day? Well that's different. You can't exactly have a quickie at lunch time (can you?) I quite like the idea of lunch with him, suggests he likes my company. Does it?

I think about it. I don't text back straight away. Although, with me, it never takes long, I don't think I've ever played it cool in my life! I make one or two more notes for the salon while it's still fresh in my mind and then pick my phone up.

Lunch sounds good, when and where?

Might as well be casual, no games, straight forward answers, that has to be the way forward. Don't over think it Kate.

Tomorrow? Was thinking 'The Chiller'

Nice choice, I've been there once with Rach and it's really nice, they specialise in iced drinks, that's their selling point, but do a full menu too. Then I start to have a mild panic. What should the protocol be on this lunch date? (is it a date?) Do we pay separately? How will I be confident without alcohol? I'll have to come back to work afterwards, so I won't be able to drink anything. That would not look good to Rich. Stop, relax, focus. This will be ok. In fact, I look at it as a challenge. And if Chris doesn't like me when I'm sober then it's better to know now because (believe it or not) I am sober quite a lot of the time. I reply,

Great, 1pm would be good for me thought I'd have a little bit of control in the arrangements.

Great. I'll book it xx (kisses again!)

Just then Rich comes in,

"What a conceited, fake, arrogant cock of a human being." Oh dear, maybe the meeting with said cock didn't go well? "Honestly Kate," he continues so I keep schtum, "…I have never met anyone quite so up their own arse before, he's like some sort of walking talking cliché, I had no idea those people actually exist, what a nob!" I'm smiling now as I've never heard Rich swear before and I have to bite my lip so I don't laugh out loud,

"Don't hold back Rich, say what you really think…" I interject in the hope that he too will see the funny side of his outburst. He laughs and looks over at me.

"Sorry, Kate," he smirks, "I just couldn't believe his arrogance, can see exactly why you didn't want to come to the meeting" he raises his eyebrows at me,

"I don't know what you're talking about," I say with sarcasm in my tone "I had a very important event to work on right here" I smile at him and look back to my work as if it is completely consuming me. "I'll make you a coffee" I say as he goes to his desk and throws his jacket over the chair and then slumps down into it.

"How are you getting on anyway? Tell me something good" I make my way over to the coffee machine,

"Have a look at my desk, think I've started with some good ideas for the salon, just need to see what they want from it all." He saunters over and glances over my scribbles,

"Looks good, what you thinking about with the caterers? Shall we aim to go with Simons again?" Seems like a logical choice, given that they have catered for the majority of our events so far.

"Was thinking that, unless Elaina has other ideas." I put Rich's coffee on his desk and go back to mine and take a quick glance at my phone. No new messages.

I spend the rest of the day working on the salon meeting and tentatively ringing our regular suppliers to see how they're fixed for dates. It's all gone well and 5pm comes quickly.

At home, I start to think about what I should wear for lunch with Chris tomorrow. I look in my wardrobe at my work gear and pick out what I consider to be the sexiest dress. I'm going to wear a black dress with some ankle boots, they shape my legs really nicely and... What am I doing? Do I really want to be having another date with Chris? What about Matt? A little devil appears on my shoulder 'What about Matt? He hasn't contacted you since the other night. If he really wants you/loves you/cares about you then he should be fighting for you, not letting you walk off into the sunset with another man!' Is that what I'm doing? No. I'm just having lunch with someone. Someone who happens to be gorgeous and really into me. How can that be wrong? It's not wrong, it's fantastic! There she is 'holiday Kate' is back.

CHAPTER TWENTY-SEVEN

Tuesday 12.45pm

I get a cab from work, don't want to look flustered or sweaty from walking when I arrive. But it makes me a bit early, does that look too keen? Maybe not, Chris is already here, so at least that saves my embarrassment. A waitress shows me to the table he is sitting at. He stands and greets me like a real gentleman, kiss on the cheek. Suddenly feels a bit formal and I'm nervous again. But then, that's how dates should be to start with. You should feel excited and nervous at the same time as neither party really knows where it's going and what to expect. I'd forgotten again just how good looking he is and he seems to look more like Richard Madden every time I see him. I can't stop staring at him. I'm feeling quite fluttery. Wonder what that means? Only really had those feelings for Matt before. (Arrgghhh get out of my head Matthew Grove!)

Lunch is lovely. We talk and we laugh and we touch hands now and again because it feels natural. But then he says:

"I wasn't sure you'd agree to meet me after the other night." I'm not sure what to say to that and he seems to be looking for some sort of explanation which I thought I'd given him in a text. I say nothing and his look is searching.

"Kate, you seem to have forgotten how much we shared in Spain. I do know that you were trying to get over another guy. It's ok, you know." Again, I don't know what to say. To be honest, if I'd met someone who was 'getting over someone else' I would have run a mile. But Chris is sitting here with me and isn't running anywhere. That's kind of sweet. I had forgotten how much we shared, it didn't seem to matter as long as it was a holiday fling. But now, I might need to remind myself what else I told him out there!

"I had forgotten that you knew that, I'm sorry, I just didn't want to…hurt you?"

"You're not hurting me, you're here with me now. Can I assume that you're over him?" Oh wow, big question and I put my best face on for it. I swig my sparkling water like it's going to save me and say,

"I'm getting there" I confide honestly and the smile leaves his face a little.

"Then, let's just take things slowly. We'll do everything at your pace." Damn he's good. Why do men always seem to know the right thing to say to get you interested in them? But he has and I'm interested. He's lovely. This is abundantly clear by the waitress's attention to him. She hardly looked at me when we ordered and she's back again now to ask if everything has been ok for us today?

"It's been fine, thank you" I say before Chris gets the chance, which means she has to look at me? Nope, still mesmerised by the apparent Adonis sitting opposite me,

"And for you sir? Has everything been ok?" blimey I think she might ask for his number in a minute,

"Yes, great thank you." He takes my hand then and puts it to his lips, "We're both very happy, thank you" and it seems to be a dig at her for her attention to him, I mean, it's blatantly obvious she fancies the pants off him, it's embarrassing, so even an idiot could see it. And Chris is far from that. I feel flattered that he's put her straight and made it clear that he wouldn't be interested in her. I feel special, as if I'm the most important person in the restaurant right now. Shit, this is how it should feel, this is how love should feel, (steady Kate!) not the stolen guilty moments or the secrets and lies. Pure, out in the open, public shows of affection. I feel liberated. And special.

Chris gets a cab for me and takes my hand again.

"This has been really nice Kate," and he kisses my cheek. Damn I want him to kiss me properly, I want him to get in the cab with me, come back to my place and… oh wow, what is happening?

I'm in the cab and on my way back to work before I really realise he's not there anymore, I was lost in a daydream, must've looked like a right airhead to him. Although, I'm pretty sure he's only seeing my good points right now, which feels nice.

My phone pings, it's Chris,

Had an amazing time with you. Let's do it again soon xx Definitely keen, I feel my cheeks redden slightly, it's good to have this kind of attention. I reply,

You free at the weekend? Maybe we could go out for dinner? my mind is working on the premise that evening and weekend means neither of us has to get up for work the next day which means…

Sorry, can't do this weekend. I'm away to Glasgow for my cousin's stag do Oh! Instant disappointment. One emotion to another, feeling slightly rejected. Another ping,

I can definitely do the weekend after? xx I don't want to appear too desperate, so I reply with,

Great x I put a kiss, just one. Seems right.

CHAPTER TWENTY-EIGHT

Wednesday

Our meeting with Elaina Sanchez is at 10am. It's at the salon so that we can see the venue and understand her design ideas. It's a really down to earth place, no pretentious signs about a haircut saving your life or creating a new you!

Elaina is a tall woman, about 50, she's been in business for years and simply loves being a hairdresser. Her enthusiasm for her work and her salon is refreshing, she wants to make a good business for her customers, they come first. We click straight away and I feel relaxed in her company. I don't feel nervous about sharing my ideas for the opening and Rich steps back and lets us get on with it (perhaps slightly out of his comfort zone). We discuss the caterers, (she's happy with the company we use), the drinks, (she wants prosecco and bellinis and then orange juice for the none drinkers, nice and simple) music (there's no space for live so she will get her son to take care of that side of things) and then we start discussing the guest list.

I'm expecting some celebrities to be mentioned here as she told me on the phone they have quite a few on their books but I wasn't expecting Jude Law! Wow! He's the most impressive on the list. There are a few others that Rich looks impressed by, mostly footballers, I think.

So overall the meeting goes well. I also suggest having someone working to get bookings on the evening, perhaps with an incentive if they book. Then she'll potentially have a full month of appointments before they're even open. She likes this idea and says she'll put together some ideas for incentives. Great. Rich is really pleased and we catch a cab back to the office discussing all the options on the way. He also explains who the footballers are, a couple who play for Arsenal and a Spurs player.

"We have a meeting with a footballer this Friday Rich. Think he said his name was Darren Bellamy. He's getting married and wants us to manage it. Forgot to say yesterday." Rich looks bemused and I'm worried for a second that he's angry with me for not telling him.

"Did you say Darren Bellamy?" he looks shocked but pleased.

"Yes, he and his fiancée Emma, we're meeting them at…"

"He plays for Palace," (Rich's team) "Oh my god Kate, this is awesome!" He's happier than I've ever seen him. I didn't even know who this guy was. But then why would I?!

For the rest of the journey, Rich just stares out of the window, trance like and smiling. Who knew it would have this effect on him? I giggle to myself and check my phone. No messages. Haven't heard from Matt for three days, not that long I suppose, but when you consider how our texting ended, maybe not good. It seems to bother me less now. But then I suppose I have Chris to keep me feeling confident. (nearly thought 'to fall back on!' bit harsh on Chris but at least he knows where I stand with it all and he wants to take it at my pace so that's good, for me at least!)

CHAPTER TWENTY-NINE

Thursday

It was crazy today at work. The phone didn't stop ringing. Word is getting out about our events and more people are wanting to hire us, it's so exciting to think I'm a real part of something that is successful and getting bigger and better every day. I finally feel like I have a work purpose, maybe even a career. Just don't mess it up Kate!

I'm glad to get home and relax. I've been lazy and got myself a microwave meal. Matt would be going crazy if he could see me eating this. Especially as I haven't even put it on a plate and I'm eating it out of the plastic! How plebeian! I chuckle to myself but also think, 'up yours Matt, I can do what I want, we're not together' which my brain is happy with, it makes sense to be talking myself out of any relationship with him, but my heart feels like it's been torn apart again.

I take a deep breath and turn the tv on. I'm sure there's some mindless trash on to take my mind off the obvious. I settle into an episode of Eastenders, at least that always makes me feel better, my life is definitely not as bad as any of the characters on there.

I haven't heard from Chris today. We've sent the odd text back and forth since Tuesday's lunch. Just nice stuff. A bit of flirting and a bit of getting to know each other, I guess. A nice balance, especially as we're moving away from the holiday romance into some other territory. So far this week, I've learnt that he doesn't like Indian food, says he's a wuss and just can't take the spices; he supports Rangers (football is really not my thing) and he used to have a dog called Zebra! It was stripy, so…ok. He now knows that I love Indian food (oh dear!); I hate football;

(well dislike, I'm not bothered by it) and the only pet I've ever had was a gold fish which died after two weeks (not really a pet person!) On reflection, maybe not a perfect match? But they do say opposites attract. To be honest, the more I think about it, maybe we're not meant to be anything other than a holiday fling. The age is clearly an obvious sticking point, not sure how long a relationship with such an age gap could last, and it somehow seems worse that I'm older than him, for me anyway. He was starting primary school when I was sitting my GCSEs, there's just something a bit odd about that! I'm pondering all this when my phone pings. My heart is hoping to see Matt's name. It's Chris. Which doesn't disappoint me. I love hearing from him but… yada yada yada, I've said it all before.

Hey gorgeous, been thinking about you today. Wish I was seeing you this weekend xx My heart melts a little bit. And he makes me smile. He always makes me smile. That's got to be good, right? All I ever felt with Matt was pain and tears, wasn't it? I text Chris back.

Well if you have to go off for your boy's weekend, sometimes you have to sacrifice the good things in life:) my sarcasm is hopefully evident to him but I add a smiley face just so he knows.

That's true, you're definitely a good thing in my life Kate. I don't have to go, I could say I'm sick or something has come up at work?

Oh, I wasn't expecting that. And it's a question. I hope he's not expecting me to make that decision for him. So,

Yeah yeah, I know how much you Scots love a good stag do, don't give it up for me

Part of me is hoping he will, that would be a grand gesture but then I also really hope he goes, I'd hate to be the one who is stopping him from having fun on a weekend that will (I'm guessing) go down in history as 'the best stag do ever'. Don't they all! If he misses that and then can't join in the future conversations with his family and friends about it, then that would be a shame for him. I'm pretty sure I'm over analysing again and starting to sound like his mother rather than a girlfriend (age thing again) but hey ho.

You're probably right, I should go. They'll never let me live it down if I'm the only one that doesn't turn up. Can I see you before I go? Oh, um, not sure, hadn't factored that in but I guess there's no reason why not but, wait, does he mean tonight?

When? I ask

Now :-) he replies. And I have to think about this. I don't want to be his booty call, I've done enough of that. Part of me would love him to come round tonight and the thought of his hands on me and looking at his glorious body again almost makes me reply with a quick *come now, I'm ready and waiting* but instead, I behave like a grown up and say,

I don't think I'd be the best company tonight, I've had a big day at work and I'm knackered and I'm slobbing in front of the telly in my worn out pjs and granny slippers and I'd rather not have to make an effort right now.

OK Have I upset him?

Sorry I reply

Don't be daft, it's fine Kate, it'll just make the next time I see you even better Is this how proper relationships start? It's so nice to be flattered and feel good about it and not feel guilty. It's a bit of a revelation to me. Weird how one relationship, however it went, can shape the person you become. I reply with exactly what I'm thinking, *You're lovely Chris x*

So are you beautiful xx

And my heart flutters again, and it feels nice and right and I feel giddy and excited. I like it.

CHAPTER THIRTY

Friday

Rich and I make our way to The Shard for the meeting with Darren Bellamy and his fiancée. Rich is nervous. He's talking too much and is quite frantic. Is this what hero worship looks like? I hope he manages to hold it together when he meets him.

"You ok Rich?" I tentatively enquire, "you seem a bit on edge."

"Yes, sorry Kate, I'll be fine, just got a lot on my mind." Oh, maybe it's not this meeting that's making him nervous, he does seem distracted. His phone rings. He answers quickly as if he was waiting for this call.

"Yes?" abrupt. He listens and his face seems to drop, "No, it has to be what I asked for, please try again and let me know how you get on." A reply from the other end and then,

"I know, I know you will. Thank you. Talk later." He hangs up. Then looks at me a bit sheepishly and smiles but then looks away. I've never seen him like this before, and it worries me a bit.

The cab pulls up at The Shard so no time to ask him what's going on, it'll have to wait for later.

This is an unusual potential client in that normally if you're holding your wedding at The Shangri-La, then the events team there would take care of all the arrangements. So, if we get the gig, we'll be in charge of certain parts of it only, which can make it quite complicated especially as teams don't always work well together when someone else is doing a part of their job, which would be true on both sides in this case. Anyway, it could still be very lucrative for us so it's a no-brainer, we have to try.

167

Darren Bellamy and his fiancée are already on Level 34 talking to the manager who weirdly scuttles away when we approach. Already a bit awkward then, an introduction and 'looking forward to working with you' might have started things off on a better foot.

As we get closer, I recognise Darren Bellamy. I've seen his face in the papers and perhaps on tv a few times. He is very good looking, has very pronounced cheek bones, gorgeous blue eyes and is about 6'2". Not my type but I can see the attraction. Emma, his fiancée seems a bit mousy in comparison. I expected more of a WAG with heaps of make-up and perfectly coiffured hair but she actually seems quite down to earth. Rich begins,

"Mr Bellamy," his voice cracks a bit as he reaches out his arm to shake Bellamy's hand, "Nice to meet you. Thank you for considering us for your wedding." Usual greeting for new potential client, well done Rich, holding it together so far. "This is my partner Kate Carlin." Darren Bellamy looks at me and shakes my hand. He's got really soft hands, must moisturise a lot, he holds on to my hand for a little too long and smiles at me. I look to his fiancée and make sure she gets a look in too. Rich seems to have forgotten about her in his star struck footballer man crush,

"And you must be Emma," I say, removing my hand from Bellamy's and offering it to her.

"Yeah, hi, nice to meet you," she shakes my hand and then Rich's. It's not a completely relaxed atmosphere. Something doesn't feel quite right. Maybe they've already been talked out of hiring us as well as the Shangri-La team. Fair enough, but just tell us. Darren Bellamy takes charge by leading us over to the window,

"Just look at this view, it's stunning isn't it." We all look out across London. It's spectacular! St Pauls looks stunning in the morning sunshine and my eyes then follow the Thames as it passes through the City. If this is what you want for a wedding, it certainly is impressive. Rich gets into business mode,

"So Mr Bellamy," he is cut off,

"Please, call me Darren," Rich looks elated. Like he's just made a new best friend and it's like the bestest best friend you could ever hope for, little boy in a sweet shop moment, but he manages to carry on.

"How would you like us to help with your big day?"

"Let's take a seat and have a chat shall we?" and Darren, ever in control, leads us back to the big settees, we all sit. Immediately, a waiter brings over a tray of drinks. We didn't order any but it seems there is something for everyone and then some.

"I hope you don't mind, I took the liberty," this phrase doesn't sit well with him, it's like he's trying to impress, "of ordering a few drinks before you arrived. Please help yourself." I look down at the selection and really fancy the glass of champagne but probably not a good idea so I grab a sparkling water and take a sip. It's elderflower water, very nice. Rich takes an orange juice and Darren goes straight for the champagne. Emma doesn't take a drink.

We're all a bit more relaxed now but it feels a bit fake to me. I take a long look at Emma and try to work her out. She seems a bit lost in all this, almost like it's not her wedding. In the little experience I've had of planning weddings, it's usually the bride that takes the lead and enthuses and charms, or it's a joint effort at the very least. But Emma is almost mute and I'm starting to think the awkwardness is nothing to do with us and it's actually between the couple. Rich and Darren are talking and I'm nodding but not really listening. I concentrate, start to make notes. They've heard about our bespoke style and want us to make the wedding unique. It's that extra style they want that reflects them as a couple and individually. Ok, that's a nice compliment for us. Feels nice to know they've heard about how good we are. I look over at Rich and feel really proud to be working with him. We're a good team.

After about twenty minutes, Darren suggests we take a walk round to get a feel for the place. They want to invite 130 guests but still make it a very personal experience for everyone. Rich focuses on Emma now; he walks with her and starts chatting. He'll be trying to gauge her so that we get a sense of her character, particularly as they want such a personal feel. I look out across London again and I'm suddenly aware that Darren is right beside me. A bit too close.

"Amazing isn't it." I can feel his breath on my hair, definitely too close, so I consciously take a step away and say,

"It certainly is a great view of London". I look at him and attempt a smile but he's looking at me strangely and I think I know that look. I've seen it before. It's a smarmy look that indicates someone is about to hit on you...

"Kate, you have the most beautiful eyes" there it is. What is this? The man is meant to be planning his wedding for god's sake. I don't know what to say. I look away to where Rich and Emma have walked, partly to make sure they are far enough away that she can't hear her fiancé chatting me up. He knows why I'm looking in their direction,

"Don't worry, they can't hear." Well that's ok then! "You really are gorgeous you know. I'd love to see you later." Oh my god! What is this man playing at? What a complete and utter prick. I'm hoping my face says it all as I am completely shocked by his advances! But apparently not as he moves closer to me and touches my cheek saying, "You feel it too don't you" This isn't a question, he's telling me.

"Feel what exactly?" I finally speak. I've never wanted to punch someone so much in my life. No wonder it's awkward between them, what the hell is she doing

170

with a man like this?

"Come on Kate, let's have some fun, meet me later?" He actually thinks I'm going to say yes to this. Is this what he does? Just comes on to women and then sleeps with them? Maybe this is what celebrity status does to a person, they get so big-headed that they think they own everything or can have anything or anyone they want. I try to keep calm so that Rich or Emma don't hear and I say,

"I really don't know why you're saying any of this. I am here planning your wedding so I think it's a little inappropriate that you're coming on to me."

"Yes," he says like he's scored a goal, "I knew you'd be one of those sorts, plays hard to get and then when you put out you shag like a hooker." I don't have any words for this man except,

"I see you have me all worked out" again this is sarcasm but this guy is never going to understand that. I was right, he reaches in his jacket and pulls out a card with his name and number on it.

"Ring me babe, you won't be disappointed" shit the confidence astounds me. He has no concept of other people's feelings. I am so close to walking out of this place, I feel insulted and a little bit violated, the way he's looking at me is gross.

I take the card out of his hand and get my pen out,

"I tell you what," I say as I'm writing on the card, "you ring me", I use my best sultry tones and he almost snorts with excitement, I hand him the card back and he looks down at it. (I'm really hoping he can read otherwise this will be lost on him) He's still chuckling to himself but then as the words sink in, he stops and looks at me.

"You silly bitch, you've just passed up the opportunity of a lifetime." Still doesn't get it, does he.

I walk away. Towards Rich and Darren's 'fiancée'. Poor girl. She must see it, mustn't she? As I'm getting closer, it hits me that I might've just blown this opportunity for us. I can hear Darren following me towards them and feel like I might have gone a bit far with what I wrote, he could say anything right now and if I've blown this deal, Rich will be fuming. Crap.

Rich and Emma are deep in conversation about the ceremony. Not on our agenda at all but she seems more enthused about it all now. Darren must see that too (maybe) as rather than throw me out, he just puts his arm round her and kisses her cheek.

"Well," Rich says, "I think we've got enough to work on right now. We'll put some ideas together and Kate will ring you next week to arrange another meeting if that suits?"

No hesitation from Darren, "That's great mate" and shakes his hand again, "Look forward to hearing from you" He clearly wants us to leave. Rich takes the hint, we do the customary goodbyes and we're out of there, not a moment too soon. I'm seething all the way down in the lift. Rich is checking his phone and doesn't say anything. There's a cab waiting so we jump in and head back to the office. Rich seems obsessed with his phone again.

"Rich? Are you ok?" he doesn't look up, seems to be busily texting someone as I can see the message box.

"Yeah, yeah," he dismisses "just making notes on everything they said. But he wasn't. He was definitely texting someone. He's lying to me. What is going on? I don't say anything else. But I will.

Twenty minutes later, I'm back at the office by myself. Rich stopped the cab and got out, said he had another meeting. He didn't, I made all his appointments this week so why is he lying? I'm really worried for him but also for Rach. I don't know where he got the money to set up the business and still never asked but now I'm worried he's in deep with something, he's not been himself all morning. I ponder on texting Rach but think better of it, I don't want to cause more problems.

I try to get my mind back into work and write up my notes from the meeting with Darren Bellamy. Just his name makes my skin crawl now. I google him and he seems to be a real ladies man according to the newspapers. At one point, it seems as though he had a different woman on his arm every week. And he's loaded so I guess if that's what you're charmed by…

I feel uncomfortable about the way he treated me but that leads to guilt. My relationship with Matt wasn't that different when you consider the basics. Both men in a relationship and trying it on with someone who is not their partner, both men willing to hurt their partner to get something they want, both men relatively rich – and with Matt, I let it happen. It played out well and truly. Mind you, Matt didn't just want sex and I'm pretty sure it was 'for one-night only' with Mr Bellamy. On the other hand, maybe Matt has only ever wanted sex from me. I guess I could look at that as a compliment, I mean, I must be really good in bed for him to keep coming back for three years. I'm lost in my thoughts again when my phone rings. It's Rich.

"Kate, sorry but I'm not going to make it back to the office today, not feeling great so I'm heading home. Sorry to leave you on your own." I'm a bit stunned. Rich never has time off so now I'm really concerned about what he's got himself into.

"Rich, you're worrying me, is everything ok?" I ask, trying to sound concerned more than panicked.

"I'm fine Kate, must have eaten something that's disagreed with me, nothing that a bit of rest won't cure." He's lying. I feel a bit of our friendship drain away.

"Ok," I try to sound normal, "let me know if you need anything".

"Thanks Kate. Bye" And he hangs up. Now should I

text Rach? No, that maybe wouldn't be fair to either of them. Awkward work/friend moment. I guess it was inevitable at some point.

Right, I make an executive decision that it is not my problem so I absolutely do not need to get involved. I make another executive decision that as it's only me in the office, and it's Friday, I'm going to finish early. I make a few phone calls which takes me to lunch time. Get the paperwork sorted for next week and I'm out of the door by 3pm. Home and in the bath for a lazy soak by 4pm. On my sofa drinking wine by 6pm. Just me. No men. No texts. No problems. Finally.

CHAPTER THIRTY-ONE

My weekend

For the first time in a long time, I feel like the weekend belongs to me. I know I won't be seeing Chris or Matt and it's kind of nice. It makes me realise that I'm always sort of waiting for approval and attention, bit sad really but at least I'm realising it.

On Saturday, I get up late. I laze around the flat for a bit and then decide to do some shopping. I haven't bought myself any new clothes for ages and I could do with some new underwear too. (Something for Chris instead of for Matt – still trying to please others!) I spend loads of time trying on clothes and end up with new work clothes more than anything for 'myself'. At least I'll look good at work. I find a couple of matching bra and knicker sets, the type that say confident but sexy and in control, at least that's what I'm hoping.

I decide to have an early night (Rock and Roll) but it doesn't quite go as planned!

I climb into my bed (fresh sheets, smells great) about 9pm and, yep, my phone pings. It's Chris. Now just bear in mind here that he is on a stag do in Glasgow and it's 9pm so he's probably pretty tanked up by now.

Hey beautiful Kate, missing your beautiful face, missing your hot body to be honest it's the lack of kisses that disappoints me but I go with it.

Take it you're having a good time then I remain light-hearted,

Fuckin great time yeah but wish I was coming home to you which is the last thing I would want, a drunken man coming into my freshly washed bed linen and falling asleep before anything happens (due to alcohol, not my company) and dribbling all over my lovely fresh linen, so glad the stag is in Glasgow.

Have a great night I figure it's best to try and end it before he starts texting things he might regret.

Can I call you? oh shit really Chris? Just go have fun.

Just want to hear your voice, oh dear he really is drunk. I remember how young he is. The immaturity shining through. Or maybe we all behave like this when we've had a drink. Age is probably irrelevant. Maybe? My phone starts ringing. Don't really want to talk to him when he's like this but,

"Hey", I answer the call. I can hear music and loud voices, shouting really.

"Hey beautiful" he does have a sexy voice, even when drunk. "How are you?"

"I'm good. Are you having fun?" not really sure how long this conversation can continue with all the noise in the background. I'm screwing my face up trying to hear him.

"Yeah it's a right laugh, some of the things the boys have done to Andrew are just ridiculous but he's taking it well." He actually sounds relatively sober. "Hope you don't mind me ringing, can't stop thinking about ya." I get the fluttery heart feeling again and cuddle into my duvet a bit enjoying the feeling. I'm not really sure what to say but I don't have to,

"Kate, I know ya no sure about uz yet and maybe we're no exactly in the same emotional place right now but I just want ya to know..." maybe he is drunk after all, "I just want ya to know that, I think ya amazing, ya beautiful, I really like ya" his accent is stronger than ever and what with the music and shouting, it's difficult to hear. But what I do hear, is lovely. He's good at making me feel good about myself. Which has got to be right.

"You're pretty gorgeous yourself Chris. Even if you're a little bit drunk?" I giggle.

"I ken, I must sound it with all this in the background and I have had a few. Mean it all though. Can't wait to see you next weekend." There are shouts of 'Chris you tight git, it's your feckin round, get off the feckin phone',

"Sounds like you're needed," I holler down the phone, feeling like I've got to shout so he can hear me.

"Yeah I'd better go. Have a good night Kate."

"You too. Bye Chris." And I hang up.

Unexpected but quite nice. He thinks I'm amazing and beautiful. I'll take that. I've got the biggest smile on my face and don't even realise to start with. This is the effect he has on me. He makes me feel great. This is how it should be. I haven't heard from Matt all week. That's not how it should be.

CHAPTER THIRTY-TWO

Sunday

I go for my run first thing on Sunday morning and it makes me feel great again. I honestly can't believe I let this slip. I stop for a bottle of water at the little café in the park and then take a slow pace home, feeling satisfied that I've already achieved something and it's only 9.30am.

I decide to have a good tidy round the flat after that. Best to keep busy. I put my music on shuffle and the first song that blasts out is Justin Timberlake's Can't Stop the Feeling so I dance my flat clean. (Can't stop the Cleaning) Then a few more upbeat numbers come on and because my energy is sky high, the flat is clean in no time. I leave the music playing as I finish up and decide I should have some lunch. But, as it turns out, I should've just turned it off because the next song is a Matt song, 'our song' if you like but it feels cheesy to think it. It's Hold My Girl by George Ezra. I run to my phone to turn it off but stop myself, I slump down at the kitchen table and just listen. The memories of Matt flood my mind and my heart and then my cheeks are streaming with tears and I can't stop. (Can't stop the crying) The song reminds me so much of the times we shared here in this flat on Sunday mornings. It was bliss, at the time. Looking back now, it feels a bit sordid, but I guess when you're in the middle of all those feelings, you put reality aside for as long as possible. I know that doesn't make it ok but for a while there, Sundays were the best and most important day of my week…

"Kate, come back to bed, you can do breakfast later," I hear his dulcet tones from the bedroom where I've not long left him, "in fact, I'll do breakfast, I'll make you my best omelette" he says with a giggle. I turn the hob off and

make my way back to the bedroom. "Yes," he says in triumph, "now come here gorgeous" and he pulls me down on to the bed, over his body and on to my back so that he is lying by my side and facing me. He looks at me and runs his hand down my cheek, it sends shivers all over my body as his fingers finally stop and rest on my neck and his thumb gently strokes my jaw bone. "You are so very beautiful Katie Carlin." He can't take his eyes off me and he kisses me tenderly and slowly and it feels so natural and right to be lost in each other like this. And then we make love. And nothing matters more to me than this moment and this man.

The song ends and reality hits. My cheeks are still wet but I'm smiling from the memory. There's part of me that wouldn't change our relationship for the world but there's another part of me that wishes I'd never met him because then I wouldn't feel this devastating pain right now. This feeling of loss. I make a deal with myself to leave it until Friday and if I still haven't heard from Matt by then, I will text him. I'm not sure what I will say, yet, but I still need some closure and if it's me that needs to instigate it, then so be it.

CHAPTER THIRTY-THREE

Monday Monday

The rest of my Sunday passed relatively quickly. Rach rang for a general chat which we try to do once a week, especially when we don't see each other. She seemed fine and although I was dying to ask if anything was going on with Rich, I didn't. Better to keep work and social life separate. (Unless I get really suss about Rich and need to protect Rach from something).

I didn't hear from Chris again over the weekend. I went with the hangover theory and figured that was fair enough. He was probably trying to remember if he actually spoke to me or not, and if he remembers calling me, he was probably panicking about what he said! (I know I've made drunken phone calls and lost friends the next day, haven't we all?)

So, Monday comes with surprising speed (Del Amitri's 'I won't take the blame' is going round my head, suddenly the lyrics mean more to me than any other song when I think about Matt.)

Work is always slow first thing on a Monday morning. Usually because I've tied up loose ends on a Friday and we're either waiting for new appointments or preparing for a meeting. This Monday is no different. Which gives me time to think. But this time not about me (shock horror!) and the woeful existence I lead but instead, my mind is on Rich. He's not turned up for work and he hasn't let me know why. I'm not his boss or anything, it's not like he has to call in sick but just a courtesy call would be nice, polite. And that's what worries me the most. Rich is so courteous that this behaviour is really strange. I start to worry that he is actually ill but when I spoke to Rach, she didn't mention anything, except to say that they went out for lunch and shopping on Saturday. So, he can't have been ill since Friday!

I make a few phone calls to confirm appointments. I try Darren Bellamy's number but get his answerphone, can't say I'm sorry. At 10am I make myself a coffee and then really start to worry about Rich. Where the hell is he? I try his number again but straight to answerphone. Nobody is answering their phone today, (perhaps it's actually Sunday and I've totally miss-timed my weekend, that would be hilarious!) I have a little laugh to myself as I settle back at my desk when Rich walks in, massive smile on his face,

"Hi Kate, how are you? Thanks so much for being so reliable. I knew you'd be running things in my absence," the worried man and furrowed brow of Friday has vanished and Rich is back, normal but more excitable Rich. It's such a drastic change that I can't help worrying even more. What is going on with him? I decide to grab the bull by the horns, (the bull being the situation, not Rich and the horns being my concerns, just so we're clear)

"Ok, enough Rich, I can't keep quiet anymore, what the hell is going on with you?" This stops him in his tracks and he swings round to look at me.

"What? Nothing is going on with me" when he says 'going on' he does the finger quotation marks and is still smiling as if I'm being ridiculous and he can sweep this under the carpet without any further questions. Well, he underestimates me,

"Rich, I'm not stupid, you're behaving totally out of character, you were shifty as hell on Friday, then said you were ill, and now you're over an hour late for work on a Monday, which you've never been before and you're on some sort of high, I mean… are you on something?" maybe that was going a bit far, but it's out there now. Rich looks a little uneasy and I worry that maybe I've hit the nail on the head, (shit he's got a cocaine habit that he's managed to hide from us all or worse, he's actually a drug dealer and this is how he's made his money... my brain really needs to slow down sometimes...) I stare at him and wait for some sort of response and he stares back and then, takes a deep breath and walks to the door, I think he's leaving, he's just going to walk out again now I've confronted him but instead he locks the door, (shit, he's a serial killer, a hitman and I'm next – please stop brain!) He goes back to his desk and from his inside jacket pulls out a little bag, (at least it's not a gun, or a knife, I wonder which one would be the worst way to be murdered...ffs brain!)

"OK Kate," he moves closer to me, "I obviously can't hide anything from you and you clearly know me far too well so," he keeps walking towards me and from the bag produces a little ring box, (shit he's going to ask me to marry him, what will I tell Rach, oh no wait...)

"Oh my god Rich!" I almost whisper,

"I'm going to ask Rach to marry me" a nervous smile appears on his face and I realise it's probably because I'm staring at him with my mouth open in shock and what I should be doing is telling him how fantastic this news is. Which it is of course, it's the best thing I've heard in ages.

"Oh my god, Rich, that's amazing!" I suddenly feel guilty for prying, he probably didn't want to have to tell me as she's my best-friend. "I'm sorry, I shouldn't have pushed you, but you were acting so weird on Friday, it's been playing on my mind." I admit.

"I know, I'm sorry about Friday. Rach saw this ring when we were in Oxford and she didn't say anything, obviously, but I knew by her reaction that she loved it. That was really early on in our relationship so I didn't think much of it at the time but in the last few weeks, I've realised it's her I want to spend the rest of my life with and I knew I had to try and get that ring." He takes a breath and then carries on, "I got hold of the jeweller last week but he said the ring had gone and he couldn't get another one. So I was really pissed off. I told him I'd pay double the price if he could get it for me, and." He stops, come on Rich…

"And what Rich?"

"And he found another one, exactly the same in a Jewellers in town so I've just been to get it and," he opens the box, "this is it"

"WOW!" is pretty much all I can say, the ring takes my breath away, completely Rach's taste and I can see straight away that she would love it. "Rich, it's stunning, she's going to love it"

"But will she say 'yes'?" he looks hesitant and nervous, like this is the most important thing he has ever done in his life, and I can see his love for Rach all over his face, and I know that she is the luckiest girl alive to have bagged a man like Rich, definitely a keeper. I stand up and give him a hug. For anyone watching this little scene outside, it would literally look like he's just popped the question and I've accepted,

"Rich, of course she'll say yes, you two were made for each other." I stand back and look at the ring again, "that and the fact that she'll definitely want that ring whether she wants to marry you or not" I giggle, trying to take the seriousness out of the moment having just hugged my boss, again. Well, boss and best-friend's soon-to-be-husband! Oh my god, my best friend is going to get married! This is huge. The first thing I want to do is ring Rach and tell her how excited I am…Obviously, I won't but it seems Rich isn't so confident,

"Kate, you won't say anything to her will you?" I do get the etiquette of proposing.

"Don't be crazy, of course I won't. When are you doing it?" I will want to talk to her about it asap though.

"I'm planning to do it this weekend. I've booked us a weekend away. She knows nothing about any of it yet" He is so excited. And nervous. "She will say 'yes' won't she, I mean it's not too soon?" They have only been together for a few months and I guess for most couples, that might be too soon, but not for Rich and Rach. It was obvious they were meant to be from the start. I feel a pang of jealousy. Why can't I find a man like Rich? A decent, caring human being who would do anything for me? (Maybe I have found one.)

"Rich, she loves you, she's going to say 'yes'" I have no doubt in saying this, she will absolutely say 'yes'.

The rest of the morning passes slowly. We both have paper work to be getting on with so we don't speak much. I occasionally look across at Rich and he's smiling like the Cheshire cat. He's put the ring back in his jacket, and now and again he pats the outside of it to make sure it's still there, as if some sneaky little mouse has crept in and stolen it right from under his nose. I wish I could be there when he proposes (weird!) I would love to see the look on Rach's face, especially when she realises he remembered the exact ring she fell in love with. That's real love right there. I'm welling up. Back to work Kate. The office phone rings and Rich gets to it first.

"Rich Events" he listens and then frowns and then says,

"Ok, I'm very sorry to hear that." He struggles to say more but the person on the other end cuts him off and then eventually Rich says, "Well thank you for considering us.", another pause to listen, "Goodbye." He hangs up the phone and looks across at me. "Well, I wasn't expecting that!" he says in astonishment, "that was Darren Bellamy's agent. He says they won't be requiring our services," oh shit, I messed up and we've missed out on a lucrative job, what do I do, should I tell Rich?

"They've decided to let the Shangri-La manage the whole thing?" I ask gingerly,

"Nope," he raises his eyebrows, "the wedding is off!" Oh shit, well that's not my fault, (I won't take the blame – song of the day apparently).

"Why, what happened?"

"His agent just said the relationship had come to an end! Pretty abrupt end if one day you're planning your wedding and the next you're splitting up. Although, thinking about it, they weren't exactly love's young dream, that whole meeting was strange, and he totally fancied you Kate, he couldn't take his eyes off you, that's not what should be happening when you're marrying someone else." I feel a little relieved at Rich having noticed the attention Darren was giving me. It makes it easier for me to say,

"He wasn't just looking Rich, he hit on me! Told me to meet him that night." Rich's eyebrows move even further up his forehead in shock and I consider my next words carefully, don't want him to think I had anything to do with this split, "I told him I thought it was inappropriate to talk to me in that way considering why we were there"

"Shit Kate, why didn't you tell me?" I look at him with a knowing glance, "I know, I didn't exactly stick round for long on Friday. I guess you would have told me today."

"Absolutely" I lie. I had no intention of telling Rich as that would have made the job awkward for both of us. But it's irrelevant now. I'm really pleased for Emma though, I hope it's her that's called it off.

Well, one job lost but plenty of others to keep us busy. I get stuck into the enquiries. Make a few phone calls. Eat my lunch. And almost forget about the fact that my phone hasn't made a sound all day. In fact, it takes until I get home for anyone to contact me. And it's Chris.

Hey beautiful, hope your Monday has been ok? Mine has been long, still a bit hungover I think. I chuckle and assume he's covering himself as he more than likely can't remember what he said to me on Saturday night.

Had a great day thanks. Must have been a good night if you were still suffering this morning I'm prying for a little bit of information.

It was a blast of a night, literally! Long story, I'll explain when I see you, talking of which…I would love that to be soon xx There's that fluttery heart feeling. He wants to see me, who wouldn't feel good after hearing that. I wonder if he means before the weekend as we had planned, I reply,

How soon are you thinking? I'm quite keen to see him too, I think I've missed him, it's been nearly a week since we had lunch.

Do you want to meet for a drink tonight? that's pretty soon and I was hoping he might say tonight but I don't fancy going out so,

Why don't you come to mine? my urges have got the better of me. But, well, if I'm honest, as much as I'd like him to sweep me off my feet and carry me to the bedroom, I also just want to see him, to be in the same room as him, to feel his eyes on me…

I can be there in an hour?

Great xx And then realise I'd better take a quick shower and put some half decent clothes on, I don't want to look like I've dressed up for him but I also don't want to look like a slob. I shower quickly, making sure I use my expensive shower gel so I smell good and then get dressed. I put on a pair of figure-hugging jeans and a short but sloppy jumper, casual but sexy is the look I'm going for, (don't know if it's working.) As a last-minute thing, I quickly clean my teeth but then decide to pour myself a glass of wine and take a swig of it so I don't smell quite so freshly prepared for him.

He's here in less than an hour. I answer the door with my sexiest smile (again, don't know if it's actually sexy but I'm trying) and once again that Richard Madden smile and accent take my breath away, "Wow, hello beautiful" I smile and he leans in to kiss me. I let him. I want him. Shit he's good looking. The kiss ends.

"You coming in then?" I say with a cheeky smile on my face as I open the door wider and stand back to let him in. I can smell his aftershave as he drifts past me and it's like some sort of aphrodisiac, (get a grip Kate!)

I pour him a glass of wine and we sit on the sofa, both perching on the edge so we can reach our wine.

"Tell me about this weekend then? Was it a good stag?" he looks at me a bit sheepishly,

"It was really good, pretty much what you'd expect for a stag. Andrew's best man is a complete loon, and really put him through his paces. Andrew ended up naked and tied to the bonnet of a vintage ford capri – turns out this is Andrew's wedding present to him." Chris is giggling to himself as he tells the story, like he's reliving it a bit in his head.

"He bought him a car as a wedding present? That's kind of extravagant, isn't it?" Chris turns to me, (oh those eyes) and smiles,

"Aye, but that's what those two have always been like, best pals since school, they'd do anything for one another. It was a pretty special night." He's still looking at me, "I meant what I said on the phone, you know." Oh, he does remember. "I wasn't so drunk that I can't remember," he winces a little bit, "I hope that's ok?"

"What, that you weren't that drunk?" is my quick retort. He grins and lovely little dimples appear, one at each side of his mouth,

"No, that I think you're amazing and beautiful and I really like you" wow, he definitely remembers things well. Bonus, good looks and I might get a birthday present! When someone says something like that to you and they're sitting right next to you (and obviously if you like them a little bit) then there's really only one thing you can do.

I move closer to him, frame his face with my hands, look directly into his eyes and I kiss him. A kiss that feels different to all the others, this one doesn't say, 'come on then, let's go to bed', it says, 'I also think you're amazing and beautiful and I like you'. Chris's arms fold naturally around my body, I feel his fingers working their way up my spine to my neck, he already knows me well, knows how to touch me. One hand stays on my neck, teasing me with his touch and the other moves into my hair. It feels fantastic. When we stop kissing, I look at him and beam,

"I'm really glad you're here, I missed you" he looks thrilled at this and we both know our relationship has just turned a big corner.

CHAPTER THIRTY-FOUR

Tuesday

I'm smiling all the way to work. Chris stayed the night and left early so that he could get home and be on time for work. We had such a lovely evening. We watched a film, cuddling and kissing on the sofa whenever the mood took us. I love being in his arms, he makes me feel safe and wanted. When we went to bed, we made love. It was perfect. And we lay together after, whispering to each other and teasing each other and giggling together. At one point, he got up to get a glass of water, and when he came back to bed he wrapped me up in his arms again and we slept like that until his alarm went off at 5am.

"I've got to get going", he whispered into my hair, and I replied with a little,

"Nooo, just stay a bit longer," so he did. He kissed me again and held me and then at 5.30am, he got quietly dressed. I woke properly to find him sitting on the edge of the bed looking down at me.

"Morning beautiful,"

"Morning" I replied.

"I've got to go. I'll ring you later." He touched my cheek, and bent down to kiss me. A really loving, tender kiss. I listened to him leaving, waited for the front door to close and then did a little silent and victory 'yes' to myself.

My week passes pretty quickly. There's lots to do at work. We have a couple of daytime events this week so I'm running about sorting those out whilst keeping our future events ticking over by ringing clients and arranging the next meeting. And while I'm doing all of this, something hits me, I'm happy for the first time in ages. I mean, happy in every aspect of my life. I have a brilliant job that I love with a great boss/partner. I'm seeing Chris, who seems to worship the ground I walk on and I finally feel like I'm moving on from Matt. (who still hasn't contacted me and in fact I've decided that I won't be contacting him either!)

Rich might as well not be in the office this week. He is so nervous about getting everything right for the big proposal that he's constantly on the phone to the restaurant and hotel where he's taking Rach. At one point I hear him talking to someone on the phone,

"No you don't understand, if you don't get this exactly right, it could ruin everything!" Maybe he's a little too obsessed with the perfection of it all but I guess he's only doing it to make Rach happy.

We have work on Friday night this week, a last-minute conference that got passed to us through Rach as the company she works for (Rich's previous employment) couldn't take it on at such short notice. For Rich Events, still up and coming in the world of Event Management, we have to take anything we can like this, it could make us. Not financially but most of this business comes through word of mouth so the more people you can impress, with taking on short notice jobs or going above and beyond the remit, the more successful you become. This is how most of our work has come to us so far. A lot has come from Matt's relaunch, rather annoyingly, it's like he's still lingering in the background somewhere taking some sort of credit for a part of my life. But I can't think like that. Although I still think of him and hope his name appears on my screen every time it pings, it's becoming less.

Anyway, work on Friday means I can't see Chris until Saturday night. He's making a bit of a thing of it all. Text me to say he wants it to be like a first date because we didn't really have one of those and due to the shift in our relationship, from holiday romance to 'seeing each other', he wants us to have an official start to our relationship. He's sweet like that. Makes me smile when I realise how hard he's trying to impress and look after me. All he's told me is to wear something classy and be ready to be picked up at 7pm. Exciting and mysterious.

The conference on Friday takes a few frantic phone calls to get everything in place. It's difficult to get catering at such short notice but we have a useful list of contacts now and some who are in the same boat as us, small businesses in their early years and so they'll go out of their way to get a job done well. We're building up positive relationships with these companies. It's always about the people. Whatever business or job you're in, if you get people on your side, you're more than half-way there. Although, Lord Sugar might disagree. I'm not saying you have to be nice to everyone and kiss ass, but common courtesy and transparency go a long way.

Friday night is uneventful. The company are pleased with what we put together, Rich and I both attend to make sure it all runs smoothly and so we don't have to pay any external staff. We finish about 9pm. Rich is taking Rach away in the morning so he didn't have to postpone that. He probably wouldn't have taken the job if it meant his perfectly planned weekend was messed up.

I get home about 10pm and feel knackered. It's been a busy week and I need to relax and sleep. I get my comfies on straight away and curl up in front of the telly. No wine tonight though. Just a hot chocolate and a bit of Gogglebox. This programme makes me laugh so much. I always used to think I wanted the job editing the episodes, some of them are so funny.

My phone pings and it's Chris.

Hi Kate, how did your conference go? xx We've text every day. And he was fine about me moving our date to Saturday.

Was good, pretty painless. Home now, tired, having a hot chocolate, rock and roll I press 'send' but then think I maybe shouldn't have shared the hot chocolate comment. Then I'm reminded (for the first time in a while) that the age gap is still a bit of a worry. Surely men in their mid-twenties don't want to hear that their girlfriend is having a quiet night with a hot chocolate. Surely they want to be going out clubbing, or drinking at the very least, on a Friday night. But his reply reassures me,

I'm tired too. Slobbing in front of the telly at the moment. Glad it's Friday and I get to see you tomorrow xx

Me too. Kind of excited about the mystery of it all xx

Just giving you what you deserve xx and I worry a little about that statement. I have a feeling, and that's all it is, that Chris is trying to make up for how I've been treated in the past (by Matt) and is a bit too conscious of it. I don't want Matt to be a shadow that hangs over us. But maybe I'm analysing too much, again.

I say goodnight and decide to get an early night. I need my beauty sleep so that I look as young as Chris tomorrow. Don't want people looking at us thinking I'm his mother. (Don't be ridiculous Kate, you're not that much older than him!)

CHAPTER THIRTY-FIVE

Saturday - The Date

Chris arrives to pick me up at exactly 7pm. I am ready, which is a bit of a surprise as I'm usually running late due to trying on several different outfits and then generally going back to the original choice. I've gone with simple but sophisticated (I'm hoping), little black dress. A little cliched I guess but in situations like this when I have no idea where I'm going and all Chris said was 'dress classy', I figure an LBD is safe. It has a slight sweetheart shape which I'm really hoping accentuates my boobs in a positive way and though the main material stops just above my knee, it has a lace overlay which rests just below my knee so it preserves my modesty (doesn't look too tarty!) I've put my hair up and given it a bit of height. Chris is tall, so it makes me seem less squat next to him.

I open the door and wow he looks good. He's wearing a really nice looking suit and tie. I didn't think he could get any better looking but right now I wish we didn't have to go out because I could just rip that suit off him here on the door step.

"You look stunning Kate" he whispers in my ear as he kisses my cheek. It feels incredibly romantic.

"So do you," I say as I look him up and down again. He gives me a knowing smile like he's just read my mind and says,

"Later baby," and I smile and start to fall in love with him a little bit. We sit quietly together in the cab and I feel nervous, like this really is a first date. He looks at me and puts his hand on mine,

"You ok?" I smile back and nod.

"Yeah, I'm fine, it's really nice to see you"

"It's really nice to see you too Kate." I want him to kiss me, surely he wants to. But, I think he wants the 'first date feel' to be real. And you wouldn't kiss someone at the beginning of a first date. I guess it's sweet.

While I've been lost in my thoughts, and lost in him, I've lost track of where we are. I was trying to guess where he's taking me by the route we're taking. I look out of the cab window. We're on Kensington Road, don't seem to be slowing down though. Carrying on through Knightsbridge, I'm getting even more nervous now, where are we going?

"Nearly there" Chris says sensing my nerves, I look at his face and he's anxious too. I squeeze his hand, hopefully reassuringly not patronisingly, and the cab comes to a stop. Shit, we're at sketch! This is impressive. I've heard so much about this place (mostly from Matt) I try not to get too excited. Maybe the cab is just dropping us here and Chris will lead me across the road to a crappy little greasy spoon. That would be disappointing now! We get out of the cab and he says, "Is this ok?" indicating sketch.

"Are you serious? More than ok." I beam at him. And he looks relieved and seems to relax a bit.

"Come on then." He takes my hand and leads me into the restaurant. He confirms his booking and we are taken to The Glade. Oh my god, that is so the one I would have chosen. sketch (too trendy for a capital letter) is four different restaurants, with amazing reviews (and two Michelin stars) but The Glade is the more quirky, unique one of the four. I've heard it's like no other restaurant and you have to experience it for yourself and boy is that right. We step in and floor to ceiling is just a feast for the eyes. It is literally like being in a forest, the carpets are beautiful with fluffy grass-like patches, the colours and the décor is like we've walked into another world. I'm suddenly aware of Chris' eyes on me, I'm staring with my mouth wide open. The waiter is smiling too as he leads us to our table, he must have seen reactions like mine a thousand times before.

We sit down and I'm still trying to take it all in. I look up and there is a sort of neon forest above our heads, hanging beautifully and giving the sense that we're outdoors in a warm quixotic setting. The whole place is just stunning. I look across the table at Chris,

"Nice choice." I say and he smiles and relaxes a little more.

Our 'first date' is the best date of my life. Chris is such a gentleman and asks me questions as if he's getting to know me for the first time. There are some questions he already knows the answers to and I frown with puzzlement a bit when he asks but he says,

"Come on, first date stuff, play the game" I love those dimples at the sides of his mouth. I'm totally entranced by him as well as the place. We talk and talk, no awkward moments of silence. He is very adept and confident with ordering and he shows real respect to our waiter. I'm kind of mesmerised by the whole experience.

We're in sketch for two hours and afterwards he takes me to a little cocktail bar where we sit close to each other. I can feel his thigh pressing against mine and it feels good. I really want him to come home with me tonight. But I also want to enjoy being out with him. I always seem to rush things to the 'sex part'. No need when the company is as good as this.

We get a cab back to my flat and he gets out with me but asks the driver to wait which disappoints me a little as all the way back I've been hoping he'll stay at mine. Taking my hand as I step out of the cab, he walks me to my door. (He'd better kiss me at the very least!)

I want to ask him to come in with me but the mere fact he's asked the cab driver to wait suggests I already have his answer (Is this all part of the first date romance?) and if he said 'no' that might feel like rejection and I don't want anything to spoil this night. So, I let him take the lead,

"Kate, I've had such an amazing night with you, thank you." (I'm starting to think he's read a book called first dates and he's memorised exactly what to say and when to say it.) But whatever he's doing, it's working as I have also had a wonderful night.

"Me too" I whisper and then, he places his hand on my cheek and leans towards me, his lips find mine and the kiss makes me dizzy. It's tender but sexy and I feel a little weak at the knees. When it ends, he runs his thumb along my bottom lip and says,

"You're beautiful, Kate. Can I see you again soon?" and I'm completely lost in him now so I'm totally going with the first date scenario.

"I'd like that." He leans in again and brushes my lips with his. A final first date kiss. He's good.

"Me too. See you soon beautiful Kate." And I watch him as he walks back to the cab. I shut the door and lean against it, feeling a bit like I'm in a movie and I'm the one who finally gets the good guy. I take a deep breath and make my way to the kitchen, feel the need for some water and maybe a cup of tea. I kick my heels off as I flick the kettle on and my doorbell goes. I smile to myself. He's not left, he did all the first date stuff but actually (because we're beyond that anyway) he's come back, I wonder if that was his intention all along. I rush to the door and feel the excitement flood through me and when I open it, I feel my breath almost get stuck in my throat and my hands start to shake, because it's not Chris – it's Matt.

Matt looks at me and tries to smile. He looks tired. He has dark rings under his eyes and he looks like he's lost weight. For a moment, I wonder what the hell I'm

196

supposed to do or say as this was the last thing I was expecting but then I shake my head and start to close the door,

"Kate, wait," he puts his hand on the door to stop it from closing. "Please?"

"What do you want Matt?" I'm furious, I feel so angry with him for just turning up and tonight of all nights!

"Can I come in? Can we talk?" My instincts kick in,

"How do you know I don't have someone here?" I sort of indicate my dress as if to show him I've been out and had a great time (without him)

"Because I've just watched him leave." More anger is bubbling up inside me with the fact that he has turned up now and ruined my perfect date with Chris (although at least Chris hasn't seen him, that really would have been a disaster). But then I look at him and see those eyes that I love and I've missed him so damn much and.... Be strong Kate. I need closure on this. Take control. Don't weaken.

"You've got 5 minutes" I open the door and let him in.

He sits on the sofa (our sofa) and I stand by the window. I do not need to be too close to him, and I need to have the power here. Standing up, being above him physically will make me superior to him.

"Who is he? Is it the same guy?" and I let rip,

"It's none of your fucking business! How dare you turn up here and ruin my evening. Who the fuck do you think you are? You haven't contacted me for two weeks and then you just show up expecting me to welcome you back with open arms. Seriously Matt, are you deranged?" He says nothing through my rant and I can see him clench his teeth together as I finish. He takes a deep breath. But says nothing. "Matt, what do you want?" I feel a bit sorry for him, he looks broken. I sit down in the chair opposite him and wait.

"Kate, I'm so sorry. I'm sorry I haven't contacted

you. I'm sorry I was such a dick. I'm sorry I've hurt you so much. Which I know I have by the look in your eyes, you're so angry with me." He looks right at me with pain in his eyes now, "I never wanted to hurt you like this. I've messed up haven't I?" my reply is instant,

"Yes Matt you have." I need some answers. If I'm going to get closure, I need to know what the hell has happened. "Where have you been? What is it that's stopped you calling me? You were going to call me when you got back?"

"I only got back today. I wanted to see you so I came here as soon as I got back but you weren't in. I went to the restaurant for a while and then came back." I wait for more, "I should have called you or text you after we fell out. But I was angry and… I just felt like you were trying to prove a point or something"

"Trying to prove a point, what point? What do you mean?" Christ where does he get off blaming me in all this,

"I was upset that you were texting someone else. I was jealous. You've always been mine Kate,"

"Shit, Matt, I'm not a possession, I'm not a fancy car you can just trade in when you get bored with it." But the way he said 'jealous' reverberates round my head, like it was massive for him to admit and he had to force the word out of his mouth.

"I know I took you for granted, I know I was the luckiest bastard alive to have you, to have you waiting for me, to have you give your time to me when you could have been with anyone you wanted to. I'm so angry with myself for treating you so badly and for not realising…" he hesitates and looks down, he looks like he's got tears in his eyes, "…for not realising how lucky I was to have you. All those times I should've been here with you and I wasn't, all those days when we could have been together and I just took it for granted that you'd wait, and when I was ready, you'd still be here for me. I'm an idiot. A fucking idiot and I don't deserve you Kate, I really don't. So, if you tell me that you don't love me anymore and that there's no way back then I promise I will accept that. I will walk out of here and I will leave you alone." I realise, as I'm listening to these words, these words that I would have killed to hear three months ago or even two weeks ago, that tears are rolling down my cheeks and I can't stop them. I try to wipe them away but they keep coming. "Am I too late?" he murmurs. I look at him, I mean really look at him. My Matt, the man I wanted to spend my forever with. The man who, until last week, I still thought I would. But so much has happened. So much has changed in my mind (has it changed in my heart?) because of Chris and because of Matt's lack of contact. And I consider his question…

"Kate, am I too late to save this?" I think about Chris and how good he is for me. I think about the wonderful evening he's just given me. I think about Matt and the fact that I love him and probably always will. I think of the times we've spent together in this flat, on this sofa, holding each other, and then I think about the loneliness and the pain and I say,

"Yes, you're too late."

"Kate," he moves towards me and kneels on the floor in front of me, takes hold of my hands and pleads into my eyes, "Please Kate, I love you, I'm sorry, I've been an idiot. I'm so sorry that I couldn't work this out sooner."

"Matt, you should have worked it out three years ago, we both should." Feeling him this close to me, my hands encased in his, I feel lost and for a brief second, I nearly follow my heart but I regain my composure, I inwardly remind myself that this will never work and I find some strength.

"Matt," I cup his face with my hands, "we have to end this, all we do is hurt each other, and I just don't have the strength anymore, I've moved on and you need to move on as well." He looks directly into my eyes and he knows it's over. He knows I mean it.

"I'm sorry, Kate" I shake my head and then gently kiss him, our wet, teared faces touching briefly and it takes all my strength and resolve to pull away and not kiss him again. The tingles and the fluttery heart are still there, no matter what I am saying right now. But I have to move on. I have to give myself a chance to be happy. Matt stands up and moves away from me. He wipes his face and takes a deep breath. I stand up and we look at one another, almost as if we're remembering the wonderful times that we spent here in this room, in this flat.

"I love you Kate." And he goes to the door, opens it and leaves. I fall back into the chair and sit staring at nothing for what feels like half an hour. Then I cry. Then I cry some more. Then I go and take a shower and then I go to bed.

CHAPTER THIRTY-SIX

Three months later

I'm sitting at work. It's Wednesday and I'm expecting Rach any second. She's meeting me for lunch. It hasn't been just the two of us for ages so I'm really looking forward to it.

Her and Rich are starting to discuss wedding plans a little more seriously though they haven't set a date yet so I'm really excited about what kind of wedding she'll want having arranged so many herself.

I pick up my phone and decide to text Chris. We haven't seen one another since Saturday and I miss him.

Hey, how's your day? Chris has been a bit unhappy at work recently. His job has changed slightly and he doesn't like his new boss, had a run in with her yesterday, so I want to check in with him to see how it's going. *

Hey, I'm ok but the pressure is on as usual. The witch is still making us all feel inadequate xx* His job does come with a lot of pressure (and money!) so it's no wonder he feels stressed by it but he also loves it, or he did until 'the witch' turned up.

You're brilliant at your job Chris, just try to remember why you love it and ignore her, you'll probably be her boss one day xx I try to make him feel better but, to be honest, I have no idea what the world of corporate and investment banking is like. And from what Chris has told me, I don't want to know, sounds like a real cut-throat business.

Thanks beautiful xx

Rach arrives just as I read the text and wow she looks radiant. Of course she goes straight to Rich first. Her love, her fiancé, her everything. They are still cute together though, somehow they don't seem too cheesy, they're just the right level of romantic so that people can see how much they love each other but don't necessarily need a bucket (depending of course on how cynical one might be about love).

Rach and I head out to The Loft for lunch. They do a nice daytime menu and it's usually relatively quiet on a Wednesday. We sit at our favourite table and I can't help but stare at her beautiful engagement ring. When Rich proposed she completely lost it for while, balled her eyes out and, to start with, Rich wasn't sure if she was having a breakdown because she wanted to say 'no' or if she was completely overwhelmed with emotion. Turned out to be the latter and mostly because she was so moved by the fact that Rich had moved heaven and earth to find that ring. She said 'yes' straight away of course, as I predicted. And they have been more smitten with one another ever since. I don't mind this at the moment as I'm pretty smitten myself but any other time I might start to get a little bit pissed off with their constant PDAs. (At least they don't go as far as calling each other their nicknames in public, that really would be a bit much.)

Rich has told us to take our time and he's not really expecting me back. Rach has got the rest of the day off so we'll probably make an afternoon of it. We order a bottle of prosecco and some tapas. It feels quite naughty to be drinking at lunch time on a Wednesday but I haven't seen my best friend in ages and if lunch is the only time we can get together, due to work events, then so be it.

"Have you thought about a date yet? Or even a year?" Rach has been really laid back about it all so far. I don't think either of them are wanting to rush it but nobody wants to be 'engaged' for years.

"Kind of," Rach ambiguates, "we're still trying to work it out" I feel like she's holding something back.

"Is everything ok Rach?" I question and she nods, trying to pretend everything is ok. "Rach?"

"Oh Kate, I'm sorry, it's just a bit strange. Rich and I can't agree on what kind of wedding we want so trying to set a date and find a venue that we both like is really difficult." She seems annoyed rather than upset by this. "I mean, shouldn't it be the bride's right to say what kind of wedding she wants?" I wasn't really expecting this, it sounds like Rich and Rach have actually disagreed on something for the first time which I'm a little shocked by.

"Why Rach, what's so different in what you both want? Surely the idea of being together and being married is the most important thing?" she nods as she takes a huge gulp of prosecco, (think she might be on a mission)

"I know, totally right. And we are being rational about it, we're not arguing too much but everything either of us suggests just gets vetoed."

"Everything?" I say in surprise, "Surely there must be something you agree on?"

"Not really. I think it's because we're both in the business. If you do it for a living and then try to plan your own, well, it's complicated. And it bloody shouldn't be." She chuckles to herself and sees the funny side. "Anyway, we'll sort it out. We just need to keep thinking and chatting about it. It's actually caused us to have our first argument but it was so worth it, the make-up sex was out of this world!" Ok Rach, steady, definitely gone in hard on the prosecco. "Honestly Kate, it's like you used to talk about with Matt, the tension creates a whole new sensation." I feel a bit knocked back. I haven't mentioned Matt for ages, I try not to. And a reminder of how good the sex was isn't really what I want to be thinking about right now. Rach notices my face drop,

"Shit, I'm sorry, I've done it again haven't I?" She seems to talk about Matt more than me these days, almost as if she can't quite believe it's really over. I suppose I threatened to end it so much, and didn't, that now it just seems to be a part of our lives. "How are you feeling about all that now?" Rach knows everything that happened with Matt down to his visit to my flat that night and how I ended it with him, I haven't seen him or heard from him since which is what I wanted.

"I miss him still. Really miss him." I murmur sort of absent-mindedly or involuntarily and Rach squeezes my hand.

"It's ok to feel that way Kate, you loved him for a long time" She's right of course, you've got to feel the feels but then get on with it. Her sentence shouldn't have been in past tense though, I don't think I'll ever not love Matt.

Rach seems to understand it all better since the split. Before, she was constantly angry with Matt for hurting me, just as a best friend should be, but now she seems softer, more sympathetic about it. I think she respects him more now for leaving me alone and allowing me to get on with my life. Rach was really pleased when I told her I was seeing Chris. She likes him and thinks he's good for me. We've been out as a four a few times and Rich and Chris get on well so that helps.

I never told Chris about Matt's visit that night. Didn't see the point in spoiling a lovely evening. Matt's timing was shit but maybe him turning up when he did, when I'd had the perfect evening with another man, gave me the strength I needed to finish things once and for all. And Chris and me have been growing stronger every day.

"Are you seeing Chris this weekend?" Rach enquires, obviously trying to subtly change to a more positive subject,

"Yes, he's planned another surprise date" this has become a bit of a thing, he's taken me to some lovely places, really expensive too, he totally spoils me which he says I deserve. Quite the romantic.

"Oh, where will it be this time?" Rach loves the mystery, "he still can't beat sketch for me but he set the bar pretty high with that one." She admitted to me last time we met that she was jealous of that evening, that it was such a romantic thing to do and that helped me to see I'd done the right thing choosing Chris over Matt. (Is that what I did? I guess it is.)

We're quickly on to our second bottle of prosecco and I'm definitely not going back to work now.

"At least I have an understanding boss." I joke with Rach and we both laugh. We talk about everything. I tell her how much I'm falling for Chris and she's really pleased for me.

"I must admit, Kate, I wasn't sure he was a long term prospect to start with, I mean, he is a bit young…" (my nagging doubt again) "…but I can see how much he cares about you and he's a keeper when it comes to the finances." She rubs her fingers together in a weird masculine way and I don't like the insinuation,

"Rach, don't say that, it doesn't matter to me in any way how much money he's got." I protest,

"I know, I'm only kidding," and she's starting to slur her words, I think she's doing most of the drinking. "he's so good for you and that sexy accent, wow, he's lush" I think she's definitely crossed over into drunksville and I suddenly feel very sober. I think it might be time to leave. I call a cab while she's in the toilet so she can't argue about it.

Rach lives in the opposite direction to me so I get her in the cab and tell the driver the address.

"I'll text you when I'm home Kate," she sings at me as I close the cab door. Wow, drinking in the daytime certainly has a different effect on people. Just as I'm calling another cab, I hear someone calling my name.

"Kate? Hey Kate," I swing round to see Lucy. I forgot this was one of her places too (totally lying there, can't possibly forget, think about her every time I'm in cubicle 1!) That moment crosses my mind now as I look at her and I'm reminded how stunning she is and I get a little throbbing sensation. She hugs me and kisses my cheek.

"Wow, Kate, it's so lovely to see you. Are you leaving?" I hesitate and say, I was, "Do you have to? Come and have a drink with me?" The toilet incident crosses my mind again and she beams at me, "Hey come on, it'd be great to have a catch up and I'll try not to take advantage of you this time" she gives me that sexy smile and the throbbing between my legs accentuates. Stop it Kate.

"Yeah, ok. It would be good to catch up." I walk back into the bar with her and she orders a gin for herself. I stick to the prosecco, best not to start mixing now. We know where that leads.

"So, how've you been? It must be nearly six months since…" her eyes look briefly towards the Ladies. I smile again at the memory,

"Yeah I guess it must. I'm doing ok. Work is great and I'm seeing a really nice guy who isn't married" I laugh and so does she,

"Always a bonus." She takes a swig of her gin and asks if it's serious.

"Getting that way, it's only been a few months but he's great, no complaints yet. What about you?" She takes a deep breath and launches into a breakdown of her life since we last met. She's been travelling with work and spent a while in Paris.

"Oh Kate, I met this amazing girl there, I think I'm actually in love for the first time in my life" I'm a little surprised at this; she always gave the impression that she wasn't about falling in love and relationships. I try not to show my surprise,

"That's great, what's she like? Is she French?" I want to sound interested but I'm a bit jealous. Especially because she said she's in love 'for the first time', I kind of thought she might have fallen in love with me a little, maybe I was kidding myself. And it's not like I fell in love with her so I'm not sure why I'm bothered? I guess it's the narcissist in me.

"Yeah she's French, wants me to move out to Paris, which is feasible, I could do my job from there. And it's such an amazing place." I sense a but,

"So what's stopping you?" she shrugs and takes another sip of her gin and looks at me,

"I don't know, I guess, I mean, I think, I often wonder if there's anyone to keep me here?" I frown a little and wonder if I've misunderstood but it sounded like a question. She raised her voice at the end which was definitely a question. Has she just asked if I want her to stay here? That's a bit crazy.

"How do you mean?" I don't know what else to say.

"I know it was probably just sex for you Kate, but I fell for you, hook line and sinker. From the moment we met, I couldn't get you off my mind. Should I have made that clearer? I know I said we should experiment and see where that takes us but looking back, I…"

"Shit, Lucy, I didn't realise, I'm… I'm not sure what to say."

"It's ok, I knew we were looking for different things, you made that clear, it's not like you promised me anything." I start thinking back to the few times we saw each other. For me it was just sex and the way she acted, it seemed that way for her too. We did have a connection though. She's being very nice about all this, considering. I really don't know what to say.

"Look Kate, I didn't expect to see you tonight and this isn't about you, it's about me. I guess I needed this meeting to realise a few things. I haven't committed to Paris because I wondered if there could be anything between you and me and now I've seen you, I know there isn't, and that's fine. I mean, I'm disappointed I'm never going to touch your amazing ass again" she lightens the mood, "but it's ok cos I just needed to know for sure."

I'm a bit flummoxed, this is the last thing I was expecting.

"I'm sorry Lucy." Is all I can think of to say,

"Don't be, please don't be. It's fine. I know now." She kisses my cheek. Same old feelings. She hovers for a second, her lips close to mine and I just sit still. She smiles and sits back, "Hey, we'll always have cubicle 1" she giggles and downs her drink. It's strange how you just can't read someone sometimes. I honestly thought she was all about the casual, that's all it ever felt like. I feel bad. I wonder how I would have reacted if she'd told me at the time? Maybe we should all be a little more honest with the people we care about and love. I feel like I've hurt her in a way that I've been hurt. I suddenly feel the need to get home. This has been a strange day. I need to be at home. Alone.

CHAPTER THIRTY-SEVEN

Saturday - Date night

Sometimes I wonder if my life is just a strange sequence of events that will ultimately lead to my downfall. Is that just the truth for everyone?

I'm back late from work due to a meeting overrunning and Chris is due in twenty minutes to pick me up for our date. I quickly jump in the shower but don't wash my hair as I won't have time to dry it. Instead, when I've dried off, I spray some dry shampoo and give it a quick going over with the straighteners, so I look half decent.

I'm just getting my shoes on when the doorbell goes.

"Hey beautiful" he says as I open the door and he leans in to kiss me.

"Hey yourself" I say, he smells gorgeous. And looks gorgeous and I look like a bag of crap. He seems to sense my anxiety "you ok?"

"Yeah, but was really late getting home so I've rushed to get ready and I probably have my shoes on the wrong feet and…" he stops my wittering with another kiss.

"You look amazing, as always." And I feel instantly better. Chris is very good at making me feel good, always knows the right things to say to make me relax.

We get in the cab and I do my usual questioning to see if he's giving any hints as to our destination. He's taken me to some fantastic places. And always insists on paying. But that needs to stop soon. Now we're more established as a couple, we need to share that responsibility a bit more. I watch where the cab takes us, but Chris is feeling amorous tonight and won't stop kissing me. Not that I'm complaining. My bag slips off my lap as the cab comes to a stop so I lean down to pick it up as Chris opens the door and steps out. That's when I see it, the olive green façade and the unmistakable sign in the window. It's Matt's restaurant. Chris has brought me to Matt's restaurant! Of course, he has no idea what he has done. I never told him who my 'ex' was or what he did. Matt's place is getting amazing reviews and Chris looks for places like that. It didn't even cross my mind that one day we would end up here. Shit, what do I do? Feign sickness? Tell him the truth? Act normal?

I almost fall out of the cab in shock and Chris catches hold of my arm so that I don't hit the deck.

"Thanks" I say, still looking at the restaurant front. "Um Chris…" he seems oblivious to my panic.

"Apparently this place has the most amazing Seafood Fettuccini and I know you love that" He's right, I love it because Matt has cooked it for me several times, in fact he tried the recipe out on me, while he was developing it, before putting it on the menu. That's why it's my favourite. This is crazy. But Chris is so excited about being here and is already at the door before I can think of any excuses. I follow him.

Inside, it's pretty much the same as the last time I was here, for the relaunch, when I got drunk. Shitty memories come flooding back to me. Matt rescuing me, Fay intervening, Tom getting kicked out by Rich. I feel my palms sweating and my breath quickening as we are shown to our table. I try to keep my eyes down, so nobody makes eye contact with me. But as I look around, I don't really recognise any of the staff and Matt will be in the kitchen (if he's even here – he has two chefs working for him now…so I've heard) so in theory I should be safe.

We are seated at a table to the left of the restaurant which makes me feel a little bit safer. Down the side, not in anyone's sightline. I take the menu off the waiter and hold it up in front of my face, virtually hiding behind it like an amateur spy in a comedy film. Chris's voice brings me out of my panic,

"You ok Kate? You seem a bit flustered." No shit. Oh this is rubbish, why did you have to choose here Chris?

"I'm fine" I lie, "just starving" I lie again, I'm not sure I'll be able to eat a thing! Chris orders a bottle of Sauvignon and I nod along with whatever he is saying but my brain is seriously elsewhere. I can see the kitchen door from where I am sitting and I can't help glancing over to see if there's any sign of Matt in there. Please let this be your night off Matt.

Right, get a grip of yourself Kate, Chris is going to get suspicious if you behave like a freak all night. I take a deep breath and try desperately to compose myself. Which works until I see the kitchen door swing open again, not Matt, just a waiter. Focus on Chris, Focus on Chris. I can do this.

"So, what do you think? It's had some great reviews recently. It's got a great atmosphere hasn't it?"

And it really has, Matt has made this place into something wonderful. I look round and see how busy it is, how happy the staff seem and how well the business appears to be doing. I feel proud of Matt. Is that weird?

"It's a lovely place Chris, really lovely." Focus on Chris. "How was your day anyway? I haven't even asked what with all my wittering on". I smile across at him, willing him to give me something else to concentrate on.

"It was a bit better. The witch seems to have calmed down. I can see her point on a few things not running smoothly enough but she has such a shitty way of saying it, putting people down all the time and making them feel useless. The other analysts are feeling it too though, so it's not just me." Chris is an analyst in an investment bank. I don't really get it and it's a very high-flying finance world which goes completely over my head, so we don't really talk about it much. More because he likes to leave work at work. Which is fair enough.

We order our mains, I decide not to have a starter, the sooner the meal is over, the better. If one course is the way to get us out of here, then so be it. I have the fettuccini. It is my favourite and it would seem odd not to have it now Chris has said that's why he's brought me here. I think I'm acting relatively normal whilst keeping half an eye on the kitchen door. Chris holds my hand across the table,

"It's so good to see you Kate, I've missed you this week." We normally see each other mid-week too but with all the evening events I'm now running and Chris having to work all hours as well, it's becoming more and more difficult to meet up.

Our meals arrive and Chris withdraws his hand from mine. I can't tell if I'm behaving normally but he seems relaxed so hopefully he hasn't noticed my angst. The food looks amazing. Of course. I think of Matt in my kitchen cooking me this for the first time.

"So," Matt frowned, "what do you think? Is it ok?" I jokingly screw my face up as if I'm going to spit it out but then laugh at the last second and tell him it's wonderful, which it totally is. "But what about the garlic, too much?" Bless him, he looks so nervous about my reaction.

"Matt, it's delicious." I declare and he seems to relax a bit. He smiles at me and I feel my cheeks heat up, I love how he looks at me, like I'm the most important thing in his life.

I snap out of my memory and remember I'm here with Chris. Here in Matt's restaurant with Chris. Could this be more awkward? The answer is obviously yes. I hear the man on the table next to us asking if he can speak to the chef. He would like to compliment him on his wonderful Beef Bourguignonne. The waiter nods and heads towards the kitchen. This can't be happening. This cannot happen. Just as I think my way out of this is to head to the toilet and hide there for a few minutes (as long as it takes this man to say his piece) Matt strolls out of the kitchen and if I move now, he will definitely see me. The only chance I have now is sitting completely still and hoping to god he does not look at our table. I keep my head turned away and try to carry on eating. Chris seems oblivious to what is happening behind him so I just keep schtum and eat, keeping my head low. Matt is right there, I can hear his voice, I glance up to catch a glimpse of him and he looks…well… he looks like my lovely, gorgeous Matt and my eyes are glued to him, I find myself unable to look away. Chris becomes aware of the chatter behind him and turns to see Matt. The movement makes Matt look towards our table, first at Chris and then at me. He does a sort of double-take, his eyes skim over me as he's smiling at the comments and compliments he is receiving but then they shoot straight back to me when he realises it's me. Our eyes lock and I can't turn away. My heart starts pounding and I simply don't know how to behave anymore. Matt focuses his attention back on the man who is praising him and says thank you. He makes a turn as if he's heading back to the kitchen and I feel relief come over me but then,

"Excuse me," it's Chris, he's calling Matt over, "Can I just say how wonderful your food is. Absolutely fantastic." Matt can't avoid it, he has to come over now to appear polite. Will he pretend he doesn't know me? I'm sweating, I don't know what to do. Matt's eyes are on me again and I feel my cheeks reddening as they always do when he looks at me in that way. He turns to Chris and says,

"Thank you, I'm glad you're enjoying your evening." Eyes back to me. "Wow, Kate, it's great to see you!" What the fuck are you doing Matt? Why didn't he just walk away?

"Oh my god, do you two know each other?" Chris

says excitedly. I still say nothing. Not sure where this is going now. "Kate, why didn't you say?"

"Kate did the relaunch on this place, she's part of the reason it's so successful." Matt is still staring at me. His beautiful eyes gazing at me like there's nobody else in the room. Get a grip Kate. Come on.

"Our company did the relaunch, it certainly wasn't all down to me. But, I'm pleased to see business is good for you." That's it, keep it professional. "We do so many of these things, sometimes I forget." Maybe a bit far-fetched with that one, Chris is now looking at Matt and then his eyes flick to me and then back to Matt. He frowns as if he's thinking. Shit is he working it out? He can see straight through me. There's an awkward silence as we all just stare, me at Matt then Chris, Matt at me constantly and Chris at me. They're both just staring at me. WTF? Take control Kate.

"Well, thanks again for a lovely meal." I sound final in the hope that he gets the message and leaves us alone. He blinks to break his stare and says,

"Enjoy the rest of your evening". I look back to Chris and he's frowning. He then watches Matt as he talks to a few other customers before making his way back to the kitchen. His eyes then return to mine.

"Oh my god, it's him isn't it?" he says in a tone I've never heard from Chris before, kind of sinister and threatening. "Chris, just…"

"Is he your ex?" slightly louder now, "Is he the man you were getting over when we got together?" I say nothing, "Kate?"

"Can we go please? I'd like to leave now." I have done nothing wrong so why do I feel so guilty. Everyone has exes who they occasionally bump into so what's the big deal? Well right now, I'd say the look on Chris's face is quite a big deal. He's fuming. He's really angry with me. Shit.

In the course of the next five minutes, Chris asks for the bill, pays the bill and we get up and we leave. He calls a cab and we sit in silence all the way back to my flat. For a second, I think he might just leave me here and go home but he pays the driver and follows me inside.

"Chris, I'm sorry, I should have told you" I try, "When I realised you were taking me there, it was too late to say anything and I could hardly tell you once we'd gone in. It would have been fine if you hadn't insisted on talking to him.." oops, was doing ok until that last slip up,

"Oh so it's my fucking fault that you've just seen your ex and totally made eyes at him across the table…"

"Made eyes at him, what the hell are you taking about?"

"You two, you couldn't keep your eyes off each other, he clearly still likes you and you seem pretty taken with him too. I mean what the fuck was that? You were there with me Kate." He seems hurt now. And if I'm honest, I can see why. It must have looked like that from where he was sitting but I was in shock at seeing Matt, I felt awkward.

"I'm sorry Chris, I know what it must have looked like but I didn't know what to do, I didn't know how to handle the situation, shit it was really awkward,"

"You're telling me, I felt like a gooseberry in my own relationship." His Scottish accent is getting thicker the angrier he gets. "You couldn't take your eyes off him Kate?" he slumps down in the chair, despair in his voice, he rests his head in his hands. I've hurt him and I feel terrible. This was the last thing I wanted.

I find myself kneeling in front of him. "Chris, he means nothing to me now. I acted like I did because it was awkward to see him. I'm with you now. I don't want to have anything to do with him so seeing him was unexpected but that is all." I find myself searching for words to try and make him feel better. "I'm angry that I've

215

seen him because it's kind of ruined what I was going to say to you tonight." He looks up and frowns,

"Why, what were you going to say?" What was I going to say? Ummmm...

"Well, I'm not sure it's right now, maybe it should wait for another time."

"Kate, please tell me?" Oh shit...

"Well, I just thought we should talk about things a bit, talk about where we're at with our relationship." What am I doing? "We hardly see each other in the week now because of our jobs and I miss you. So, I was thinking...what if we...live together?" What am I doing?

"Really? Is that what you want? How would it work?" He's smiling now, god I love those dimples,

"Well I was thinking, maybe, you could move in here?" He raises his eyebrows, (I have literally never thought this!)

"Really, you sure?" No, I'm not, so why are these words still coming out of my mouth.

"Well, it makes sense doesn't it. My flat is slightly bigger than yours, and still easy to get to both of our jobs, so why not?" He looks round the flat as if taking it all in and considering the offer, he beams down at me,

"Do you think you can put up with me?"

"Do you think you can with me?" and he says,

"Hell yes" and kisses me, passionate and powerful. He pulls me up on to his lap and continues kissing me. I rise up on to my knees and put one leg each side of his so I'm straddling him. I can feel how hard he is underneath me and it turns me on. All other thoughts of the evening have evaporated and right now all I want is him. He is the right one for me, not Matt, Chris. I climb off him take his hand and lead him to the bedroom. The sex is amazing, we've never really argued before so it's hot and heavy and I can feel the tension in him but it just turns me on more. When it's all over, and we're lying side by side, he says,

"Wow, Kate, I guess this is my bedroom now too" I smile and smirk and think 'what the hell have I done now!'

CHAPTER THIRTY-EIGHT

Sunday

I go for my run early the next morning and leave Chris asleep in bed. I didn't sleep much. So confused by what I still felt for Matt when I saw him and the fact that I've asked Chris to move in with me. What a night! I decide to run it off.

I get halfway round the park and take a seat on a bench. I take my phone out, open a new text and put Matt's name in. Never did get round to deleting his number. I feel like I owe him an explanation for last night, at least I think that's what I feel.

Matt, I'm sorry about last night, I had no idea that's where Chris was taking me until it was too late. I don't know what I'm expecting, probably nothing would be best, shouldn't really be opening up these channels again but what my head is saying and what my heart is thinking are two very different things. The reply is quick,

It's fine, we were bound to bump into one another sooner or later. How've you been? oh dear, he's asked a question, that means I should reply, so I do,

Really good. You?

I'm ok, throwing myself into work. You looked beautiful last night. He's obviously good for you. that sounds like a weird searching statement,

He is good for me

So pleased you're happy. Not sure how to respond to that so I leave it there, probably enough said. No need to open any more old wounds. I continue my run and when I get back Chris is up making breakfast for us. I wrap my arms around him and kiss him,

"Oh you're all sweaty" he murmurs,

"I know, sorry, better get in the shower" I turn to go

but stop at the kitchen door, "joining me?" he smiles, turns the frying pan off and follows me to the bathroom.

CHAPTER THIRTY-NINE

"You've done what?" Rach shrieks down the phone when I tell her I've asked Chris to move in with me. And when I tell her it was a panic reaction because of seeing Matt she says, "oh shit Kate, that's crazy!" I'm looking for answers from her really. Either to tell me how to get out of the situation I'm in with Chris, maybe give me a brilliant reason why it's not a good idea for Chris to move in with me, one I can share with Chris that he will totally understand…or…she needs to tell me that Chris moving in with me is the best idea I've ever had and this is exactly what she was expecting (even if I wasn't!)

Instead, she says, "How did you feel when you saw Matt?" that is not something I should be thinking about so why has she gone there? I consider how I felt, lost but excited to see him. It's true, I got all the old feelings, I felt pleased and frightened to see him. But not frightened because I was with my new boyfriend and I didn't want Chris to get hurt (that is obviously a part of it though, isn't it?) but because I knew how I'd feel, I knew that as soon as I saw Matt I would want him again, need him again, love him again, but then that has never stopped.

"Oh Rach," I mutter into the phone, "you shouldn't ask me that." There is silence at the other end for a few seconds before she says,

"Are you still in love with Matt, Kate?" She sounds surprised and I don't know why. Maybe I've sold my feelings to her so well that she truly believed I was over him. I know in everything that I told her I was trying to convince myself of that, must have convinced her too. I'm surprised she's even asked the question because somehow, her asking that, has given me some sort of false hope with Matt. It's almost like if Rach thinks there is love still involved then maybe it could still work with Matt.

I snap myself straight out of my thoughts, I'm falling into a pit of Matt despair. Do not go there Kate, too many times you have let those feelings lead you down the wrong path – this is what Rach should be saying to me right now. But she isn't. Why? Her voice focuses my thoughts,

"What about Chris?" yes what about Chris? Lovely, gorgeous, caring Chris. "Are you in love with Chris?" These questions are driving me a bit crazy, I don't know how to answer them. I feel if I answer them out loud, even if it's only Rach listening, then that sort of seals my fate in some way. That, if I say 'yes I'm in love with Matt', I will instantly lose Chris and that's not what I want but if I say 'yes I'm in love with Chris' then it's definitely over with Matt and what if that's not what I want either. Shit!

"I don't know Rach, I'm so confused." I whimper.

"Kate, do you want Chris to move in with you?" Do I want Chris to move in with me?

"Well, it's not exactly what I envisaged so early on in our relationship but if we're going to keep moving forward and getting more serious then I guess it makes sense."

"Kate this isn't a business deal, it's bloody serious when two people live together, you have to really want it to happen, especially as he's going to be moving into your place. Your flat is going to become a 'couple' place, no longer yours and yours alone. Do you realise what that can do to a relationship?" I now think she may be talking more about herself and her moving-in issues with Rich. Rich has suggested several times they live together but she always comes up with a good reason (excuse) why they shouldn't and Rich buys it. I'm not even sure they'll live together when they're married if Rach can't get her head round space sharing.

I look round my flat and imagine Chris living here

with me. I do quite like the idea of him being about all the time, knowing when I finish work at night, I'll be coming home to him, to cook for him or to have him cook for me and then cuddling up on the sofa together. We could still have date nights but now we just get ready together, he would probably still want to surprise me (although he might have gone off that idea after last night's surprise was on him!)

I feel good about the thought of him being here with me. I do love him, I am falling in love with him. That's a funny thing to say when you think about it. Falling in love. It's almost as if you're not quite there yet, not quite 'in love' and something he does could change that at any moment but play your cards right and before long, I won't just be falling, I'll have fallen. So maybe if you think you're falling then actually, you have already fallen, oh it's complicated this love crap. Maybe if you're with the right person, you never stop falling.

As I say goodbye to Rach, a text comes through, it's Chris,

Hey beautiful, are you absolutely sure about me moving in? I can give notice on my place and slowly start moving things across if it's definitely what you want xx

I find his tone really sweet; he's always checking I'm happy with things, always making sure I'm ok. That's love I think, caring so much about someone else that you put their feelings before your own. I know Chris really wants to move in, I could tell by the look on his face when I suggested it and now he's being considerate and making sure I'm happy… decision made, I have to give this a chance, a proper chance.

Yes more than sure. Let's do this xx

And so, we do.

CHAPTER FORTY

Chris pretty much moves in with me over the next two weeks, slowly moving stuff across from his place which was a furnished rental so he doesn't have any big furniture to bring across, just clothes, shoes (so many shoes!) kitchen stuff, a few house plants and some sort of games console (did not see that one coming!) a record player, (very retro) and a couple of boxes of LPs. It's amazing what you don't know about a person until the day they move into your space!

It's all good though. We actually have fun deciding how we're going to fit his stuff into the wardrobe as it's already full of my stuff but he's fine with it all. Makes me realise it's time for a clear out. In the meantime, some of his stuff will just have to live in a suitcase.

There's no real 'moving in' day. It's more of a gradual thing so when we finally sit down together and he realises there's nothing left at his place, it feels really good. It feels like we're committed and solid. We cuddle up on the sofa and watch some telly. My eyes fall to the Xbox that is now looming ominously under the tv. I'm not sure I really like the idea of losing my telly time to gaming, never been my thing, but maybe he doesn't use it that often. Although, he was pretty insistent on having it in the lounge on a permanent basis. When I suggested he just gets it out when he wants to use it, he looked at me like I was stupid, so it's under the telly. Might be harder than I thought to surrender my space. We'll see.

CHAPTER FORTY-ONE

Tuesday

"How's it going with you and Chris living together Kate?" Rich asks as we're sat having a coffee at work. He seems genuinely interested and maybe a little envious.

"It's great so far." I say, ever optimistic with the 'so far'. "It's really nice to see him every day and lovely to go home to someone rather than an empty flat"

"Do I sense a 'but'?" Rich is very intuitive or I'm really obvious,

"Well, not so much a 'but'…but you never really know someone until you spend all moments of life with them do you? You know like toilet habits, cooking, tidying… all that stuff doesn't come into it when you live away from your partner, but when you suddenly have to share all that and sort of be responsible for one another in some way, well, it sort of changes things."

"I would imagine it does" Rich looks pensive, as if he's imagining all this with Rach, longing for that shared responsibility perhaps.

"Don't get me wrong Rich, the good stuff outweighs those bits. Although, then there's the gaming!"

"Yeah Rach said you didn't really like that idea. But it's just a hobby, like fishing or playing football."

"I guess," I ponder, "but he's like a child when he's playing games, he sits there killing zombies and fighting aliens, it's like I'm watching a different person…maybe it's the age thing!" I mutter the last bit under my breath. "Have you and Rach moved any further forward with the wedding plans?"

"Sort of, we've decided we would like the ceremony and the reception all in one place, no churches or anything like that. So, I think we're finally getting there." He smiles as he says this, even their disagreements seem to draw them closer together.

"Are you still ok for Saturday?" I ask knowing they will be, once Rach commits herself to something, she sticks to it.

"Yes of course, looking forward to it." Rach and Rich are coming to my, I mean 'our' flat for a meal. It's the first bit of hosting we've done in the flat as a couple and I'm quite excited about it. In fact, I'm going all out on the cooking. Even going to the market to get fresh veg on Saturday morning.

The phone on my desk rings so Rich and I get back to work. The phone call is a potential client. Quite an exciting one. It's an enquiry for a themed gala night for a charity called ALL (Altogether Learning for Life). Charity events always get celebrities and socialites in attendance so potentially, if we get it, it could open up some more doors for us. I arrange to meet Hannah Scott, the Creative Director for the Charity on Thursday. She's keen to get going straight away so wants to meet this week. When I get off the phone, I tell Rich all about it and see the pound signs flash up in his eyes. I do some research on the Charity straight away so I've got some good knowledge to go into the meeting with. They're a global charity who work in several different countries putting money into education. Their testimonies speak for themselves. They have built schools and learning centres in eight different third world countries in the last five years. Their latest project is a focus on educating youngsters in the more deprived areas of London. That's what the gala night is for. This could be the biggest thing we've done yet and I feel nervous and excited all at the same time. Rich is already planning the meeting. And we both work on it for the rest of the day.

CHAPTER FORTY-TWO

Saturday

I start cooking about 3pm. It's probably a little early but I'm really excited. This is the first time I've done anything like this. I mean obviously I've cooked for friends before but not like this, me and my boyfriend inviting another couple round for a meal. Very grown up and it's only taken me until I'm in my thirties to experience it! Chris is working but will be back by 5pm so plenty of time to get showered, make himself look presentable and help me with laying the table and sorting the drinks out. I want to impress him as well as Rich and Rach. This is a new experience for us and I'm determined to make it a good one. Might even make it a regular thing if it goes well.

I put some music on to get me in the cooking and socialising mood. Matt always used to say that listening to the right music when cooking a meal can make the meal a success. He reckoned if you're happy while you're cooking then that will come through in the food.

I walk into the kitchen and the opening riff of Mr Brightside by The Killers is streaming into the room. Matt is standing at the hob with his back to me and is starting to nod his head along to the song and wiggle his bum a bit. He turns to see me standing in the doorway checking him out. I smile at him and raise my eyebrows as if to say 'nice moves' and he takes the encouragement. He grabs a wooden spoon from the utensils pot, holds it like a microphone and starts singing to me. He's right in front of me, dancing like a mad man, smiling and laughing and I can't help but join in. He chucks me a spatula and I sing the chorus with him, we're in each other's faces and I realise how much I love him and I love how much fun we have together. I don't think I'll ever feel so relaxed and free with anyone else. We end up laughing so much that Matt nearly burns the sauce but it's totally worth it. He pulls me into his arms and kisses me before saving the meal. I love these stolen moments we have together. I love him.

Rich and Rach arrive bang on 7pm. Chris has only been back an hour, he had to work later than he thought so only really had time to jump in the shower and get changed before they arrived. Which means, all of tonight's delights are completely down to me! I hope they're delights, I neglected a crucial part of 'chefing' – to taste as you cook! Oops. Might taste like shit, too late to worry now!

Chris plays the host, taking their coats and offering them a drink.

"Kate's in the kitchen, still working on her masterpiece," he says. I hear Rach's voice getting louder as she makes her way to me,

"Wow Kate, smells amazing." We hug and I indicate the bottle of wine on the side,

"There's an empty glass there, help yourself and top me up." Rich is close behind and kisses my cheek.

"Hey Kate, this looks great, I hope you haven't gone to too much trouble" well if you call getting up at 6am to go to the market just so that I get the best veg, agonising over which aubergine looks the best while I'm contemplating whether to make a chocolate fondue or a cheesecake neither of which I have ingredients for which means another stop on the way home then yes I guess you could say I've been to a lot of trouble but instead I say,

"No, don't be silly, no trouble". Rach smirks at me as she knows exactly what I'm like and has probably already realised the 'trouble' I've gone to based on my rosy cheeks, the mess in the kitchen and the amount of wine that is already missing from the bottle.

"Is there anything I can do to help?" she says as she gulps her drink and pours Rich one. I shake my head and reply,

"Nope, it's just about ready so just take a seat at the table and relax." We've moved the kitchen table into the lounge tonight, there is space for it in there and I have considered getting another table to go there for while so thought we'd try this out as an experiment to see if it'd be worth it. I watch them all go back through, take a gulp of my wine and start plating up (plating up, lol, I think I'm on masterchef).

My garlic and cheese stuffed mushrooms seem to be going down really well. They're more of an amuse-bouche than a starter, something to get their taste buds tingling for the main event. The conversation is good too. Chris starts by asking Rich and Rach what they've been up to and a whole conversation about wedding venues opens up as they have viewed three different places today.

"And did you agree on any of them?" I pipe up half laughing as I know how many things they haven't agreed on yet. "Well Rach likes the more modern venue," he looks at her and smiles, "which is fair enough, but we viewed this gorgeous old country manor out in Kent and I really like it."

"And Rach, did you like it?" I enquire, not sure they've properly discussed this yet judging by the looks going back and forth so I try to retract, "sorry, I'm prying, don't answer if you don't want to".

"Actually Kate, you might be surprised to learn, that I loved it." Rich smiles and takes her hand. She continues, "We're going to talk to them next week and start discussing dates!"

"Oh my god!" I exasperate, "this is huge! A venue

and a possible date next week, I might have to start getting a little bit excited now."

"Well that's worth a toast," Chris says, "to Rich and Rach and the perfect wedding venue" we all raise our glasses and clink.

"Thanks guys," Rach says shyly, "It is pretty exciting now we've seen the place we want." She smiles at Rich and he leans in for a kiss.

"Alright, you two, save it until after the main course." I get up and clear the table of the starter plates. Chris helps and we make our way into the kitchen. He puts the plates down and pulls me towards him,

"Come here," he kisses me and holds me tight, I can hardly breath,

"Wow, what was that for?" I smile back at him,

"Just because," he says and kisses me again. Think we all might be hitting the wine a bit much but we're having fun, and I love that Rich and Rach's love for each other is maybe rubbing off on Chris a bit.

Ten minutes later, we're all tucking into my main course. I just eat, slowly and patiently, I have literally sweated over this and would really like just a little compliment. I keep my head bowed over my plate but my eyes are raised and watching for reactions as they all dig in,

"Wow," it's Rich, "this is amazing Kate, "who the hell taught you to cook like this? It's like proper restaurant food!" and then the awkward silence as Rich realises what he's just said, Rach kicks him under the table, (really obviously, even if it wasn't intended that way) and Chris looks at me and I watch those dimples disappear. I'm trying to think of something to say when Rach saves me,

"Nobody taught her, Kate has always been a brilliant cook, for as long as I've known her." Thanks Rach, not true but hopefully it's calmed the waters. Blimey, Kate, be careful what you wish for when it comes to praise.

Chris seems to relax a bit but he's never quite got past the fact that he knows who my ex is. It's like he feels threatened. The meal goes well and the conversation gets back on track. We talk about work a bit, Chris tells us a little about his job but mostly about the witch he is working for now and Rich talks about our new charity event which we confirmed on Thursday following the meeting with the CEO of the charity. It's a massive event for us, could really put us on the map.

I serve the pudding and hope that my chocolate fondues are the right consistency in the middle, they should be gooey and silky. I make my apologies before anyone has even cut into them but as it turns out, they too are pretty successful, (another training session I had with Matt). God he's everywhere, I didn't realise how much of an influence he'd had on me, (who am I kidding, of course I did!)

Nobody makes any comments this time, just a few 'this is tasty noises' from around the table and that will be just fine for me this time.

Chris opens another bottle of wine (we're on our fourth now) and fills everyone's glass up. The talk moves towards what we like doing in our spare time and Chris starts to talk about a new game he's just started playing. I flinch a bit and see Rich glance at me (probably remembering the conversation we had at work this week about my hate for all things gaming!) But Rich seems genuinely interested. I can't tell if he's being polite until Chris suggests they have a go right now and Rich is totally up for it. Great, another evening where Chris is killing zombies.

They make their way over to the tv (games room) and Rach moves seats so that she and I are now next to one another. I suppose the boys heading off does give us a chance for a chat.

"Do you really like this venue then?" I ask excitedly.

"Oh my god, Kate, it's so beautiful. I honestly hadn't imagined my wedding in a place like that but as soon as I saw it, I knew it was perfect. Will you come and see it with me?" I've never seen her so animated, she really does love it.

"Of course, I'd love to."

"Cos obviously, I need my maid of honour to ok the place?" she says a little cheekily and as a question. She hasn't officially asked me yet and though we've always said we would be one another's bridesmaids, I didn't want to assume anything too soon.

"Ahhh Rach, Yes, I'd love to see it and I'd love to be your maid of honour." I hug her and squeal. The boys look across at us but they're clearly not bothered enough to ask what's just happened, too absorbed in the game. "So when shall we go…" just as I start to speak, my phone, which is on the table in front of us, pings and we both look at it together, we both see Matt's name appear on the screen and we both turn to look at each other, mouths open. I grab my phone, trying to pretend she didn't see who the text is from but her face says it all. Her head stays facing me but her eyes flicker towards Chris. She raises her eyebrows and lowers her voice,

"Kate, what the…"

"Don't Rach, I have no idea. I haven't heard from him for ages. That's a complete shock to me as well as you." She looks at me in disbelief. "Honestly, you read it then, you'll see it's nothing that I was expecting." It can't be, I haven't heard from or text Matt since before Chris moved in two months ago. I don't expect her to actually read it but she says,

"Ok then and takes my phone off me" She knows my passcode and types it in, I have nothing to hide from Rach (at least I don't think I do!)

I watch her read it and try to gauge her reaction. She shakes her head and hands me the phone.

Just wanted to let you know, I gave Rich Events' number to a friend who works for the charity ALL. Think they're going to contact you, hope that's ok.

Of course, they already have, about five days ago so why leave it until now to tell me? Why did he feel the need to tell me at all?

"Why is he telling you that?" Rach asks as if reading my mind.

"I've no idea," and I am a little confused by it and maybe a little bit pissed off. Why did our biggest client yet have to come from Matt. Rach can see my anger.

"You annoyed?" she asks.

"Kind of," I reply, "it pisses me off that *he's* given the client our name…but I guess that's how business works, one client word-of-mouths to another. Just be less annoying if it wasn't from the man I'm desperately trying to forget." I feel Rach's eyes boring into me, "What?" Her eyes flick across to Chris again before she says,

"You are still in love with Matt, aren't you?" I stand up quickly, too quickly as I make a glass fall over on the table and catch it before it smashes. We both glance over to the boys but they're oblivious. I gather the plates and carry them into the kitchen, Rach follows.

"Kate, what are you doing?"

"I'm clearing up, what does it look like?" but I'm not going to get away with that. I dump the pile of plates in the sink, turn around and lean against it. Rach is still looking at me. "I'm not doing anything. Yes, I still care about Matt, I can't help it, I loved him Rach, it's hard to forget that or pretend it never happened. But, I'm with Chris now and I'm happy. That's all that matters to me now."

"But you still have feelings for him Kate, I didn't realise how deeply you still felt."

"I don't Rach, it's just getting that text, it's a reminder of old feelings and maybe I get a bit nostalgic. But that's all." She doesn't look convinced but she doesn't look angry either, which is what I thought she would be. She hated what Matt did to me. She always had to pick up the pieces.

"Just tell me one thing Kate, when he came here that night, he was single and you and Chris weren't serious at that point so, if you still loved him, why did you tell him it was over?" It's a question that goes round my head a lot, whether I made a mistake that night. Chris had swept me off my feet and Matt was still just turning up whenever it suited him. Maybe I acted on the wrong emotions, anger rather than love.

"It was the right decision, Matt and I would never have worked, too much had happened between us for it to be ok"

"Or too much had happened between you for it to end!" She shocks me with this. It's like she thinks I shouldn't have ended it with Matt.

"Shit Rach, stop it, you're making me have doubts about everything and I can't do that now. I'm with Chris, we live together for fuck's sake,"

"But do you love Chris?" I hesitate in answer to this and she sees it but,

"I do love him, yes,"

"Really?"

"Rach can we just leave it?" I plead. "I love Chris, I'm with Chris. That's what matters now." She looks at me and nods slowly,

"Ok, I'm sorry, I just want you to be happy Kate, that's all."

"I am."

She smiles but still doesn't look convinced. She hugs me and then pours us both another glass of wine. I glance through to the lounge. Rich and Chris are still playing games. They yell and high five each other. It's like they've regressed to teenagers. Rach and I look at each other and drink our wine.

They leave about 11.30pm. Rach and I chatted about wedding plans for the rest of the evening and Chris and Rich continued to kill zombies. (I really don't get it!) As soon as they've gone, Chris says,

"Do you mind if I carry on for ten minutes, I've just got to a really good bit!" he's like a little kid.

"Really?" I sound like his bloody mother! He does the cute dimple smile, "OK, I was going to get the washing-up done anyway." Better to do it tonight than face it in the morning. Chris is straight back into his game and I make my way to the kitchen. There's something not right about it all.

Chris is still playing forty minutes later when I come back into the lounge. I sit next to him on the sofa and watch the game for a bit. Maybe if I watch I will see the fascination. Mmmmm. I have another glass of wine and start to fall asleep. I jolt awake and Chris turns to me. He pauses the game.

"Hey sleepy," he puts his hand against my cheek and I feel comforted, "Why don't you go to bed, I won't be long." I'm so tired so I nod, kiss him, and make my way to the bedroom. I look at the clock as I climb into bed a few minutes later, it says 0.23. At least I made it to midnight, makes a change.

I wake suddenly at 2.02am. I feel for Chris next to me but then hear the death rays from the lounge. Bloody hell, he's still playing? I'm awake now and want him here with me. I lie still for a couple of minutes and then go into the lounge. I plonk myself with a thud next to him on the sofa so that he can't possibly miss me.

"Hey babe, thought you were asleep" wow so he thinks this is fine. Interesting.

"I thought you were coming to bed" is my retort.

"I was but then I got on to this level and if I could just

kill this one," he's still playing as he's talking to me, emphasising the words as he pushes buttons (not just on the controller!)

"I thought we might, you know, have some fun," I use my best sultry tones on. Clearly not that seductive though as he says,

"Oh babe, don't nag me, I'll be there in a bit" Wow, that's… that's…really pissed me off! He's not coming to bed any time soon and I don't actually want to do anything with him now so I stomp back to bed.

I think about texting Rach to tell her what's just happened, I'm in disbelief! Don't 'nag' him? Don't fucking 'nag' him? I have a little silent scream to myself, is it so wrong of me to want my boyfriend to come to bed with me? I pick up my phone to text Rach. I don't care if it's late, I'm fuming and need to share.

As I open my texts, I see Matt's name again at the top. I open it and read it again.

Just wanted to let you know, I gave Rich Events' number to a friend who works for ALL Charity. Think they're going to contact you, hope that's ok. I hover over the reply box and then think, 'I might as well, he'll be asleep now anyway so won't reply'.

They called us this week, it was good of you, thank you. How are you? Send. The reply comes through in seconds.

I'm ok. And, you're welcome that's it, then,

p.s. you're up late! I consider telling him the truth, that my boyfriend is more interested in zombies than me but I decide that could open a can of worms so instead,

We've had friends round, they've just left bit of poetic licence on timing.

Wow, a social life, I've forgotten what that's like! Only people I see at the moment are my staff and my mother

Is he trying to tell me that he's not seeing anyone?

Don't read into it Kate. I reply again,

Oh dear, sounds like a sad existence :-) I add the smiling emoji at the end so he knows I'm joking.

It really is. Just me, sitting in my lonely flat, no one to talk to... I'm sensing the humour but maybe there's a flirtation too?

You never were very good in your own company maybe I should be less familiar,

No, I was always much better in yours Shit. What's he doing? What am I doing? I'm shaking a bit and it's for the wrong reasons, for those feelings that I shouldn't be having. But I'm smiling. And remembering. Again. Get a grip Kate, change the subject (or just don't reply?)

You never said why you're up so late?

Just working on some new menus. It's good to hear from you Kate. I can't help myself so I say,

You too Matt and his reply,

Kate, I still miss you The bedroom door opens and Chris comes in.

"You still awake." He almost sounds pissed off.

"Just playing candy crush" I lie.

"Ah see, we're all gamers really." We are Chris, just not sure what game I'm playing right now. Feeling a bit disappointed in myself as he cuddles up to me.

"I'm knackered babe, all this socialising has worn me out." He kisses my cheek, says goodnight and rolls over, away from me. How quickly things change! Last week we were ripping each other's clothes off and now we're like an old married couple – kiss on cheek and sleep. I light up my phone again and look back to Matt's last message. 'I miss you too Matt' I think to myself but I don't reply. There are already worms everywhere.

CHAPTER FORTY-THREE

Sunday Morning

I wake up to the smell of bacon wafting in from the kitchen. Chris is already up. I feel a bit woozy as I sit up and swing my legs round to find the floor but more because of a lack of sleep than too much alcohol. I get my running kit on straight away, if I don't go now, I won't go at all.

Chris is in the kitchen, frying bacon and singing along to Marvin Gaye's 'I Heard it Through the Grapevine', the lyrics seem apt after I text Matt last night.

"Morning baby, you want a coffee?" he sings at me,

"No, going straight out for a run." I still feel a bit angry with him for the way he behaved last night.

"Kate, before you go…look, I'm sorry I got so obsessed with that bloody game last night, it just hooks me and before I know it, it's 2 o'clock in the bloody morning. I'm so sorry. I could have been with you…" he moves closer to me and pushes a loose bit of hair behind my ear, "making love to my beautiful, incredible girlfriend and instead I'm killing stupid zombies." I'm kind of glad he has realised all of this… "I can be such an idiot sometimes" he puts his arms round my waist and gives me that cheeky, gorgeous, dimpled smile, "Forgive me?" I put my arms round his neck,

"You were a bit of an idiot" he looks really sorry and a bit worried, "but I forgive you." He leans down and kisses me, a warm melting kiss and my anger goes away. Still holding me, he says,

"Kate, why didn't you say something, tell me I was being a dick?"

"That would have gone down well, and anyway, I'm not going to 'nag' you to come to bed if you find something to do that's more of a priority than me…" I emphasise the word 'nag' to remind him of what he said to me last night. He looks slightly ashamed.

"Nothing is more of a priority than you, Kate." I smile and giggle a bit and try to turn my comment into a joke. But I know, in my heart, I mean it. I've come second to someone's wife and business before, I won't come second to a bloody zombie game. I think I made my point?

"Right, I'm off for my run." Need some time.

"Ok babe, have fun."

And I go – half in love with him for realising that last night wasn't ok and half…?...well, half not in love with him for not realising at the time. Living together is actually a lot harder than I thought.

CHAPTER FORTY-FOUR

The next few weeks pass with relative calm for once. Chris is more attentive than ever following zombie-gate and I have reassessed how angry I felt with him. I was perhaps a little selfish in expecting him to devote every second of the evening to me but he should have been a little more aware at the very least.

Last night we had a surprise date night (first one since the Matt incident) and it was just perfect. He even went out of the flat and knocked on the door to pick me up like it used to be. He can be so thoughtful at times.

"Chris, can you get that?" no answer, "Chris, I'm halfway through getting my make-up on, please can you see who is at the door," the doorbell keeps ringing so I go myself, "Alright, I'm coming…" and I answer the door to find him standing there, with that gorgeous, dimpled smile on his face. I laugh and smile at him,

"Hey beautiful, sorry I'm a bit early," he kisses me and pushes me back through the door.

"That's ok" I say and pull his face to mine once more. I miss the mystery that we had in our relationship, but this brings it back so he must feel the same. The kiss continues and I can feel how turned on Chris is as he pushes himself up against me. I don't really want to stop but if this is going to be a real 'surprise date night' we'd better try to maintain the magic a while longer. "Come on," I whisper, "let's at least try to get to the restaurant before we start ripping each other's clothes off." He grins and waits on the sofa while I finish getting ready.

The restaurant is lovely, Chris has chosen well. It's in a little side street, well-hidden but clearly very popular as Chris explains how he had to twist a few arms to get a booking at short notice. I wonder what he means, not sure who he knows that could have helped him to secure this booking, but I don't ask.

Everything about the evening is perfect from the food to the company. It makes me feel content again, like we're back on track after our little wobble and I feel, well yes, I feel completely in love with him. I'm smiling at him across the table,

"What? Why are you looking so pleased with yourself?" he asks as he tucks into his gourmet burger.

"Nothing," I say, attempting my seductive look, "just like what I see in front of me." He flashes his beautiful smile at me and I'm taken back to Spain and the fun we had out there. It's a shame it can't always be like that…like this. I'm only now starting to realise how much you have to work at a relationship for it to last. But that's ok, there's fun to be had in the making up.

When we're on our way back to the flat, we maintain the mystery and romance.

"Hey Chris," I say, as the cab pulls up outside, "would you like to come in for a bit" I catch the cab driver's eyes in the mirror, he raises his eyebrows as if to say, 'go on mate, I think you're in there'.

"I'd love to" Chris swoons and kisses me again. It's a perfect evening and life continues with this feel afterwards. We're both still working hard but the evenings together are really special. Even when we're just cuddling up on the sofa, it's almost like we've started again or maybe come to an understanding about how to live together. He still plays his zombie games but usually when I'm in the bath or cooking tea or when I go out for a drink with Rach, so it works for us. It feels right at last.

CHAPTER FORTY-FIVE

Thursday

It's been a mad few weeks at work. We're busier than ever and Rich is thinking of employing someone else. 'Thinking' at the moment as we have a great dynamic and we're both a bit worried about how another person could change that. He keeps considering it but I think there will come a time when he has no choice if work continues like this.

"Do you think male or female?" he pipes up randomly.

"What?" I question,

"Well, if we were to hire someone else to work here, do you think we'd work better with a man or a woman?" Controversial!

"Careful Rich, surely it's the quality of the person we'd be looking at and the experience and expertise that they could offer rather than what sex they are." I say this slightly tongue in cheek and make sure he sees I'm smiling.

"God, you're right, that sounded a bit sexist didn't it? Can't be seen to be like that these days. Especially if we decided to hire a man because he's a man! Can you imagine the feminist uproar?"

"We are allowed to hire men Rich, just for the right reasons though. If a man fits the dynamic then there's nothing wrong with that." He looks a bit nervous and unsure now,

"Yeah, you're right, sorry just being stupid"

"You ok Rich? You seem a bit distracted today." He does seem miles away again. And I know he can't be planning another proposal but I'm pretty sure it's something to do with Rach. "Rich, what's happened? You know you can trust me? I'm not going to blab to Rach just because she's my friend." He shakes his head a little and shrugs his shoulders, then takes a deep breath and says,

"I'm just confused Kate. One minute Rach is really keen for us to live together before we get married and then she's totally against the idea. I want to live with her more than anything, I mean I want to be with her, look after her, look after each other and we can only really do that if we're living together, otherwise it always seems like we're not quite complete, like we're still living separate lives, or at least a part of our lives is separate. I just don't get why she can't properly commit to it. She says she wants to marry me and yet, she has doubts about living with me, I mean, how is that going to work?" I really feel for him, I understand why Rach is so hesitant and I'm not sure if she has told him everything.

"Have you asked her about it? Does she ever give you a reason or explanation?" I try to sound searching rather than knowing.

"I've asked why but she won't tell me much. Is there something behind it? Is there a reason she's like this?" Oh shit. Difficult. I've asked him to open up to me and now I feel like I can't actually tell him anything.

"Rich, just ask her again, it's not really my place to say anything but I will say there is a reason, and it's not you, so you shouldn't be worried about that. She loves you more than anything."

"What's happened that's so bad, Kate?" I look down and he knows he shouldn't ask anymore. I feel like I've already said too much. "Sorry Kate."

"Don't be daft Rich, it's fine. I asked you, remember. She loves you more than anything and this will all be fine, she probably just needs to adjust to the idea. You'll be living together before you know it and then probably wondering why the hell you wanted to!" I try to sound like I'm joking but my tone doesn't convince Rich.

"It's not that bad with you and Chris is it?"

"What do you mean 'that' bad? Do you think it's bad?" I wonder whether he and Rach have discussed it. I'm sure they must have had something to say about it after they came round.

"No not bad, but you seemed a bit pissed off with him when we came over. Is it just the gaming?" I snort a bit at this comment and picture that evening again, Rich was just as much into 'the gaming' as Chris was. "It was good fun that game" he murmurs, reading my expression accurately.

"I think we're ok now. We seem to have come to a middle ground. He knows I'll never be into that stuff and I know he really likes it so we just have to work round it. But, if I'm really honest, living with a partner is nothing like I imagined it to be. You always think about the romantic side, the support, the fun…but the reality is dirty washing, hairs in the bath and unreciprocated hobbies!" Rich looks a bit taken aback. "In fact, he's going away on a lad's weekend tomorrow and I'm really looking forward to having the flat to myself. How bad is that?" I giggle.

"I hadn't thought of it like that, might remind myself of that next time I beg Rach to move in with me!" We laugh and he jokes, "shit she'll probably want to now and I'll be like, 'do you know what, maybe we should wait'" more laughter. Rich checks his watch, "Shit!"

"What?" I gasp as he stands up and grabs his coat,

"I've got that meeting in 20 minutes. Was gonna get the tube but it'll have to be a cab now, bloody hell!" He makes his way towards the door just as someone opens it. I look away but then hear a familiar voice.

"Hi Rich," I look up and watch Rich shake his hand and then turn to me with an 'oh fuck' look.

"I'm just heading out, did you want me or…Kate?"

"I'm here to see Kate." I'm watching this as if it's not happening. Why is he here? What is he playing at? Rich looks at me again as if to say sorry, I know he's got to go to his meeting but he can see the panic on my face.

"See you later Kate, shouldn't be too long." I think he added that last bit as a sort of warning.

I stand up. Rich closes the door behind him and mouths 'sorry' at me through the glass. I shake my head to reassure him it's ok (is it though?). I take a step closer and look at Matt, his strong arms, his beautiful brown eyes, that face…and all those feelings, that I've locked away, come flooding back like a tsunami drowning me and my stupid naïve heart.

"Hi Kate."

"Matt." I try to sound business like and calm but inside I'm quivering.

"I'm sorry to just turn up like this but I needed to see you." (what?) "That is, I need to ask you something, make sure you're ok with something before I agree to it and upset you. I don't want to upset you." What the hell is he going on about? I can't speak.

"Kate? Are you ok?" I take a breath and try to speak but I just open my mouth and close it again. Why the hell are you here Matt? What is this? I don't want to see you. Are things I really want to say but nothing comes out of my mouth.

"Look Kate, I'll get to the point," (oh god, my heart is racing, is he going to tell me that he's met someone else and is getting married again? Is he going to tell me that he wants us to plan the wedding, because I don't think I can handle that. I don't want to know he's fallen in love with someone else, when he should be loving me!)

"Kate, Hannah has asked me if I'd be interested in doing the catering for the fundraiser. She knows nothing about us and what happened," (us – me and Matt) "but I didn't want to say yes until I'd run it past you. It could mean us spending some time together and I wasn't sure how that would sit with you." I'm still just staring at him.

He's wearing a blue shirt with a casual blazer and jeans. I can see his chest going up and down as he breathes deeply and I want to touch him and hold him. He looks nervous. I wonder what he'd do if I just put my arms around him. It's weird when you split up with someone, they sort of belong to you when you're together, you can touch them whenever you like and then you split and you almost have to pretend that none of that ever happened. Back in the room Kate, get a grip. So, he's not getting married, I feel relieved all of a sudden and I feel my shoulders drop. But I still can't speak. He'll be starting to think I've become mute if I don't say something soon. Now Kate, anytime you like…

"Um, I…" GET A GRIP. Rage takes over, "Did you really have to come all the way over here to ask me that? Couldn't you have just called or something?"

"Ouch!" he says. Good. "I could have just called but I wanted to ask you face to face so you could make a decision without being polite and I think I've got my answer."

"No you haven't! Do you really think I'd say 'no' Matt," my tone is curt but professional and maybe a little bit spiteful but I'm desperately trying to hide any emotion. "I wouldn't stop you doing the catering for a second. If we have to work together at some point then it'll be fine. Christ, it's not like I lose it every time I see you," (I do, I completely and utterly lose it!) he smiles at me, reassuringly and in agreement, as if he's accepting what I'm saying. "We've moved on, both of us, and we need to be professional." I consider my words carefully. "the only reason I'm taken aback by your being here is because I'm…worried what Rich will think." (A lie, I know what Rich will think, he'll be worried about me getting hurt!) "He knows everything about you and me, and I don't want him thinking I'm going to make an idiot of myself again like I did at the relaunch." I take a breath.

"Kate, you didn't make an idiot…" I cut him off,

"We both know I did but that's in the past and Rich trusts me and this job is important to me, it's the best thing that's happened to me in ages." He gives me a searching look as if that was a dig at him.

"Ok, I'm sorry. And in truth…I came here because I wanted to see you, I needed to see you." We stare at each other. "Kate," he starts to move towards me but I put my hand up and he stops. "Kate, I thought after our text messages that maybe, I don't know, maybe we could be friends. I know you're with someone else now…"

"Chris, my boyfriend's name is Chris" I remind myself as much as Matt.

"Ok, I know you're with Chris now and you're happy and he's good for you, better than I ever was…"

"much better" I say a little too smugly and he winces a little bit,

"but do you think we could try to be friends? Or have I hurt you so badly that you just can't stand the sight of me?" He's frowning at me, almost pleading with me to say something positive to let him off the hook of being the bad guy in all this. "I meant what I said in the text, I miss you, I miss us. But I also miss our friendship. I know it can never be the same, but I feel so sad to know you're in the world and I'm not allowed to talk to you ever again." Bloody hell, what does he want from me? (I desperately want to touch his skin and feel his arms around me, I start to wonder what he'd do if I just walked over to him and kissed him right now, right here in this office…) grip grip grip, get a grip!

"No" I say it and mean it. "No Matt, I don't think we can be friends." He looks a little broken by my response.

"Kate…"

"No Matt, you asked and I've answered. Yes, we can work together because it's important that we are professional but there can be no friendship. You must know that. The text messages were just alcohol and nostalgia, I'm sorry if you thought it was anything more."

"Kate, I didn't come here with the intention of winning you back but now that I've seen you, that's all I want to do!" (Oh Matt) "but I know you've moved on, I shouldn't have come. I can see now it was the wrong thing to do." He's looking at me as if he's waiting for me to stop him and ask him to stay. He looks miserable. I keep my composure and his tone changes. "I'll go. I'll keep my distance with the event. Maybe Rich can handle the catering aspect of it if you don't feel you can talk to me. I'm sorry." He walks to the door and leaves. He's good at that. He's good at leaving me wanting more of him. He's good at leaving me. I've done the right thing, I have. We could never be friends, not after everything that's happened, not after the way he's treated me, not when I still love every little bit of him. I make my way back to my desk as the tears roll down my cheeks. Pathetic Kate, just pathetic.

CHAPTER FORTY-SIX

Chris is cooking for me tonight before he goes off for his lad's weekend. I think he sees it as some sort of romantic gesture before he leaves me all by myself like some poor maiden unable to fend for herself! It's amazing how quickly men become the hunter gatherers. But I am genuinely looking forward to some time on my own. I miss my flat just being mine. Not sure that's a good sign, shouldn't I be wishing he wasn't going anywhere and then pining for him when he's gone, I'm sure that's how relationships are supposed to work?

We're having steak. It's his go-to dish. I think he feels a little intimidated when it comes to cooking, he made a comment once about being nervous cooking for me because of who my ex is. I tried to reassure him but, well, I'm not sure he believed me.

He's bought me roses and placed them in the middle of the beautifully set table. He's certainly got an eye for presentation. My favourite Orla Kiely place mats are out and he's used the grey table cloth but mixed it up with the red napkins to highlight the roses.

We sit down to eat at 7pm.

"This looks perfect" I say and smile at him. He looks a bit apprehensive, "What's the matter?"

"I don't know," he says as we start to eat, "I just feel a bit strange about going away this weekend. It's our first time apart since I moved in and I kind of wish I wasn't going." I tease him a little,

"Oh Chris, are you going to miss me that much?"

"Alright smug," he giggles, "if you must know, yes I am going to miss you. I'd much rather be here with you this weekend than getting meaninglessly drunk with the lads." He pauses and looks directly at me, "I love you Kate and the more we're together, the more I fall in love with you." Wow, that's taken my breath away. I stand up and go round to his side of the table. He pushes his chair back a bit and I sit on his knee. I kiss him and for the first time I say,

"I love you too Chris" I think he gives a visible sigh of relief and then kisses me back. Being here in his arms, feels right, this is exactly where I should be. The kiss ends and I move to get up, he pulls me back to him and kisses me again, I move again and he pulls me back, we're both laughing,

"Chris I love you but I'm not wasting this steak." I tear myself away from him limb by limb and return to my food. He smiles,

"So, how was work today?" and I feel myself redden as the memory of Matt's visit flashes into my mind. I finish my mouthful and try to sound normal, there's no way I'm telling Chris that Matt turned up. (maybe I should, not now, wrong time)

"It was ok, lots going on with this fundraiser so plenty to keep me busy." I load my fork up again, "What about you?"

"It was ok," he grunts, "Still trying to please the witch but nothing is ever good enough or quick enough, but that's the job, they're all power hungry jerks, she just never shuts up with all the insults, it's even starting to get personal."

"Well that's not right Chris, it's one thing to have a go at someone for not doing the job to their standards but getting personal is just rude." I feel angry for him, "What has she said that's personal?" he can see I'm not impressed and tries to play it down a bit,

"Honestly, it's fine, it's just that type of job"

"Chris, nobody deserves to get treated badly at work, whatever job you do!" I feel really strongly about this and

249

can't quite believe he's taking so much shit off this woman.

"Kate, you don't get it, it's such a cut-throat world, if I put one foot wrong with someone like that, I'll be out, career over. Goodbye Chris." I'm shocked but he means it, he seems happy to take the shit if it means he keeps his job and eventually gets promoted, I guess. Can't imagine being happy with that.

"I'm not happy about it Kate, but for now I just have to live with it." He says this in quite an 'end of conversation' tone and I leave it. Don't want to argue with him, not tonight.

We sit in silence for a while and eat. The steak is great. The wine is great and Chris is great. I look at him across the table and smile as he eats.

"What?" he smirks,

"Just looking," I say, "thinking about what I'm going to do to you later" he raises his eyebrows,

"Really?, I like the sound of that." He finishes his steak, puts his knife and fork down and says, "Careful though, we won't get to dessert at this rate." We both laugh and smile, way too much innuendo and suggestion in our faces to ever get to dessert now. Chris clears our plates away and walks round behind me. He massages my shoulders and then bends down to kiss my neck, I rest my head back against him as he moves his hands down over my breasts and my nipples instantly react. I stand up and take his hand and start to lead him to the bedroom but he pulls me back into his arms and kisses me hard and long. He moves me back against the table and lifts me on to it,

"Really?" I ask, "kitchen table sex?" he nods

"It's always been a bit of a fantasy of mine, I just sweep everything off the table and make love to you right here." I'm a bit conscious of all my lovely tableware but I'm also pretty lost in the moment so I say,

"Go on then, sweep away."

"Really?" he seems surprised but I'm lost in him and don't care about Orla Kiely right now,

"Do it!" so he does, pulls at the cloth like a magician trying to leave everything on the table but it all goes flying, everywhere! There's a moment of uncertainty as we wait for everything to stop clanging, (thankfully it's just condiments, spoons and table mats) and then laugh together. He pushes me further on to the table and then kisses me again, it's not the most comfortable place I've ever had sex. I'm wearing a skirt, so Chris easily removes my knickers. He also removes my top and kisses me through my bra. There's something so erotic about just having that one piece of cloth left between you and your lover, the final piece of mystery to keep them guessing. His breath is heavy and I can feel how turned on he is, I bring my body up to meet him. His kisses are sweet and hot and then the kisses stop and he's just looking at me,

"I love you Kate" I smile and kiss him as he holds me, wants me, loves me.

CHAPTER FORTY-SEVEN

Saturday night

Rach and me are sitting on the sofa in my flat drinking wine. We're having a girly night while Chris is off on his lad's weekend. (starting to hate that phrase!) He went straight from work yesterday so I spent my Friday evening in comfies in front of the telly. It was absolute bliss! I made myself a simple bowl of pasta and then tucked into some Chocolate Fudge Brownie Ice-Cream, it was heavenly. There's something quite liberating about eating when nobody else is around, no judgement.

I had a lie-in this morning. Not unusual for a Saturday but the last few Saturday mornings have pretty much been filled with sex. I think because it's the first time in the week when me and Chris feel relaxed after our hectic weeks at work. Not to say we don't have sex in the week, it's just a bit more…I want to say 'laboured' on a Saturday, but that doesn't make it sound great, and it is…great, I mean.

Rach arrived an hour ago with two bottles of wine, a plethora of snacks and an overnight bag. We haven't had a sleep over for ages. Not since she's been with Rich really. We used to have them all the time, especially when we were both single. We would sit and chat about men, their giant egos and small minds!

Tonight, however, we seem to be quite grown up. We're steadily getting through the wine and snacks and we've watched a couple of episodes of Peaky Blinders, seen before of course but sometimes a bit of Cillian Murphy is what you need when your man's away.

"Kate, what did you say to Rich about me?" oh this sounds like a loaded question. "Only, he asked about my past, said that you'd tried to reassure him about my not wanting to move in just yet." She looks at me and smiles, she must see the worried look in my eyes, "Don't panic, it's fine whatever you said, he seems much more relaxed about it all now." Relief.

"I just said that there was a reason you weren't sure but that it had nothing to do with how you felt about him, I think he was worried you were having second thoughts. Have you told him yet?" She frowns,

"No, I don't want him to think I'm damaged in some way."

"For god's sake Rach, he's not going to think that. I know this is a massive part of your life but Rich loves you and you need to explain this to him. You're going to marry him, he deserves to know. And, to be honest, I think he'll be relieved when you tell him." I pause, "Sorry I hope that doesn't sound callous, I'm not trying to belittle what you went through but I think Rich has built it up to be some sort of monster."

"I know, it's just something I don't talk about with anyone…except you obviously. And I didn't realise it was an issue for me until we started talking about living together and getting married. And now the longer I've left it, the more difficult it is to tell him because it's something I probably should have said ages ago. Does that make sense?" She screws her face up and raises an eyebrow for some sort of reassurance,

"No fucking sense whatsoever, you nutter!" we both laugh, "Just tell him."

"But what am I supposed to say, 'Rich, the reason I am apprehensive about moving in with you is because my Mum and Dad spent their lives arguing with each other and hitting each other and I'm scared that's how we will end up!'"

"Exactly that Rach. He will understand, just be prepared for some questions. He'll want to know how it affected you. Like I did. The first thing I asked you was 'did they hit you?' so just be prepared for a bit of emotion." She looks down at her wine and shakes her head. "Hey, it'll be fine. He loves you. Nothing's going to change that."

"I know, I'm just not good at the emotional sharing stuff!"

"No shit" we both laugh and I fill up our glasses again. "Here's to honesty and the relief it will bring" we clink and drink.

"Talking of honesty Kate, when were you going to tell me that Matt turned up at the office?"

"Never, next question." I have been trying to keep this off my mind so would rather we didn't discuss it. Not sure Rach is going to accept that though,

"Oh come on, Rich said he had to leave you alone with him, what did he want?" Bloody hell, really didn't want to relive the whole thing but Rach wants a blow by blow account so I explain word for word what happened.

"Shit," she exclaims when I finish, "Did you really tell him that you can never be friends?" Why is she so surprised by this bit?

"Yes of course, how can we be after everything that's happened? Plus the fact that Chris would never be happy if I was friends with him so it's just for the best."

"It's for the best? Have you heard yourself?" She shakes her head at me. "Telling him you can't be friends is basically admitting you're still in love with him. It's like saying that you can't bear to see him because every time you look at him you want to throw your arms round him. It's like…"

"Ok Rach, I get it. Enough." She's right. That's exactly the reason I don't want to be friends with him. Friends is not enough so it has to be complete avoidance. (Complete denial of feelings!)

"I don't get you Kate, you loved him for ages, you wanted to be with him, in a proper relationship and when he offered you that, you told him to piss off! I've never understood why you made that decision. I know I didn't approve of him but that was because you kept getting hurt. He was married and you deserved better than that but why turn him away when you did, when he was single?"

"Rach we've talked about his before, it was the right thing to do, I was with Chris by then and, that night, me and Chris had just had the most amazing evening. Matt turning up, out of the blue as usual, and expecting me to just drop everything and fall into his arms just made me realise that I'm better off with Chris…"

"Better off? Shit Kate, I'm not sure that's how love is supposed to feel!"

"You know what I mean, Chris spoils me, he treats me well so actually Matt turning up at that point, when I'd just had a wonderful evening with Chris was perfect timing because it made me realise how I should be treated in a relationship. So, it was a good decision I made that night." I'm desperately trying to convince Rach and myself that this is true.

"Ok, I get why you think it might have been a good moment to make that decision but what if…what if it was the worst moment because you were blinded by the idea of romance with Chris, what if it was really bad timing Matt turning up like that, what if he'd turned up the night before or the night after, would we be sitting here having this conversation now?" I'm not sure where she's going with this. "Just be honest with me, Kate, even if you're only ever honest with me and nobody else. Are you still in love with Matt?" I take a deep breath and linger over the question, we both know the answer,

"Yes, I am. I'm still in love with him and it hurts every day. I'm in love with him and I have to work with him on this bloody event. I'm in love with him and I've convinced him I'm not. But it's too late, Rach. I'm with Chris and Chris loves me so it's too late." And so, I've said it out loud, admitted it. But that doesn't mean I've made a mistake, does it. Does it? Rach is just staring at me. She thinks I've made a mistake. But she doesn't know what it was like.

"I waited for Matt to text me Rach, again and again, he had plenty of opportunity and he didn't bother and, in that time, there was Chris. He took me out, he made me feel amazing and he loves me. Matt only wants me when he can't have me, that's what it feels like."

"Ok, ok, I'm sorry, don't get upset. I just want you to be happy."

"And you think I'll be happy with Matt?" she shakes her head,

"I don't know, I just know how much you love him. I know that you thought he was the one for a long time and I think that he must love you too because he's still around, he still wants to be in your life. If you were just an easy shag for him, then why is he still trying? Cos he is trying Kate, isn't he?" I shrug my shoulders. I've never been so confused. I know Rach is trying to help but I feel lost again. Right, get your head straight Kate.

"Rach, I'll maybe always love Matt a little bit but I've moved on. I'm with Chris now and he makes me happy." I'm hoping that sounds final as I just don't think I can take any more of this tonight. She seems to get the message.

"Sorry, that was all a bit heavy wasn't it! Shit, let's open another bottle and get wasted." I smile and go to the fridge for more wine. Desperately trying to tell myself that Chris is the right choice. Desperately trying to tell myself that I'm happy.

CHAPTER FORTY-EIGHT

Sunday

I say goodbye to Rach on the doorstep as I head out for my jog and she gets a cab home. We didn't talk anymore about men. We just drank wine and listened to shit music and danced and laughed. When I eventually went to bed, Rach had already fallen asleep on the sofa so I covered her up with a blanket and went to my bedroom. I text Chris and told him I missed him. I have missed him. I've really enjoyed some time by myself but I'm also really looking forward to seeing him. Having time apart somehow makes me think about him more and care about him a little more. Is this what they mean by 'absence makes the heart grow fonder'?

As I jog round the park, I feel good. This has been my regular Sunday morning exercise for a few months now and it's definitely starting to show in my fitness and stamina. I can run for much longer without feeling like I'm going to keel over and I'm really toning up muscle wise. Feels great to be honest. And I love that it's my thing, something I do on my own. I look forward to this time in the week so much.

As I run this morning, I'm planning Chris's return. He loves a fry-up at the weekend, especially after he's had a few drinks, so I figure a welcome home brunch will be perfect. I've even managed to find some of that square sausage, that he raves about, so hopefully he'll be impressed with me for that. He's not due back for at least another two hours so I'll have time to get a shower, tidy up a bit and then get cooking so it's ready for him.

I decide to really push myself for the last few hundred metres and start to sprint right to the exit of the park, I'm so determined that I don't notice the woman walking

257

round the corner and I crash into her (like Rachel into the horse!) and fall back...

The woman is a bit angry:

"What the bloody hell..." she screams as I try to get my balance and it is completely my fault,

"Oh my god, I'm so sorry, are you ok?" I blurt out in the hope that I haven't damaged her in any way and as I get my vision back I realise who it is, I realise I know her, and oh my god...

"Kate?" It's Fay. It's Matt's wife (ex-wife?)

"Oh god, I'm so sorry, I was so lost in running that I wasn't looking where I was going." I feel the guilt swarm back. I haven't felt it for ages. This is messed up. She seems less annoyed when she realises it's me,

"Kate, wow, I haven't seen you for a while" she looks thinner and prettier than I remember. She seems less strained somehow, the rbf seems to have disappeared. We stare at each other for a while not really sure what to say. We both start at the same time...

"How have you..." I stop my sentence first and apologise, like one of those awkward moments in a film when you just know these two people don't really like each other but now they've bumped into each other they have to be polite. What they're both actually thinking is 'get me the fuck out of here'. Or at least, that's what I'm thinking, it seems Fay has other ideas?

"Listen Kate, have you got time for a coffee or something, it would be good to catch up?" What am I supposed to say to that? Whatever it is, think quickly Kate, say you'd love to but you have a lunch date, say you're on some radical diet and coffee isn't allowed, say something, say anything but don't say:

"Of course, that'd be lovely" Noooo, why do I do this to myself. There's a coffee house just at the North end of the park so we make our way there. We don't say much on the way except to comment on the weather and how lovely it is to get out of the house. This isn't going to end well. I can just feel it.

Five minutes later, coffees on table, we're sat staring at one another. I must have a sympathetic look on my face because she starts with:

"You know what happened between Matt and me in the end? Of course you do, who doesn't what with the press putting it out there. I mean he's not even that much of a celebrity but if there's any negativity or something bad happening in someone's relationship then you can be sure they'll put it out there for the world to see." She has a point. She takes a sip of her mushroom coffee (sounds revolting but it's a thing now apparently!) I'd better say something,

"I did read about what happened. I'm sorry." I choose my words carefully. I'm not sorry they have split up (she made Matt miserable) which probably sounds selfish but I'm trying to show some sort of honesty in my words, even if it's only me that realises it. She looks at me searchingly which makes me think she knows more than she's letting on. I move a little awkwardly in my seat and lean forward to take a sip of my coffee (a regular latte, boring? There was a time when that was pretentious but now it's all about nitro coffee and coffee spritzers – I mean, fizzy cold coffee? What is that about?) I realise I'm drifting off and Fay's words snap me back to reality,

"If I'm honest, I knew our marriage was over years ago. We were both just clinging on to something because we felt we should. But there was very little emotion from either of us for a long time. It was more like a business arrangement." I really feel like I shouldn't be listening to this. I'm not the person she should be confiding in but something compels me so I ask,

"What made you stay with him?" she raises her eyebrows at that, almost like she hasn't thought about it before.

"I'm honestly not sure anymore. Do you remember that time I asked you to check up on him, to find out if he was seeing someone behind my back?" I remember only too well, that was the night it all began. I nod and frown a little like the memory is insignificant to me. "Well, he was and had been all that time." I can feel myself starting to squirm, does she know it was me? "and the thing is Kate, all that time, I didn't actually care! He could have been sleeping with a different woman every night and I don't think it would have bothered me." Well that was unexpected. I can't help myself,

"Why not?" she looks me direct in the eye, oh god, is this it, the big 'I knew it was you all along', she takes another sip of her coffee and winces at the taste, pretty sure she hates it but must be seen to be drinking on trend.

"I don't think I've been in love with him for years. I mean I care about him and I think he's a brilliant chef but I was so wrapped up in making a success of the business that he was like an employee to me" Shit, brutal. But that's pretty much how she treated him, looking back. "I treated him badly and he treated me badly by cheating on me. And as long it was just sex, as long as he was just using his celebrity to work his charm on women, I could handle that and I could get on with the other parts of the business" I felt a 'but' coming,

"But" yep, "when we finally sat down and talked it all through, after he ran out on me at the renewal ceremony, he admitted it all" Oh god, my heart is pounding now, I can almost feel the blood draining from my face, she does know, here it comes…

"And that's what really got me more than anything." She went quiet. What did he admit? Should I ask? Is that what she wants me to do? I can't not ask…

"What did he admit?" again looking directly at me,

"He told me that he'd been seeing another woman for several years, that he's in love with her, and has been since the day he met her" I could feel my heart pumping out of my chest and a little tear forming in my eye, "He told me that he thinks he might have lost her because he's treated her so badly and he looked so broken by that, he looked like he might cry and it was like he was being honest with me for the first time in our relationship. And that's when I knew. I knew right then and there that he had never loved me the way he loves this other woman. And he never would and for some weird reason, that's ok with me. It was like I was off the hook or something, like I didn't have to carry him anymore." She sat back in her chair and smiled at me. "Does that sound cold to you?" I shrugged my shoulders and tried to consider it from her point of view but all I was thinking was that he'd told her he loved me. He'd told her he'd been in love with me since he met me. (Be less selfish Kate, just for one second).

"It doesn't sound cold at all. It sounds like you wanted a way out of the marriage, and you got one?" Was that too much? Should I have perhaps kept that thought to myself.

"That's exactly it Kate, I knew you'd get it. Until he admitted it, I didn't have a clue what I wanted, I was just being a wife and behaving in a way I thought a wife should behave but I was unhappy. I was so unhappy. Thinking back, I was almost disappointed when you told me he wasn't having an affair, I think I wanted him to be found out so that I would have a reason to leave him." Wow, this was seriously big revelations and it was making me frustrated more than anything. Why couldn't she have worked it out years ago? Why didn't I tell her he was having an affair when she asked me to interrogate him? Why? why? why? I'm still not sure if she's building up to the big reveal, that she knows it was me? She picks up her cup and starts to lift it towards her mouth but thinks better of it and puts it straight back down again. We've kind of come to an end of conversation moment so I say,

"So what's next for you?" She takes a big breath which lifts her shoulders and straightens her back, as if telling me this has been another weight off her shoulders.

"Well, I'm going travelling" she smiles and waits for my reaction.

"Wow," I exclaim "that's really exciting" I'm genuinely surprised.

"All this has made me realise that there's so much more to this world than business and marriage. God Kate, Matt and I got married way too quickly, we saw something in one another that would help us get further in life, Matt saw my business connections and money and I saw a project to manage, and we both got lost in all of that for far too long. It was crazy, looking back, and we can both see that now." She looked at her watch. "I should go, I'm going to my sister's for Sunday lunch, she's taken pity on me since the split but listen Kate," those searching eyes again, "thanks for listening to me, it's really helped. And, if you find someone you love Kate," she takes hold of my shoulders as if to make sure she has my full attention, "I mean really love Kate, hang on to them for the right reasons, don't waste your life with the wrong man." She stares at me and smiles and there's a moment when I wonder again if she knows it was me. "Anyway, it's been lovely to see you, take care won't you." She air kisses me and turns and she's gone. I sit back down in my seat and wonder what the hell just happened. I'm a little confused. What with Rach making me doubt everything last night and now Fay telling me this, it's all a bit much when I know I love Chris. I do love Chris. And Chris loves me and that's where my life is, Chris is the one. Not Matt. Chris. Matt and I missed our chance. I have to accept that.

I walk slowly back to the flat and on my way try to refocus my mind on Chris and how much I've missed him this weekend. I put my key in the door and think I can hear voices inside. I pause, the door slightly ajar, and listen. Chris is home already but he's not alone. I push the door open a bit further and hear what I can only describe as banter alongside cheers and the occasional frustrated 'argh'. As I walk into the flat, I see Chris is standing in front of the telly and to his right are two men I've never seen before. They all have their backs to me and they're all clutching an Xbox controller. What the…? Chris is back early and his first priority is to play on his Xbox?! They are so engrossed in their 'game' that they haven't even noticed I'm here. I make my presence known,

"Er, hi, Chris?" he turns his head quickly and doesn't even make eye contact with me.

"Oh hi babe, thought you'd be out for longer running." He doesn't take his eyes off the screen as he says this. He's completely transfixed on the game. I take a look at the screen and it seems to be a football game as far as I can make out. And even if he did think I'd be out longer, I'm back, I'm here in the room and he hasn't even looked at me properly. Maybe this is ok? Is this normal? I'm feeling a little bit pissed off, well, a lot pissed off actually. And he's still not bothered his ass to turn around and look at me. I'm still standing in the same place and I can feel my rage building. I need to chill. Maybe I'm over-reacting because I was looking forward to seeing him and him getting back early has scuppered my plans a bit. Ok Kate, take a minute, have a shower. Maybe this isn't so bad.

"I'm going for a shower," I shout across the noises of the game, and get some sort of grunt in reply. Charming.

In the shower, my emotions go from calm to confused to raging pretty quickly, I can't really get past the fact that he's out there playing games before he has even said hello to me. I'd imagined our reunion to be romantic and passionate, I wanted him to have missed me like he said he was going to on Thursday but from what I can tell, he missed his Xbox more and now he's brought his besties round to show off. Here was me thinking he would have been pining for me all weekend, talking about me to his mates but the reality seems to be that he was pining for his bloody Xbox. I finish my shower and dry off in the bedroom, getting dressed slowly in the hope that it gives Chris enough time to have got rid of them now I'm back.

No such luck. I go back into the lounge to find all three of them in the same position. Christ, I haven't even seen the other twos' faces! They don't even have the common decency to turn around and say hello. I go to the kitchen and put the kettle on but I'm still feeling stunned by this whole situation so I walk back into the lounge.

"Chris?" I say it gently but loud enough for them all to hear.

"Yes babe?" he still doesn't look at me. What do I have to do? Maybe I should take my clothes off and go and place myself between them and the tv screen, although I have this horrible feeling that they'd just casually peer round me so they could still see the screen!

"Can I have a word please, babe?" I emphasise the babe, I've never called him that before and I think maybe now he senses my frustration as he looks at me, looks back to the screen, looks at me and then puts his controller down and walks towards me. The other two sort of groan as he walks away.

"What's the matter, Kate? You ok?"

"Am I ok?" Now I'm really cross, "No I'm not bloody ok! Are you taking the piss?"

"Alright Kate, calm down," he says as he ushers me into the kitchen. "What's going on?" I can't quite believe his reaction. Am I really the only person here that thinks this is not ok? This is how teenage boys would act towards their mother when they bring friends round but at least the friends might have the common decency to acknowledge the mother.

"I can't believe you're asking me what's going on.

You've just got back from a weekend away, the first weekend we've spent apart since you moved in and you bring your mates back with you to play games! Are you serious Chris? Is this some sort of joke or something?

"Alright, keep your voice down," he looks through to the lounge, "I thought you'd be out for a while so I didn't see the harm. It's the kind of thing we do when we get back, normally we would have gone back to my flat."

"Really? But you don't live alone anymore and I've missed you Chris, didn't you think that I might want you to myself or that maybe I'd planned something special for you coming home."

"Christ, Kate, I've only been away for the weekend. What's the big deal?" He might as well have put Mum at the end of that sentence. I feel like crying. He's clearly not in the mood to see my side (am I being selfish, can I see his side?)

"You might have only been away for the weekend Chris but you seem to have come back a different person, what happened to all the 'I'll miss you' crap from Thursday night?"

"I did miss you, I really did Kate. You're blowing this all up out of proportion." Maybe I am but he's not even kissed me.

"I was looking forward to seeing you Chris, I didn't expect you to bring people back and they haven't even looked at me they're so ignorant."

"Oh don't be like that, they're not ignorant, they're just into the game. You know what it's like."

"No Chris, I don't know what it's like. I don't understand the fascination with it. And I certainly don't understand why the first thing you want to do after a weekend away from your girlfriend who you 'love' and 'miss' is to play on that fucking machine. You're just as ignorant as they are if you think any of this is acceptable." I storm past him, grab my bag and coat and head for the door. I need to get out of here, I need to get away from him for a while before I say something I might really regret.

I walk for ages, walk and walk. At a pace too, pounding out my anger through the soles of my shoes. Am I being completely unfair? Selfish? Irrational? I don't think so. Am I? I am trying to see it from his point of view but I just don't get how he could have thought the whole thing was ok. I've turned it over so many times in my head now that I'm going round in circles. Had I just built up our reunion too much? Maybe, just the mere fact that I'm calling it a reunion probably sounds a bit over the top! It's not like he's been away for a month. Ok so maybe I shouldn't have expected so much. I guess we both saw his coming home as a different kind of celebration. And maybe, if I'm really honest with myself, I'm trying so hard to make this work because it isn't working. Maybe when you have to work this hard at something, it's just not meant to be. Christ what am I saying?

I get back to the flat about an hour later and Chris is alone in the lounge. The tv and Xbox are off and he's sitting with a cup of tea. I throw my keys on the coffee table and sit on the sofa. For a few seconds, we both just sit. Then,

"Kate, I'm so sorry." I'm taken aback, wasn't expecting this. "I get stupidly carried away with it all and we'd been talking about that game all weekend, I got so wrapped up in it with the lads that I…I…

"Forgot about me?" I finish for him. That is what he was going to say but it must have sounded pretty harsh in his head.

"I didn't forget about you Kate, I just got wrapped up in it all. I'm sorry. I shouldn't have brought them here, it was a ridiculous idea. I'm such an idiot sometimes." I can feel my anger subside a bit as he apologises, I can't really stay angry when he realises how much he's hurt me.

"I just can't believe you thought that would be ok for one second Chris, I mean, after all the romantic things you've done in our relationship, I honestly thought having been away from each other, you would be more excited to see me." I feel sad about it now, like this should have been really romantic and now it's ruined. Maybe I'm just too much of a romantic. He moves next to me on the sofa,

"Kate, can you forgive me? I know I'm stupid sometimes, I know you deserve so much better than what just happened. Can we start again, can we pretend I've just got back? Please babe." I don't know what to say to this, I can't pretend it didn't happen. Not right now anyway.

"I don't know Chris. I'm just a bit surprised by it all I think, I feel quite gutted right now so just give me some time. I'm not sure what I want right now."

"What does that mean?" he looks worried, "that sounds like you're not sure if you want me?" I look into his eyes and bring my hand up to touch his cheek.

"Don't be silly, I'm just not in the best of moods right now, just give me a few hours to calm down a bit." He frowns at me. "Chris, don't worry." I kiss him and go to the bathroom. I decide to have a bath, mostly because I know that I will be on my own and it will calm me down. But my brain is still flitting all over the place. Am I looking for a way out of this? I feel like I'm making something out of nothing and it's making me question my feelings for Chris. Ultimately, I'm questioning the age difference. Never in our relationship have I felt more like his mother than his girlfriend, but today all that changed, and those few years between us suddenly seem like a gaping void.

CHAPTER FORTY-NINE

Saturday - Day of the Gala

It's been two weeks since the incident with Chris and we're mainly back on track. We had a long talk about what happened and were really honest with each other. Although, I didn't tell him that the whole thing had made me concerned about the age difference again, not sure why I didn't. Maybe there would be no way back from that and I decided I don't want it to end. I just wish that Xbox wasn't such a big part of his life.

I've spent most of my time since, getting the Charity Fundraiser sorted out. It's such a big event that it's taken over the office and we've had to turn other jobs down. Thankfully, Rich has spoken to Matt when needed and because Matt is so efficient and knows exactly how these things work, we haven't needed to contact him much at all.

So, tonight's the night. I'm nervous but excited and Rich is the same. It's taken a lot of blood, sweat and tears to get everything perfect for this and it will really put Rich Events on the map if we get it all right.

"We can get into the venue to set up from 4pm" I remind Rich, "so can you get there no later than that to work with the staff, they'll want the organ grinder not the monkey" Rich laughs at me,

"If only they knew who really makes this place tick" but I haven't got time to smile or appreciate the compliment, still lots to do. The evening kicks off at 6pm. It's an early start and an early finish due to the strict noise policy, the event will all be done and dusted by 10.30pm. I'm making the last-minute phone calls to ensure the smooth running of it all: flowers, displays, music and staffing (there's always someone who drops out at the last minute so I have to get a stand by).

"Rich, is everything sorted with the catering? Does he know what time he can get in?" I ask nervously, trying to sound business-like but can't actually bring myself to say his name.

"Yes Kate, I spoke to him this morning, he's already there, knows someone who works there so they've let him into the kitchens early." At least I don't have to worry about the quality of the food, if there's one good thing I can say about Matt, he does know his job.

"Kate, in case I don't get the chance later" he enthuses, "thank you for being so amazing with all this, you've put so much into it and I really do appreciate all of your hard work." I carry on flicking through the paperwork, a little embarrassed as I'm not too good with praise (maybe comes of not having much!) and quietly respond,

"Just doing my job Rich, this is what you pay me for."

CHAPTER FIFTY

The Gala

We have a red carpet leading up to the huge doors of the venue. The old church looks majestic. The early evening sun is blazing through the north window, its stained glass creating beautiful colours inside the main building. The guests have started to arrive and I'm so pleased to see the effort that has gone into their appearances. We have a select few paps waiting outside, snapping the celebrities and socialites as they arrive. A third of the guests tonight have been invited. These are the mega rich, the ones that we know will come here tonight with the intention to spend a shit load of cash. The rest of the attendees have bought tickets at £500 each. They're the sort who want to mix with the Beckhams of this world and will go to any length to socialise in the same circles. You can instantly tell the ones who have real class from the ones who got famous on some sort of reality tv show. Doesn't matter tonight though, they're all loaded and we need them to be generous. The charity have a target of making £100,000 from the auction which will be easily surpassed with the amazing items we've got going up. They range from a river cruise on the Thames to a four-week cruise in the Pacific. Rich couldn't believe it when I told him a company had donated that and I was pretty shocked myself, only really suggested it so that they could barter me down but they agreed straight away. I regretted I hadn't started my bartering with a bigger prize but still, it looks pretty impressive on the list of auction items. We've also got lots of 'can't buy' items like a football used in the last game Arsenal played at Highbury in 2006 (it's just a football but Rich reckons it'll go for thousands!)

The auction is scheduled for the second part of the evening after the meal. Matt has put together a heavenly five course dinner. I've tried desperately not to have anything to do with the catering but I needed to know what food would be served and it looks amazing as usual.

The courses are:
Starter: Creamy Cucumber and Avocado Soup
Salad: Mixed Spring Greens with Champagne Soaked Pears, Candied Walnuts, Goats Cheese and Honey Vinaigrette
Entrée: Seared Scallops with Butternut Squash Puree
Main: Pistachio and Chive Crusted Lamb Cutlets with Chargrilled Broccoli and Parsnip Mash
Dessert: Honey Yogurt Panna Cotta with Blood Orange Sauce

The evening begins. The meals are served. Rich and I watch and make sure everything is going well. He seems a bit stressed and no wonder, this is a huge deal for him, for us.

After the meal, it's essential that the auction gets started straight away due to our time restrictions. It has to start at 9pm and the compere is going to have to be pretty swift with each auction item. We have a Plan B which, if time is getting on, means we will remove a couple of items and move straight to the big hitters. I start to panic a bit, maybe two and half hours, to serve two hundred people five courses, was pushing it. The last few desserts go out at 8.45pm so we might have to do a bit of switching around of auction items. I ring Rich, as he's moved down to the other end of the building and explain my concerns about timing.

"Ok Kate, if we have to we'll switch to Plan B but I reckon we could start the auction while people are still eating." Makes sense I guess. The VIPs have all finished and that's where we're counting on the big money coming from.

The auction starts bang on 9pm. The compere doesn't miss a beat, he has the audience exactly where he needs them, the right amount of encouragement for people to bid more but he keeps the pace going and all items are sold. I haven't been adding up the bids but I'm sure we've surpassed the 100k. The biggest bid of the night was for Golf Lessons with a professional golfer I've never even heard of (sport is not really my thing!). Rich managed to secure the prize through a friend of a friend. (I do have to wonder about his connections!) The lessons went for £21,000. More money than sense, some people, but as long as the Charity is benefitting, that's all that matters.

The auction is over in an hour and ten minutes which is perfect timing to get everyone out of the building so we can be cleared of people by 10.30pm. I look around and can't quite believe we've pulled it all off. We really have! Security makes sure the last guests have left and that's it. All done. I sit down at a table for the first time all evening and take a deep breath. Rich creeps up behind me and enthusiastically pulls me up out of the chair for a hug.

"Bloody hell Kate, we did it!" He's so pleased it went this well and so am I. This will be the major step forward we need to not only secure the future of the business but also to expand, hire more staff and have more than one event running at a time. It's really bloody exciting. Rich hands me a glass of champagne and we have a quick toast. Hannah Scott approaches and shakes Rich's hand and then mine.

"This has been an amazing success. You two have done a fantastic job." Her eyes gaze past me and fix on someone at the other end of the hall, "Matt, come and have a drink with us. Let the others clear up." Shit shit shit. Matt don't come and have a drink with us. Keep clearing up. I tentatively turn to see Matt approaching. He looks sheepish, like he knows how difficult this will be but he joins us and grabs a glass.

"Matt, your food was outstanding, so many people have commented on it. Thank you so much. All of you. You make a great team." Awkward. We all clink glasses but I'm so conscious of standing this close to Matt it makes me shake slightly. I try to steady my glass but I need to get out of this situation. I take a sip and make my excuses, say I need to check something, and head for the back rooms. If there is nowhere else, at least I can hide in the toilet for a few minutes.

When I come out, it's quiet. I start to gather my stuff together and plan to leave discretely before anyone else sees me. I'll text Rich later and say I was tired and just needed to get home. But as I make my way through the lobby, he's there. Matt. And he's waiting for me.

"Kate, I just wanted to say how amazing tonight was, you've done a fantastic job. I mean, you and Rich. You must be so pleased." He wanted to say this? Really? Could he really not see how awkward I felt? Why couldn't he just leave? "Kate, are you ok?" I'm standing still, but rocking on my feet, looking for an escape route and if I rock then it means I'm ready to make a quick exit in any direction at any moment. So I do, there's a door to my right so I head towards it (really hoping it's not a cupboard, although I would literally walk in and hide in it for a while) I open the door, it's a small ante room and there's no other exit. Not my best plan but Matt will get the message now and leave me alone. Or not. He follows me in.

"Kate, what's going on?" I can't look at him. The sound of his voice is enough to make me want him. "Kate, I'm worried, say something." After a few seconds, I finally turn round and look at him.

"What are you doing Matt? Why are you talking to me? You said we wouldn't have to see each other, and we haven't in all the time we've been working on this so why, now, are you in this room with me? What are you doing?"

"Kate I'm sorry, I didn't want to make you feel uncomfortable, I genuinely wanted to tell you how amazing tonight was and how…proud of you I am." I don't think I can handle this. This is my biggest fear right now, being left alone with him. And here we are. I should have walked out of the building, not into this room and yet, here we are.

"Kate, what are you so afraid of?"

"Bloody hell Matt, isn't that obvious?"

"No it's not, it's like you can't stand to be near me, do you hate me so much that you…

"Hate you? Shit Matt is that what you think?" I'm moving towards him and stop myself. I can hear my words and I'm scared what I might say next.

"So what is it then Kate? Surely we can have a civil conversation, you said yourself we need to be professional." I look down at the carpet, it's bright red with a gold swirling pattern going through it at intervals. Probably worth a fortune. I keep looking down.

"That's just it Matt, I can't be professional around you, I fail every time. Because…" I should stop speaking, now! I'm still looking at the carpet when Matt's feet come into view. He's moved closer to me, he's still moving closer to me.

"Kate" his voice is soft, I want him to hold me. I keep looking down. If I look at him now, he'll see everything in my eyes, he'll see how much I still love him. He'll see and I'll be shattered again. Broken. He raises his hand and touches my cheek, I close my eyes and take a deep breath and feel myself relaxing into his touch. "Kate" his voice is a whisper now. I look up at him. He lowers his head and kisses me. I don't stop it. I want this more than anything. I want Matt more than anything. He brings his other hand to my other cheek and kisses me gently. I let him. And as he moves his face away I open my eyes and look at him. My Matt. Those beautiful eyes burn through my skin. I can't stop loving him. He leans in to kiss me again and this time my response is more obvious, I willingly open my mouth and let him in. Right back into my heart. I feel his hands move slowly down my body and stop at my waist. He pulls me closer to him and our bodies are touching again and it feels…No! I push him away. I have to stop this. I have a boyfriend and I'm cheating on him. I won't do that. I love Chris. I get my head together and move away from Matt.

"Kate please, I'm sorry, I just thought" he looks broken now.

"That's the trouble with you Matt, you're always sorry. That's all I ever get, apology after apology." Oh dear, here comes bitter and angry Kate, "You're nothing but a manipulative, cheating bastard and all you ever do is hurt people. You get them exactly where you want them, make them fall desperately in love with you with all that charm and then you break them apart bit by bit. I won't let you do this to me again Matt, I won't give you the chance to ruin my life twice." I storm out of the room before he has the chance to respond and I get out of the building as fast as I can. I'm running along the pavement. I don't want him to catch up with me. I don't think he's following me but I'm not risking it. I keep running.

After about five minutes, I relax to a walk and take a quick look behind me to make sure he's not there. Of course he's not. Why would he be? Too much like hard work. (Macy Gray's I Try is going round my head, has fate brought us here? Should we be together?). I'm a terrible person. I let him kiss me, I cheated on Chris. Chris who worships the ground I walk on. Chris who I live with and love. I'm such an idiot. I'm going to have to tell him what happened. I won't be able to live with myself if I don't. What did happen? Matt kissed me. I let him. Matt and I kissed. I feel the shivers down my whole body. Matt kissed me. I think I told him I was desperately in love with him, is that what I said? Christ Kate, way to go. I get a cab and decide, on the way home, that I will tell Chris everything.

CHAPTER FIFTY-ONE

The Confession

The flat is dark when I get back. I knew Chris was working late but I thought he'd be back by now. I turn the light on in the lounge and nearly jump out of my skin. Chris is back but he's sitting in pitch black.

"Jesus Chris, you scared the life out of me, why are you sitting here in the dark?" I throw my bag down on the sofa and then I sit. Lingering in the back of my mind is how on earth I'm going to tell him what just happened with Matt. But something is wrong. He looks as white as a ghost, "Chris what is it? Are you feeling ill?" He doesn't say anything but lifts his head to look at me and he looks devastated. I have a sudden panic that he already knows what happened but I get a hold of myself, he can't possibly know. (unless he was there!)

"Chris? What is it?" Silence. He looks at me again and almost looks like he might cry. "Chris you're scaring me, what's going on?" He covers his face with his hands and holds his head like it's a dead weight,

"Kate, I'm so sorry, I've…I've…done something…" his face is still covered by his hands. I move from the sofa and kneel in front of him,

"Chris, you're scaring me, what is it?" I move his hands down from his face and he has tears in his eyes. "Chris?"

"Oh shit Kate, I'm so sorry" a tear rolls down his cheek, "I had sex with someone else" I freeze. What?

"You what?" he looks at me now, "who?" I sound calm but I'm starting to shake,

"Does it matter?"

"Yes it fucking matters!" Does it? My boyfriend has had sex with someone else, does it really matter who? All

277

I can think is, 'this is what it feels like to be cheated on, this is how bad it feels and I did it to someone for three years'.

"My boss!" that stops my self-pity,

"Your fucking boss, the witch who you hate?" I get up now, I really don't want to be that close to him anymore. "When?" I ask

"Tonight." He whimpers, "At work?" I say in astonish-ment.

"Yes" he looks ashamed. I'm backing further away from him.

"Kate, I'm so sorry, we had a few drinks as we were working late and one thing led to another and…"

"Oh well that's ok then," sarcasm engulfs me, "if it was just alcohol then you're completely forgiven."

"Kate, I'm trying to be honest. I regretted it as soon as it happened, I never meant it to happen Kate, I just…"

"Get out." I say with surprising calm. I can't stand to be in the same room as him right now. He doesn't move,

"Kate please, we need to talk about this."

"Really? You think we need to talk about the fact that you shagged your fucking boss over the photocopier. Ok then, let's talk, is she a good kisser? How long did it last? Did you enjoy it?"

"For fuck's sake, Kate, stop it." He stands up and starts to move towards me, "Babe, I'm sorry, I'm so sorry."

"Just get out Chris. I can't talk to you right now. I don't want you to be here. Please just get out." I shout so he gets the message and he goes. I hear the front door shut and I collapse on to the sofa, I curl up in a ball and hold my aching stomach and I cry. I can't believe how much this hurts. I can't believe after everything, Chris has done this. I thought he loved me. I thought this was it. My tears don't stop. And my mind is racing. Matt crosses my mind and I wonder if I'm crying because of Chris or Matt. What a mess. What a fucking mess!

CHAPTER FIFTY-TWO

Decisions

I'm still lying on the sofa an hour later when Chris comes back. I hear his key in the door, sit up, dry my cheeks with the palms of my hands and steel myself.

"Can I come in?" his voice is quiet. I nod and he comes in. As he walks past me, I can smell alcohol on him and I wonder if he's been to the pub or whether it's the alcohol he drank at work, with his boss, that I can smell. I have no idea what this woman even looks like. And that feels weird. Chris has been with another woman and I'm wishing I knew what she looked like. Is she prettier than me? Is she younger than me? What does it matter?

"I'm sorry Kate." He looks at me as he sits down. I'm so sorry."

"I know you are Chris" I'm calm now. I know what I need to do. "I know you're sorry and I know you want us to try and work through this, but we can't." I look directly at him and make sure I don't blink, so he knows I mean it.

"Kate, please don't do this, we can work this out, I love you, I know it probably doesn't feel like it right now but I do. I don't want to lose you."

"I'm sorry too Chris. We can't. If it hadn't been this, it would have been something else eventually. I know you love me and I love you too but we can't carry on, not now. And we can't work through it because when you were…" I can hardly bring myself to say it, "…having sex with your boss tonight," he winces at my calm way of saying this, "I was letting another man kiss me." Chris frowns.

"What do you mean? Who?" He's not going to like this,

"Matt." He raises his eyebrows in disbelief.

"He kissed you?" he murmurs, "Yes, and I let him, I kissed him too. But, then, I stopped it. I thought about you and I stopped it because I felt so terrible, I knew it would hurt you and that hurt me so I stopped it." I look at him waiting for some sort of response. I have no idea what he's thinking. "Chris?"

"You must love me Kate, if you stopped it. So maybe we can work through this."

"That's what I was hoping in the cab on the way home, I was working out how to tell you about it and I was hoping you would forgive me and we could work through it, but…"

"Please don't say but,"

"But you didn't stop, you had sex with your boss Chris. You've had sex with another woman and I've kissed my ex. What does that tell you about our relationship?" He looks dumbfounded,

"Kate, we can get past this, we both just need some time, please don't make this decision now, sleep on it and see how you feel in the morning. I love you." His eyes seem to well up again and I feel a bit sorry for him. But not in a 'I love this man and I would do anything to fight for this relationship' way, in a way that makes me know it's definitely over. I feel nothing but sympathy for him. Because he really regrets what he has done. But the real problem is, the thing that I can't get out of my head, is…I'm relieved. It's like a weight has been lifted and I'm free. I feel guilty feeling this way but I can't help it. There's not much else to say tonight. I stand up and watch his face fall as he realises I mean it and there's no coming back from this.

"I'm going to bed," I hesitate as I don't want to sound cruel but I say it anyway, "you can sleep on the sofa tonight." And I walk away. I'm devastated that he has done this, I feel angry at the thought of him with someone else. I wonder, now it's over between us, if he might go back for more, which makes me feel jealous and angry. Our whole relationship flashes through my mind, the lovely romantic evenings, Spain, his lovely dimples and I realise I'm going to miss him. I wonder why we had to end like this. Maybe some things just aren't meant to be forever. But underneath all this emotional confusion, I know it's the right thing to do.

CHAPTER FIFTY-THREE

The morning after

I wake at 7am and need coffee. Chris is still lying on the sofa. I'm not sure if he's awake yet so I sneak quietly into the kitchen and put the kettle on. I make him a cup too and take both through to the lounge. I put the cups down on the coffee table and perch in front of him on the sofa. He's staring at the ceiling, transfixed it seems, hands above his head. He's incredibly good looking.

"Chris?" he looks at me and tries some sort of a smile but fails. How quickly people can go from being totally comfortable with one another to awkward and silent. I break the silence, "You ok?" he shakes his head.

"I'm an idiot." His look is vacant and I know he really regrets what he has done and would probably never do it again, there's even a part of me that considers trying to work it out with him, trying to forgive him but there's too many doubts now. He has to work with this woman, he wouldn't give up his job so I'd be spending every day wondering if he's having sex with her again. The trust has gone. "Is there no way we can put this behind us, work through it and move on?" I take a deep breath and look at him. Lovely, charming Chris.

"I wish there was a way Chris but it'll never work now, you have to see that woman every day and…"

"I know," he cuts me off before I can suggest anything, he seems sickened by it, "I know, I've ruined it, I've let you down but I love you Kate. I can't just stop loving you." He sits up and takes my hands in his, "please just think about this, just take your time, don't just throw this away, we're so good together." I shake my head now,

"Are we? If we're so good together, why were we both with other people last night? Why was that even an option for either of us?" he lets go of my hands and sits back.

"Will you go back to him now?" he sounds bitter and childish.

"No Chris, me and you ending is not about my wanting someone else, it's about us not being right for each other."

"Yeah but the reason we're not right for each other is because you've never got over him have you?" he glares at me, "come on Kate, at least be honest with me now we're finished, at least be honest with yourself." I look into his eyes and I am honest with him,

"No, I've never got over Matt. I should have got over him properly before me and you started something but our holiday romance escalated pretty quickly and while my feelings for you were growing, I never dealt with my feelings for him. And I'm sorry if that hurts you. I really am. I wanted us to work Chris, I really thought we would, but when we stand back and analyse it all, there's too many differences between us." I'm trying to make this amicable, I don't want to hurt him. Even though he's hurt me. Is it worse to cheat on your partner physically or emotionally? Chris had sex with someone else; I'm in love with someone else. Either way is cheating if you're not fully present in your relationship. I take a sip of my coffee.

"So what happens now Kate? Do you want me to leave straight away?"

"It's probably best, if you've got somewhere to go." I'm pretty sure one of his mates will put him up for a while, (they'll be able to Xbox all night long).

"Kate are you sure? Are you sure this is what you want?" I hesitate and so he grabs my shoulders and pulls me to him and kisses me. I don't stop it, but I know it's our last kiss. And when it's finished, he knows too.

If my time with Chris has taught me anything, it's that I'm allowed to be happy. For so long, I've relied on someone else to make me happy (I thought that was how it's meant to be) but our relationship has made me realise that if I'm not happy then it's me who has to take action. You can work at things, (and I know that any relationship can be hard work), but if when you work at it, it still isn't right, then it's time to get out. I love Chris but maybe we should have just kept it as a holiday romance. But I don't regret it, he gave me so much confidence and I love him for that but we were never going the distance, not when I had so many doubts. And as for Matt, well, we never had to work at the feelings in our relationship, they were there from that very first night he kissed me. It was like everything suddenly made sense. It suddenly felt right. It was love. And if it had been in different circumstances…maybe, he would have been the one? My heart still hurts. All this has brought me to one conclusion. I've worked out what I want from life and it's just – to be happy. Being on my own makes me happy and if I do meet someone one day who adds to that happiness then so be it. Stop searching for love, just be me, if it's meant to be, it will be. And if it's not…well, turns out I quite like me.

CHAPTER FIFTY-FOUR

Six months later.

The place looks amazing. This is going to be the most wonderful wedding day. I have spent so much time getting everything just right, just how it should be and now the day is finally here. I clutch my flowers, smile and start walking down the aisle. A slow walk, like I've been taught, don't want it to pass too quickly, everyone should enjoy this moment. As I get to the front, I look at the man waiting, such a handsome and loving man, the perfect gentleman. I take my place and then turn towards the door.

Rach looks stunning in her wedding dress. She has chosen a traditional A Line dress in Ivory with a sweetheart bodice and a finger-tip length veil that falls elegantly down her back. She holds her brother's arm tightly and looks nervous but so very happy. I turn to look at Rich's face and he's trying not to cry, the love that beams from him for Rach is evident every day, but today it is pouring out of him.

The ceremony is beautiful and emotional. The whole room is clearly behind them and you can feel how happy everyone is to be sharing this day. As Maid of Honour, I've had several jobs to do leading up to today but I have also worked as their wedding planner as they refused to let me say no. I think they asked me to give me something to focus on after my split with Chris. And it worked I guess, although you could argue that some people might call that a bit thoughtless, asking someone who has just split with their boyfriend to plan their best friend's wedding, not me though, it was a welcome distraction and it was for Rich and Rach so it didn't take much persuasion.

I'm running around all day, making sure the transition from ceremony to photos and receiving line to wedding breakfast goes smoothly. I'll be able to relax when the evening do starts and I know the last bit of my job is done. It's good for me, though, to keep busy on a day like this. It stops me thinking about how single I am when all I see around me is loving couples.

The photographs run like clockwork, Rach didn't want this part of the day to take too long because, as an event manager herself, she knows this is the time in a wedding when the guests either drink too much and start making fools of themselves or start losing interest if they can't be near the bride and groom. The photographer appreciates this too and her assistant is super-efficient at arranging the different groups and calling up the next lot.

The speeches are brilliant. Rach's brother's speech is straight from the heart. There's not a dry eye in the room and Rich is so emotional for his that he can barely speak, but he gets through it and everyone cheers. Rich's best man is his brother Rob. He's married, unfortunately for me, so not even a bit of fun with the best man. I'm sure that used to be a given at weddings. Oh well. Rob shares lots of funny stories about Rich, and has the guests in stitches when he tells them about how Rich was asked several times to be a page boy when he was little and got so nervous that he wet his pants at every wedding. Rob is hoping that the same thing doesn't happen today. The guests all laugh and look at Rich as if to check if his trousers are still dry.

When the meal is over, there's just one more job for me to do. Rich and Rach are taking a quick break before the evening guests arrive and the final part of the day begins. I have a word with the DJ to make sure he has the music lined up and then I actually have a toilet break. I realise it's my first one today but then I haven't really been drinking much in the hope that I can keep a level head. I will be making up for that as soon as their first dance is over.

The DJ calls Mr and Mrs Gregory to the floor for their first dance as a married couple. They're dancing to Alison Krauss's version of When You Say Nothing At All which suits them perfectly. I stand in awe of them as they dance and hold each other tight. They have only ever had eyes for one another since the day that they met, and right now that is so evident, I don't think they've even noticed that there's two hundred people staring at them. When we get half-way through the song, I encourage both sets of parents to join them on the floor and slowly, as is tradition, everyone else does too. Which just leaves me. The wallflower. Nobody to share this moment with. But that's ok, I know my day will come. One day. Maybe.

I turn away from the happiness in front of me and make my way to the bar. It's time for me to relax and I need a gin. I drink it quickly and ask for another.

"You'd better slow down, I know what you're like when you're drunk" What the…?

"Matt?" I spit my gin all over his suit. "Shit, I'm sorry." He laughs and wipes it off. "Matt, what are you doing here? You're not invited." Why? What? I…?

"I was invited actually, I thought you knew." What a liar!

"Matt, I've planned this whole wedding so I know exactly who was and wasn't invited and you were most definitely not invited." I stress 'not' and realise I probably sound quite angry. I'm about to speak again when a voice behind me stops me in my tracks,

"I invited him" it's Rach. I turn to look at her and question why she would do this. "Kate, you need to stop being so stubborn and sort your life out. You're my best friend and I love you but you keep messing up when it comes to men and the reason you mess up is because you love that man there in front of you." I turn to look at Matt, who is looking quite shy as Rach points at him, he's also looking incredibly dashing and gorgeous and perfect and being this close to him still makes my heart beat out of control. "How ever you two got together doesn't matter now, anyone who knows you can see you're made for each other." I turn back to Rach, not really sure what to say. She takes hold of my shoulders and hugs me, "Kate, I married my soul-mate today and I wanted you to have yours here too. It's the right thing to do." She looks at Matt and he nods and smiles back at her with a look of gratitude on his face. Rach goes. I turn back to Matt.

"I can't believe Rach has done this, I thought she hated you!" I look at him in disbelief that he's here.

"Thanks," he smirks. "is it ok that I am here?" I take a deep breath and nod.

"I think so." I say and look at him properly for the first time in six months. There have been so many times when I've nearly text him but told myself it wouldn't work, it was all too painful but now he's here in front of me, I know I still love him. That has never gone away. But how can we…

"Kate, can we start again? We're both single. We have no reason not to be together. I think about you every day. I miss you every day. I love you Kate." (I'm pretty sure if they put a heart monitor on me right now, they'd be insisting I go to hospital).

"I don't know what to say Matt, how can we trust each other after everything that's happened?"

"Because we love each other. Kate, you're it for me. You're everything I've ever wanted. I just wish it hadn't taken me so long to work it out."

"But what about the other women, you seem to be out with someone new every week?" I have discretely followed Matt in the press. As his rise to fully fledged celebrity chef has progressed, so have the number of women on his arm.

"There's no one else Kate, all that stuff is publicity and media crap. People see what they want to see." He can see the uncertainty in my eyes, "Kate, I haven't been with anyone since you. I haven't been the slightest bit interested in anyone but you. I have been sitting on the side-lines, waiting, hoping they'd come a time when you were ready to see me again, ready to let me back in your life. So, when Rach called, I knew I had to be here tonight."

Shit, what is happening here? Matt is here in front of me. I believe him, I know he's being sincere. He still loves me. And I love him.

"The only thing keeping us apart now Kate, is you." He looks at me, searching for an answer, wondering if I'm going to rip his head off again like I have in the past. I don't. I take his face in my hands and I kiss him. I feel his arms slowly wrap around me and I feel alive again. The shivers, the heartbeats, the tingles, they're all still there. I look at him, my hands on his face, my body wrapped up in his arms and his love.

"I didn't know if you'd want me after all this time Kate."

"Oh Matt, it's always been you, it will always be you. I love you Matt."

"I love you too Kate." And he kisses me again. My fingers move up into his hair and I can feel my whole body react to him.

"Hey," he says, as he looks at me and smiles. "dance with me?" He takes my hand and leads me to the dance floor. I see him give a little nod to the dj and the music changes. Those opening guitar chords and George Ezra's voice is unmistakable, Hold My Girl plays out across the room and I feel a tear come into my eyes.

"You remembered" I say,

"Always, Kate, always. I love you so much." He kisses me tenderly and then just looks at me. Everything suddenly feels right, perfect. "Now, come here" he smiles, "and let me hold my girl" he wraps his arms around me and holds me like he's never going to let go.

Over his shoulder I see Rich and Rach watching us, smiling. Tears are rolling down my cheeks but this time, for the first time, because I'm happy.

I look at Matt and I know he's mine. Completely mine.

THANK YOU

Thank you for reading. I really hope you enjoyed it!
Please leave me a review on Amazon if you liked it (or even if you didn't!)
Sign up for new offers and pre-publication news at www.nerysmccabe.com

New from Nerys McCabe...'The One'

"To be honest, I haven't met anyone for a long time that I felt attracted to." He looked down at her and took a breath, "until tonight." and kissed her again. She felt dizzy as she felt his hands on her face and then move down to her waist, one resting there while the other felt the curves of her bum. The shivers were intense and she knew he was feeling it too. His breath was broken and stilted almost like he was nervous but desperately wanted her. The moment was intense and exhilarating. Matilda's heart was racing as she was taken over by passion and want. She wasn't the sort of girl who slept with someone as soon as she met them but this was different somehow. She trusted him completely. It was like everything had been leading to this moment. She knew she wasn't drunk. This was something else, something which was unstopp-able, something that she had to experience. It wasn't just the physical contact though, there was something electric between them. Jamie pulled away and looked down into her eyes and she knew.

Matilda rearranged the chairs for the third time in as

many minutes. She had the cosy blanket, for the smaller children to sit on, at the front with the chairs scattered round the outside but now she thought nobody would sit on the chairs if they were too close to her. Instead, she lined them up behind the blanket but then started to think it looked too much like a classroom. She wasn't sure why she was so nervous. She'd run children's story-times in her previous job but she desperately wanted to get this right and make a good impression so that they encouraged more children (and parents) into the library. She eventually decided on the lay out and made her way back to the desk to continue with her other work. Story-time was due to start at 10.30am so that gave her an hour to get the returns back to their shelves. She could, realistically, leave this task until later but she needed to keep herself busy so that she stopped her incessant worrying about story-time.

"It's only bloody story-time!" a voice behind her whispered as she put a book about Penguins back on the shelf. Ian had spotted her arranging and rearranging the chairs and wanted to make her feel better. "Don't worry so much, you'll be so great, it won't matter where anyone is sitting, the only thing you need to be concerning yourself with is where we're going for a drink after work."

Matilda smiled and felt her shoulders relax a bit. Sometimes she got so caught up in the moment that she forgot about the bigger picture and the fact that this was just a job and she really shouldn't get so worked up about it. It was right that she wanted to make a good impression but not to the extent that she had sleepless nights over it or forgot to eat properly which, on occasion, she did.

"I know Ian, you're right, but if the first session is really successful then word'll get round and we'll get more and more kids coming to the library. That's what we need, after all, if we're going to survive all these closures."

"Don't be daft, girl, this has been a library since time began, only an idiot would consider closing this place down."

"You forget who's running the country at the moment!" Matilda said with a sideways glance as she pushed the trolley along a bit further.

"Just focus on one thing at a time. You're so well prepared for this story-time that nothing can possibly go wrong."

"What if nobody turns up?" she gasped, having a panic that people won't have seen the posters, maybe they weren't prominent enough or not flashy enough. Ian shook his head and took her by the arm to the balcony.

"Just look down there, missus!" he indicated the reading area, there were already at least 5 children with parents scattered around them. She smiled with relief. Her eyes then fell to a man who was standing with his back to the main desk. It couldn't be!

"No way, it can't be...?" the man turned round and she instinctively ducked down behind the balcony making Ian crouch down next to her,

"What's the matter Tilly? Are we being shot at?" He smiled, he was used to her drama and knew how to disarm it with humour.

"It's him!" she was squatting down with her back to the balcony as if she actually was in a warzone trying to dodge enemy bullets, her breath quickening.

"It's who?" Ian replied standing up. "Who is it?" he looked down at her, she wasn't moving.

"The guy, the man I... you know, the one I told you about..."

"Oh my god 'the one'? Where? Which one is he? I need to see this god for myself." Ian was now scanning the downstairs floor so obviously that Matilda thought he was being far too blatant, as always, and decided she needed to stop him. She slowly stood up and looked down to where 'he' had been. Damn, he wasn't there now. Had she imagined him? It wouldn't be the first time. There was one time in the supermarket where she made a fool of herself to a complete stranger and then another time on the bus where she ended up getting off four stops early as she was so embarrassed for approaching a man while the rest of the passengers on the bus giggled at the sorry scene unfolding. It had become like some sort of manhunt that she was becoming a little obsessed with. But she still couldn't believe, after the amazing night they spent together, that he hadn't called her. She scanned the floor again but he had vanished, if he was ever there at all.

Matilda checked her watch.10.25.

"Shit, I'd better get myself down there for story-time." She bellowed, running past Ian, who was still looking for 'him'. She ran down the stairs so quickly that she didn't see the man coming round the corner and crashed into him, knocking the book out of his hand. "Oh god, I'm so sorry" she immediately bent down to the book, reading the title as she picked it up, and handed it back to the man she had almost knocked over. She looked up at him and for a second, she couldn't breathe. It was him. She had seen him. He was here. Jamie.

ACKNOWLEDGEMENTS

Thank you to my friends and family who have shown me no end of support in my whims and wonderings.

To my husband, who puts up with me wanting to follow my writing dream; to my son just because he is wonderful; to my Mum and Dad who have always encouraged me in whatever craziness I have undertaken; to my sister and her wife who endlessly support and counsel me and remind me to be me.

Thanks also to Nikki for always listening to my ideas and coaching me through them, to Sarah for the fantastic book cover and to Bev and Scott who gave me really useful feedback.

Thank you all for your advice and encouragement.

ABOUT THE AUTHOR

Nerys McCabe

Nerys is a secondary school teacher who is finally writing novels! Having taught Literature for fifteen years, she thought she'd have a go at it herself. She really hopes you enjoy her first foray into the world of romance.

It's Just Sex...(Isn't it?) is her first novel.

BOOKS BY THIS AUTHOR

The One

Matilda had the perfect night with the perfect man, it was love at first sight for them both, so she thought. So why doesn't he call her? Matilda isn't the type to let things lie but she has no way of contacting him and has to accept that it was just one perfect night. But then, he walks right back into her life and after that, the surprises just keep on coming!

Visit www.nerysmccabe.com to learn more about me and my novels. Join in with my interactive blog and have your say in the 'chapters' section, where you get to decide a character's fate.

Printed in Great Britain
by Amazon